the brothers torres

coert voorhees

hyperion • new york

An Imprint of Disney Book Group

ACKNOWLEDGMENTS

Much love and gratitude to Molly, Dayton, Sara, and
Emily Voorhees for their patience and support. Thanks
also to Dan O'Brien, Sara Crowe, and Arianne Lewin,
whose insight and honesty allowed this book to emerge;
and to Jorge Diaz, *que en paz descanse.*

First Edition
1 3 5 7 9 10 8 6 4 2
Printed in the United States of America
This book is set in 12.5-point Centaur.
Library of Congress Cataloging-in-Publication Data on file.
ISBN-13: 978-1-4231-0304-2
ISBN-10: 1-4231-0304-1
Reinforced binding
Visit www.hyperionteens.com

For the Daytons

one

SO, THERE'S A GUY, right? And he's known this girl forever, from back when they used to take swim lessons and throw dirt clods at cars and lift packs of Juicy Fruit from Arroyo's QuickMart. But she's all grown up now. She's sixteen and in high school, and somewhere along the line she got smoking-hot. And this dude, he wants to ask her out, but he can't bring himself to do it. He doesn't know the right words. He gets this nasty pinch underneath his rib cage when she even turns around to look at him and blah, blah, blah. I know, you've heard it all before. I thought I had, too. Until that dude turned out to be me.

And now here she is, sitting on the metal bleachers right

in front of me, leaning forward so that a little sliver of olive skin peeks out between her shirt and the top of her jeans. Damn.

My best friend, Zach, elbows me hard on the shoulder. "Wake up," he says under his breath.

"Huh?"

"Uh-oh. Was somebody dreaming?" Zach looks like a cartoon when he smiles. Round white face with tufts of blond hair like a diseased yucca plant, all floppy and shooting out in different directions. "I'm guessing you don't want to be that obvious."

"Come on, *ese*," I say through clenched teeth, pointing at Rebecca with my eyeballs.

"I was just playing."

"Go play with yourself, then." I barely move my lips, like a freaking ventriloquist. It's hard to say much when the topic of conversation is right in front of you.

Here's what you need to know about Rebecca Sanchez: she's funny and smart and all that, but damn is she hot, too. She's biracial, a *coyote* like me, but unlike me, she got the best of both worlds. Straight black hair, creamy light brown skin, a kickin' body—not too skinny. And eyes such a deep shade of blue that sometimes you want to lean in close so you can see the bottom. Cheesy as hell? Definitely. But I'm telling you.

My name is either Frankie or Francisco, depending on who's around. My mom's Latina, and my dad's Anglo. Her last name, Torres, is the Spanish word for his last name,

Towers. They took it as a sign, and now they run a little New Mexican restaurant named Los Torres. Cute, huh? At least my mom doesn't hyphenate. That would be redundant, like saying Rio Grande River or ATM machine. Mostly I'm Frankie, unless my mom's really pissed at me. Then she yells at Francisco.

A gust of wind stings my face with dirt carried all the way from the parking lot, but at least it cools me down for a few seconds. Tourists who come to the restaurant always talk about how much they love the dry heat, how it's so much better than back home, and how they want to move here to get away from the humidity, but I think any kind of heat sucks ass when it makes your pits all sweaty and Rebecca Sanchez is sitting three feet in front of you.

We play all our home games at a soccer complex near downtown Borges called *Arroyo del Águila*. In English, that means Eagle Ditch, which is a classic New Mexican name. *Eagle* because it wants to be a place where kids can come to soar in their athletic endeavors. *Ditch* because it's just a few dirt fields next to an emergency flood drain, trying to pass itself off as an athletic facility.

The bleachers overlook downtown, with Romero Mesa rising a couple miles behind it. The mesa, a flat-topped hill with juniper bushes dotting the rocky slopes like clumps of green fuzz, is a kick-ass party spot. There's such a huge network of narrow dirt roads and hidden nooks and crannies that the cops can hardly ever find the festivities, let alone bust them up. I haven't been to a party there yet, but I'm definitely going this year, now that I'm a sophomore.

Pretty much the whole school turned out for the game against Highland today, with almost everyone in green and white—Borges Panthers colors. There's also a couple college scouts here to watch my brother, Steve. I know the dude from the University of New Mexico is for sure—he's at every game—plus some other guys I've never seen before. Like always, my dad is sitting two rows behind them, pretending not to look at their clipboards.

Rebecca and her friend Katie don't seem to be paying too much attention to the game. They talk and giggle and tell each other to shut up. Once in a while, the crowd makes some noise, and the girls look up for the obligatory "Go, Panthers!" But they're mostly in their own little world. Not that I'm paying attention to the game, either.

Amid the cheers and the referee's occasional whistle, a steady throb of bass comes from a cluster of *cholos* in the parking lot at the far end of the field. These are the dudes our parents always warned us about—the tattoos, the screw-you attitude, the dark-ass sunglasses day or night—hardcore *vatos* chilling with their lowriders. Some of the *cholas* who hang all over them are dressed in hardly nothing—short skirts, high heels, low tops. A little bit of hot mixed with a whole lot of skank. I'm not saying they're all getting wasted in public, but I'm not saying they're not, if you know what I mean.

Right in the middle of the group, leaning against the

hood of a silver '51 Chevy pickup, is a tall dude named Flaco, my brother's best friend's cousin. I see him around from time to time, but I've never met him. I guess Steve has been hanging with him lately—my parents would be thrilled if they knew. From the stories Steve tells, Flaco is by far the hardest *cholo* in town.

The big news these days, aside from our undefeated soccer team, is what happened to a sophomore chick named Nicole Lawrence a couple days ago. She was home alone when some dudes busted into her house and took all her family's stuff. Rebecca and Katie can't stop talking about it.

"Hey, Rebecca," I say, leaning forward. "Did your dad say anything?"

"God, Frankie," she says. "Nice eavesdropping."

"Oh, come on. They heard you in Santa Fe."

She rolls her eyes and smirks. "Anyway. He doesn't talk about police business at home."

Yeah, Rebecca's dad isn't just a cop, he's the chief of police. Maybe that's the reason I can't bring myself to ask her. The last thing I need is to have the cops busting surveillance on me.

"I heard she got knocked around pretty good," Zach says. The whole Nicole thing kills him—he's had a crush on her forever. They almost kissed in fifth grade, playing tag during recess when Nicole was "it." Zach faked left and went right, but Nicole wasn't fooled, so their faces collided and they fell back onto the dirt. Zach sported a fat lip for a week.

Rebecca shakes her head. "Who told you that?"

"I don't know," he says with a shrug. "Some dude."

"Some dude is full of it. They locked her in the closet."

"That's not too bad, I guess," he says.

Katie's thin lips hang open in disbelief. "Not too bad? It scared the hell out of her."

"She said she's going to try to come back to school next week," Rebecca says.

"That's messed up," I say. We have break-ins in Borges, just like everywhere else. It's not like we're the 'hood, but it feels different, much worse, when it's someone you know. "Just chilling, doing your homework, and dudes bust in like that? I can't even imagine."

Zach laughs. "Which part? Doing your homework?"

I don't know why he's my friend. Here I am trying to make an impression, trying to pave the way, and he has to chop me down like that. If we were alone, I'd have a kick-ass comeback for him, or at the very least I could punch him. But with Rebecca here, everything I think of is stupid, and if I punch him I look like an ape; so all I can do is smile and make like he's the funniest guy in the world.

In the face of my silence—I'm such a *pendejo*—Rebecca and Katie turn away from us and show some school spirit. They do one of those wave things, but since there's only two of them, they have to stand up and sit down a lot. They have to know we're watching, right? And they have to know what we'll be looking at. Katie isn't anything special—red hair down to her shoulders, face all tight and pointy like a Doberman, nothing much to see from the back. But Rebecca? Either she's clueless and is just having fun at the soccer game, or she knows how into her I am and likes to torture me. I turn to Zach and mouth, "Damn."

When they get bored with the wave, Katie and Rebecca decide they need to go to the bathroom. As they walk away, Zach squints and shakes his head at me like a disappointed parent.

"What?" I say. "Here? Now?"

"Why not?"

"In front of everybody?"

"Crowd could be a good thing. The cheers might drown out her laughter."

"*Pinche güero,*" I say, flipping him the bird with both hands.

"You got to do it soon, bro."

My brother said the same thing. Even though we've only been back in school for two weeks, with a chick that fine, it's just a matter of time before the upperclassmen bust in; and I have to say, they've been circling her like vultures these days. Homecoming last year was such a disaster (I went stag with Zach because I couldn't find a date) that I promised myself this year would be different. Steve warned me that not having a date sucks even worse as a sophomore, but it's not like he ever had to stress about a date to anything.

"I will," I say.

Zach chuckles. "I mean before you graduate."

"*Ándale,* Steve!" I yell. It's like my brother can see the play develop in slow motion. He doesn't put the ball where his teammates are; he puts it where they're *going* to be. But he has such a ridiculous shot that the coach doesn't want him to pass too much. That's why Steve has three scholarship offers—and why my parents let him get away with anything—because he can finish better than anyone in the state.

"Seriously, Frankie. What do you have to lose?" Zach says.

"I know. You're right, I just—"

"Other than your dignity, I mean."

I shot him a look. *"No mames—"*

"I'm not messing with you—"

"You don't think she wants to go with someone else?" I say. "Not to be paranoid or anything, but she's been cheering for Dalton all day."

"Come on, relax. You look like you have to take a duker. All tense and—"

"You'd be all tense, too, if you had the *cojones* to ask some-one."

Zach busts out laughing. "Oh, did I miss something? Since when do you have the balls to ask someone?"

"I'm just . . . I *will* have them. . . . She's just . . ."

I'm about to smack the punk-ass smile off his face when Rebecca and Katie come back to the bleachers. We quickly act all nonchalant, and I pretend not to clock their every move as they sit down in front of us.

"Let's go, Panthers!" they yell in unison, clapping like cheerleaders.

The closest thing we have to actual cheerleaders are hot chicks rooting for their favorite players. John Dalton has his own section down in the front row by his parents. Popular girls with short shorts and tight shirts squeal whenever he touches the ball, regardless of what he does with it. A blond junior named Samantha shrieks, then stands up and takes a picture of him with her cell phone. I don't want to get caught looking at *her*, so I turn back to Rebecca.

You know how when you can see a chick's bra strap underneath the back of her shirt? And all you can think about is the clasp? You run the unhooking process over and over in your mind, just in case you ever get to complete the maneuver in real life. You want to be prepared.

"No time like the present," Zach says, following my gaze.

"Damn, *ese*. Give it a rest."

"Hey, Rebecca," he says, "you have a date to Homecoming?"

Is he freaking kidding me? To keep myself from pushing his ass off the bleachers, I develop a sudden interest in the clouds forming off to the west. Little wisps right now, but in a few hours they'll turn into late afternoon thunderheads.

Rebecca turns around. "Not yet." Is that disappointment in her face? The eyebrows squinched together, the full lips pursed to the side? It might be.

"Huh," he says.

"Why, Zach? Are you looking for someone to go with?"

Her eyes flick toward me for a split second, which is

probably enough time for her to figure out exactly what's going through my head. I'm sure it's stapled all over my face.

"Nope," he says with a dismissive wave. He wants Nicole, but he doesn't know how to ask, especially after her break-in trauma. And anyway, he's too much of a puss to admit it in front of her friends. Not that I blame him. "I've got some seniors lined up."

Rebecca smiles wide. "Oh, really?"

Katie snorts through her sharp little nose, and Rebecca hits her on the shoulder with the back of her hand.

"Hell, yeah. I'm a pimp."

"A pimp?" Rebecca says.

"Or, as your people might say, a *pimp-o*."

"That's not how you say it," Rebecca says, laughing out loud.

Katie nods up at me. "So if he's a pimp, Frankie, what does that make you?"

My mouth opens only slightly. I smile. "Me? I'm a . . ."

"Frankie treats women with respect," Zach says, leaning his elbow on my shoulder. "He's too much of a gentleman to be a pimp."

"He's a gentleman?" Katie says.

I force a laugh. It's all I can manage. "Something like that."

"Surprise, surprise," Rebecca says. "I didn't think there were any of those in Borges."

I guess that would depend on her definition of a

gentleman, but she's probably right. Although I think that's more because we're in high school than because we're in Borges. I don't want to break it down into social classes or anything, but different groups hang together, just like everywhere else. Soccer players are the top of the totem pole, so it's not like they have to be nice to chicks to get them to go out with them. The *cholos* just plain scare the crap out of people, so they don't have to be nice to anybody, either. And then there are guys like me and Zach, on the fringes, trying to figure out a way to get in.

There's an awkward silence while Rebecca and I smile politely at each other, and then the girls turn back to watch the game. I want to kill Zach right now. The last thing I want Rebecca to think is that I'm a "gentle man." Gentle men don't make chicks want to hook up with them. Gentle men get their asses kicked.

A low groan comes from the crowd when Dalton shanks the ball out of bounds for the second time this half. He throws up his hands like he's pissed at Steve for making a bad pass, but the pass was perfect. Anyway, Steve's too smart to take the bait, so he claps and says, "Come on, Borges, keep it up!"

It's amazing how different the on-the-field Steve is from the normal, everyday Steve. If Dalton showed him up anywhere else, my brother would get right in his face.

"Dalton's going to blow the game," I say.

"He is not," Rebecca says.

"Look at him! He's three steps slower than everyone else."

Dalton used to be good. He spent too much time in the weight room, though, and now he's like a tank. Slower, less athletic. He's in trouble unless he can muscle his man off the ball, but he can still kick the crap out of it.

Rebecca scoffs. "Like you can do better?"

"If they ever give me a chance," I say. I knew she was into him; why else would she be defending his sorry ass? But I can't afford to sound jealous right now, so I have to backtrack. "I guess he tries pretty hard."

Zach stares at me like I'm radioactive. "Yeah," he says in disbelief. "He tries hard."

The truth is, John Dalton is an asshole. He's easily the richest kid in Borges, and if I were Rebecca, I would hate him no matter how hot I thought he was. When his family moved to town about ten years ago, Mr. Dalton bought out Rebecca's grandmother's New Mexican restaurant just for the recipes. He bulldozed the building her family's place had been in for over sixty years and built his own: the Tortilla Emporium.

The food is just okay, but they catch a lot of tourists because they can afford to advertise on freeway billboards. Plus, they own a factory—also called the Tortilla Emporium— that supplies tortillas to most of the restaurants from Albuquerque to Santa Fe. Their tortillas are so good that the super-traditional New Mexican food restaurants order from the Emporium instead of making their own. Even my family's place uses them. You can see the factory from here, a full thirty feet taller than the five blocks of banks, restaurants, and hair salons that pass for downtown Borges.

Don't get me wrong; I don't care that the Daltons are white. But they're not even originally *from* New Mexico. They came in from Dallas and bought up most of the land by the river, and now William Dalton is like the unofficial mayor of Borges because the Tortilla Emporium is the biggest employer in town, and his wife prances around in full Santa Fe style—the Navajo rug serape, the turquoise bracelets, the silver necklaces—and their only child gets to drive a perfectly restored, midnight blue 1969 Pontiac GTO convertible. And Rebecca's family? Where the tortilla recipe came from in the first place? They get a nice cold bowl of dick.

The ref calls a hand ball in the Highland box, and we all jump to our feet. My brother grabs the ball and walks to the penalty spot. He bounces the ball a couple times and then spins it backward on the ground, searching for the perfect placement.

"Come on, Steve," Zach says. "Do something."

Rebecca glances back at us, then does a double take. "Oh my God, Zach. Not now."

Penalty kicks make me as nervous as anyone, but at least I don't have my eye in my hand like Zach does. And that's not some random expression for being nervous. I mean, he actually has his eye in his hand.

"*Órale,*" I say, "be careful with that."

"I'm not going to drop it."

Zach has a glass eyeball. But it isn't really glass, and it isn't really a ball. It's more like a slightly concave ceramic saucer. It looks so real, though. He even has his name written on the edge, in red-vein cursive:

Zachary

He takes it out all the time; it's like a twitch. I don't even think he knows that he's doing it. If it gets some dirt on it, he just washes it off in his mouth. Then he pops it back in the socket.

Katie turns around and pretends to gag when she sees it in his hand. "That's disgusting."

"You're just jealous of my tricks," he says.

"Could you please not do that in front of me ever again?"

"Jeez," he says. "Don't be such an eye-ist."

I've never been around someone as comfortable with himself as Zach is. Maybe losing his eye relieved him of the pressure to be cool. He knows who he is—he's the kid with one eye. Screw anybody who doesn't like it. The rest of us are always trying to pretend we're something else.

"Just put it back in before you crack it on the bleachers," I say.

Instead, he sucks on it like it's a breath mint as my brother lines up the penalty kick. "You think he makes it?"

"Of course he makes it," I say, even though I'm already preparing for a miss. That's probably what I should be thinking with Rebecca. Expect her to say no, and then it'll be a pleasant surprise if she doesn't.

Steve doesn't miss, though. He places it perfectly into the bottom left corner with the inside of his foot, and afterward he hardly even celebrates. He just points to his friend Cheo, the right midfielder, and jogs back to the other side of the field. 1–0 Borges. The UNM scout scribbles on his clipboard.

Everybody sits down again after Highland kicks off. Zach pops his eye back in place and nudges me with the side of his knee. "Dude, you want to come over later? Begay finally got me those M-80s."

A while ago, Zach bought some M-80s off Josh Begay, a Navajo kid whose uncle runs a fireworks stand on the big reservation every summer. Josh hoards some of the more potent explosives and sells them during the school year. I guess you could say he scalps them. Get it?

Oh, and by the way. Don't get all pissed off because I said I have an Indian friend whose uncle sells fireworks. I know a lot of Indians who don't sell fireworks. It just so happens that this particular Indian kid likes to blow stuff up as much as Zach and I do.

"Depends," I say, checking my watch. My parents make me wait tables at least three times a week, and I'm on tonight. "I have to prep for the dinner rush."

"Come on, just a few? We could take out some anthills."

Rebecca rolls her eyes at us. "Is that all you guys ever talk about?"

"Who's eavesdropping now?" I say.

"We talk about other things," Zach says. "Like you, for example."

This is my best friend. He wants me to blush, or mumble something, but I won't fall for that, so instead I stand up and scream at the referee. "Come on, ref! That's a foul!" The ball wasn't even in play, though, so everybody in the stands turns to look at me. I shrug.

Rebecca seems curious. "Us?"

"He means girls," I say as I take my seat.

"You talk about girls and blowing stuff up?" she says. "That's it?"

Zach winks at her. "Sometimes we talk about girls blowing stuff up."

One of the Highland forwards puts a move on Dalton that's just plain embarrassing. He fakes left, then right, then dips the shoulder left. Dalton buys the last juke and nearly comes out of his shoes, while the dude breaks right again, creating enough space to rip a shot just over the crossbar.

Dalton's cheering section doesn't seem to mind. Samantha starts a chant of "Johnny, Johnny, he's our man," and the rest of them stand up—tiny purses clutched underneath their arms, a few with cell phones in hand—and sing along. I can't help but wonder if Rebecca is as annoyed by them as I am, or if she's envious.

It's weird going to school with rich people. On the surface, you're jealous. You want to be like them, you want to have the things they have, wear the clothes they wear, and drive the cars they drive. But somewhere in the back of your head, you realize that you don't want to be the one everybody looks at and says to themselves, "I can't stand that fucker." So you're left wanting to be just like them and hating every bone in their bodies at the same time.

The crowd thins out pretty quickly after the game. With today's 2–1 victory, we're still undefeated, so people are feeling good. I overhear Willy Stinchcomb and some of the popular crew making plans to hang out later at the Daltons' pool. My dad, who hasn't missed a game in two years, talks with the UNM scout near the sideline. The players mill around the bench, taking off their shoes, congratulating each other, giving each other a hard time. Steve and Cheo reenact the second goal of the game, also Steve's, which was a sweet header off Cheo's far-post cross.

Rebecca and Katie have met up with a couple more friends, and they've all clustered by the corner flag. Zach and I hang out on our bikes by the bleachers, waiting for the right time for me to strike.

"Let's go, dude," Zach says, like a trainer psyching up his boxer between rounds. "Show her how much of a *pimp-o* you really are."

"I got this." I say, trying to muster as much confidence into those words as possible.

I look down at my white T-shirt and frown. I don't normally wear collared shirts, but I wish I had one on right now. Maybe she'd take me more seriously. I let the breeze cool down my pits for a second before making my way over to the flag. You know how in *Star Wars* when they go into hyperspace, how the stars all melt away and it looks like they're going into a black tunnel? That's kind of how this is, except that the end of this tunnel is Rebecca. Everything else goes out of focus.

I can feel my pulse in my earlobes and behind my eyes. I hope it doesn't look like I'm going to pass out. When I'm about ten feet away, I take a deep breath and roll the tension out of my shoulders. I got this.

"Hey, Rebecca," I say as calmly as possible. "Can I talk to you for a second?"

"Um, sure," she says, glancing at her friends. They turn away, giving us a little bit of privacy. "What's up?"

Her smile is so warm, so inviting, so *her*, that it immediately puts me at ease. She has to know what's coming, and she's probably doing everything she can to make it easy for me. I have nothing to worry about, as long as I can get the words out in the right order. "So, remember what Zach said before?"

She laughs. "About the fireworks?"

"No," I say with a laugh of my own. She's so funny, trying to make me all relaxed. "Before that. We were talking about Homec—"

Suddenly, someone pats me on the back so hard that I stagger forward, almost crashing into Rebecca. When I regain my balance, I turn around to see John Dalton staring at me with a smile that doesn't make it to his icy blue eyes.

"Hey," he says. "Steve's brother."

"Hey," I say. "It's Frankie."

"Oh, I know, Frankie-Spankie. I'm just messing with you." He's all sweaty, his wavy blond hair stuck to his forehead, with his bag slung stylishly over one shoulder and his uniform untucked, sipping orange Gatorade from a plastic bottle.

"Good game, John," Rebecca says.

"Yeah," I say, "not bad."

Dalton doesn't miss a beat. "Hey, is that your bike over there with the Cyclops?" He points with his chin.

Zach straddles his own bike while holding the handlebars of mine, an old GT Mach One BMX. The blue paint is all faded, so I've been trying to get Cheo to show me how to airbrush it. I threw some pegs on it when Steve first gave it to me, and I had to replace the crappy plastic pedals when one of them broke, but other than that I haven't put any money into it. The bike doesn't exactly kick ass, but it gets the job done. This is the first time I've been ashamed of it.

"Yeah," I say. "It was my brother's."

"That's good," he says. "Nothing wrong with a hand-me-down."

I glance over at Rebecca, but she just stands there, fiddling with one of her earrings. She gives me a look like she's sorry, but I don't think she'll be coming to my defense. Not that I blame her. The only way I can get out of this with any self-respect at all is to hit the "eject" button.

"Okay," I say, nodding. "I'll see you guys later."

Rebecca waves. "Bye, Frankie." There is sympathy in her voice. Or is it pity?

"Yeah," Dalton says. "Awesome chatting with you."

By the time I get to Zach, I can feel the heat on my face. My mouth is dry, and my breath comes in short spurts. I feel like throwing up, but at least I got out of there on my own terms.

"What the hell happened?" he says.

I hop on my bike. Given how small I feel, it's almost a miracle that I still fit on this piece of crap. "Let's just go."

In order to leave the complex, we have to ride through the parking lot, and that means we have to pass the *cholos*. It's not that I'm scared—they've never messed with me before—but there's just something unsettling about being around such badass dudes. It makes me feel self-conscious, like I should be tougher than I am, even though I don't want to be anything like them. Anyway, I just want to get through.

Right as I'm pedaling by a cherry red '77 Caddy lowrider, the driver pops open the door, and I have to slam on the pedals and swerve to avoid it. My tires slide out from under me, and I hit the dirt hard. Zach stops right behind me.

"Watchale, *ese*," the dude says, stepping out of his *ranfla* and inspecting its door. His hair is shaved close and he's got a thin goatee and dark glasses.

Zach bends over to help me up as a crowd begins to gather. One look at his face and I can tell he wants to get out of here even faster than I do. If a coyote like me is anxious,

I can only imagine what a full-fledged white boy feels like. I stand my bike up and dust myself off, trying not to make eye contact with anyone.

One of the *cholas* steps in front of me and looks me up and down. She has a teardrop tattoo under her right eye. Her black hair is gelled and wavy, pulled back with a dark blue bandanna, and it comes down to her waist. "*Oye,* you're Steve's brother, ain't you?"

"Uh-huh," I say, nodding. She's wearing black jeans and a sleeveless top cut down low to reveal some monster *tetas.*

A deep voice adds to my discomfort. "Careful where you're looking, *ese.*" Then Flaco appears at her side and puts his arm tight around her neck. He's so tall I have to crane my neck up to see him. His long-sleeved flannel is buttoned at the top, and a thick silver chain sparkles out from underneath. His laugh is bottomless.

The *chola* pulls the collar of her shirt to the side, revealing a dark red rose tattoo underneath the edge of a black lace bra. "Tell your brother that Carmenita can't wait to see him again," she says, pouting.

There is a moment of complete silence. I fight the urge to look at Zach, but I can sense his nervousness from here. I had no idea my brother was going out with this chick Carmenita, and my parents are going to have a heart attack if they find out. A tattooed *chola* is a long way from his last girlfriend, Annabelle, who just left for college in Pennsylvania.

Then suddenly everyone busts out laughing. Carmenita

spins away and giggles with a bleached-blond *chola* in a miniskirt and fishnet stockings.

Flaco leans down, putting his hands on my handlebars. "Tell Steve good game," he says with an odd, almost condescending smile. Then he steps aside and pushes the seat of my bike. Zach hops on his, and we both get the hell out of there as fast as we can.

The road takes us around the complex and up a small hill above the fields. As we pedal away, I resist the urge to look back at Rebecca. If she's looking at me, I'll feel like an ass for being caught. And if she's not looking at me, I'll feel even worse.

two

NORMALLY, I'D HEAD straight home and pretend to do my homework before going to the restaurant, but after what just happened, I really need to blow something up—a little detonation therapy—and that's where Zach's backyard comes in. It's a half acre on the outskirts of town, all dirt and sagebrush, with anthills everywhere. An old flagstone path runs from the back door to a sad adobe wall that wraps around a big fire pit. Zach's mom ran out of energy before she stuccoed the wall, so now it erodes a little every year. Pretty soon it won't even be tall enough to protect us from our homemade shrapnel.

A thundercloud gathers steam in the west, the streaks of

rain in the distance looking more like brushstrokes than actual moisture. We're hiding behind an old cottonwood tree stump, waiting for the detonation of our latest masterpiece.

"I can't believe you didn't warn me," I say.

"He came out of nowhere," Zach says, as if that explains everything. Seconds later, a tremendous *BOOM* shatters the afternoon silence. Small clods of dirt and chunks of smoldering blue rubber fly over our heads, peppering the dozens of sage bushes that surround us like bodyguards.

Zach and I had cut open a racquetball, inserted an M-80, and filled the ball with sand, making a nice little grenade. Then we dug a hole down the center of an anthill, lit the fuse, jammed our grenade to the bottom, and covered the hole with dirt. Pretty creative, if you ask me.

"That was a good one," he says, patting me on the back.

He stands and walks over to a crater the size of a large watermelon. Charred pieces of ant litter the outside rim. These are yard ants—fire ants—not the cute little kitchen ants that set up miniature highways on your counter.

"I was so close, too," I say, kneeling to inspect the results of our explosion more closely. "One more sentence."

Little globs of racquetball have fused against the inside walls of the crater, and the faint smell of burning rubber mingles with the more familiar acrid scent of exploded gunpowder. I stick my mouth and nose under the collar of my T-shirt, protecting my poor lungs from the fine cloud of brown dust we stirred up with the grenade.

Zach bends over and probes the charred dirt with a small twig. "That was sweet."

"What if we put gravel in the ball instead of sand?" I say through my shirt. "More damage?"

"Maybe," he says. A headless ant flails its pathetic little legs, struggling to climb out of the crater. "Look at this guy."

Órale, let me interrupt here. You're probably about ready to write me off as a cruelty-to-animals type. A psycho. One minute I'm blowing up ants, the next minute a crowded McDonald's.

Please. If you knew the damage fire ants are capable of, you'd pin a medal on me for taking them out.

When I was twelve, I played goalie once for my soccer team. It was the first and last time I ever played goalie, by the way. I'm a striker normally, not as good as Steve, but I can do some things if anyone ever gets me the goddamn ball. We were playing such a crappy team that our coach put me in the box and gave the regular goalie a chance to score.

Anyway, this other team really sucked, and I was bored because all the action was on the other end. About halfway through the second half, I felt a tickle on my legs inside my goalie pants. Our "field" wasn't grass—not even close—it was packed dirt. And when I say packed, I mean packed. Hard enough to give you a concussion if you hit your head against it.

Of course, fire ants live in dirt, and I'd spent most of the second half standing on top of their huge-ass mansion, so they decided to take their revenge by swarming up my legs. I ran to the sideline as soon as I realized what was happening. But when I started running, the *chingones* started biting. The ants were deep red and huge, each one the size of my middle fingernail. It felt like my legs were on fire, and I managed to take off only one pant leg before I fainted.

I still have the scars on my calves—deep pockmarks, like I had a massive case of lower leg acne—so forgive me for taking a little revenge of my own from time to time.

Zach wanders over to a stump near the wall, away from the anthills, and takes a seat. "The question is, can you get it together soon enough to ask again?"

"I have a month."

"A month?" He shakes his head. "You're retarded."

Normally I'd disagree, but when it comes to Rebecca, it may be true.

"What if she wants to go with some upperclassman, like Dalton?" I say, collapsing to the ground. I lean against the wall and wrap my arms around my knees. "What if she doesn't want to go with me?"

Zach whacks me on the side of the head. "That's your problem. You have to figure out a way to *make* her want to go with you."

"How?"

"Most people would tell you to just be yourself." He pauses dramatically and scratches the yellow fuzz on his chin. "But I don't think that's such a good idea."

I'm on him before his next breath. He tries to push me

away, but he doesn't have much balance on the stump, so he falls backward onto the dusty ground. Maybe his lack of peripheral vision gives me a slight advantage, but I don't want to hear excuses. I have him in a full nelson and I'm just about to feed him a mouthful of gourmet dirt when his mom comes out of the house holding an ice tray filled with grape Kool-Aid cubes on toothpicks.

"Boys," she says. "You're going to ruin the bushes."

"Yes, Mrs. Mason," I sing out. We've rolled right up against a sage. "How ya like me now?" I whisper to Zach before letting him go, jumping to my feet, and raising my arms in triumph.

Zach pushes himself up and dusts off his shirt. "Sneaky Mexican," he says under his breath. He wipes little pieces of dried sticks from his hair and tries to craft a part, but the dust has mixed with his forehead sweat to form a kind of gritty mortar. His hair isn't going anywhere.

Mrs. Mason holds out the tray. Her face, one of the most patient I've ever seen, breaks into a smile, and her sun-worn skin instantly fills with lines. "It's hot out here," she says.

I have no idea why Zach's mom still lets us blow stuff up. Tell me the truth; if your only child had lost his left eye playing war with his cousin—the way Zach tells it, the knife only went in two inches. *Only* two inches!—would you just stand by while he and his stout Latino friend detonated high-powered explosives in the backyard?

Maybe she thinks we're doing a service, taking out all the

anthills. Or maybe she's just given up the hope that Zach will ever stop putting himself in danger and has come to peace with it. Whatever the reason, she's almost supportive.

"I'll leave this for you boys," she says, placing the tray on our stump. "Remember not to—"

"—blow our hands off," Zach and I say.

"Good boys." She wipes her own hands on her blue jeans and goes back inside.

I only met Zach's dad a couple times, but he seemed like a nice enough guy. He was really loud—he didn't yell or anything, but he didn't have what my mom used to call an "inside voice." A couple years ago he left a note saying he was going back to St. Louis, where his family was originally from. Zach and I never talk about it, but my brother told me that Mr. Mason took off because he owed the Santo Domingo casino over a hundred grand.

Zach tosses a used toothpick to the ground and helps himself to another cube. "Promise me one thing."

"What's that?" My ice cube is melting fast, dripping purple sugar water down the back of my hand. I slurp.

"Next time you get the chance, you have to take the shot."

"Yeah, yeah, yeah. It's easy to coach from the sidelines. Maybe if you got in the game."

"You know the funny thing about high school chicks?" he says. "They like dudes with two eyes."

"Lame excuse." He could get dates if he wanted, but his problem is that for him it's Nicole Lawrence or nobody. He spent all last week convincing himself that what a hot chick like Nicole really wants, deep down, is to go out with the funny guy who makes her laugh. But now that she's all freaked out from the B & E, he doesn't know what to do, so it's probably going to be "nobody" forever.

I shrug and lick my ice cube at the same time. "It's like, I have the perfect thing to say, and then I'm in front of her, and I forget my lines or something. But then as soon as she turns away, I remember everything."

He sits again and considers me, like my father searching for the right words during The Talk. "That's perfectly normal, my little half-breed."

There are many benefits to interracial friendships, and one of my favorites is the freedom to call each other nicknames that other people consider racist. I think everyone has a natural urge to say the wrong thing. It's like standing next to some dude on the sidewalk and suddenly wanting to push him into oncoming traffic. Don't even try to tell me you've never had that feeling.

Zach has a bunch of names for me that would get his ass kicked if someone misunderstood, such as: Half-breed, Moistback, and *La Mezcla* (the Mix). I call him Great White, Wonder Bread, and *Güerito* (Little Whitey). He likes to call himself The Caucasian Sensation.

"So, what's your brilliant advice, then?"

"I say you kick Dalton's ass."

I let loose one of those snort laughs. "Dudes like me

don't kick the asses of dudes like Dalton." Not exactly a news flash, I know.

"Your brother could," he says. "How sweet would that be? He'd beat him down old-school."

I get this almost every day. As soon as I say I can't do something, everyone reminds me that my brother could. The thing is, Zach's right. Especially now. It's like Steve's more ripped every day. He came home two weekends ago with a black eye and a cut on his cheek, which totally freaked my parents out. He told them it was from a midnight pickup soccer game, but they couldn't have believed him. Anyway, it's almost like I'll have to start working out just to survive in my own home.

Not only that, but Steve is probably the only one in town who could get away with kicking Dalton's face in. People would forgive him. Captain of the soccer team and everything.

"Old-school," Zach says again. He frowns and nods at the same time. I get the feeling that if he had a pack of cigarettes, he'd light one and take a long slow drag, contemplating the beautiful vision of John Dalton's neck trapped under my brother's cleat. There are no smokes, though, so he punches me in the shoulder instead.

A couple of years ago, Zach and I went through a little phase when we sneaked cigarettes from his mom's purse. We thought we were so cool, smoking out in his backyard after his mom had gone to bed. We would inhale, squat down, pop back up, and exhale—the nicotine combined with the head rush gave us a crazy buzz. That fun lasted almost a month. Right up until Mrs. Mason noticed her smokes were missing and stayed awake one night to catch us in the act.

I thought I was toast, but she didn't tell my parents. Instead, she bought two packs of Marlboro Reds for me and two for Zach and sat next to us, watching while we smoked each cigarette to the filter. I threw up after only two-thirds of a pack—Zach lasted into the second pack before he booted—but she made us smoke every last one of them. I can't even look at a cigarette now without wanting to puke. To this day, Mrs. Mason has never said a word to my mom or dad.

Zach grabs an M-80 and tosses it from one hand to the other. "You ready for more?"

Of course I'm ready for more. I'm always ready for more. But I make the mistake of checking my watch before answering, and the news is not good. "Nah, I have to get to the restaurant."

"It's still early," he says, looking all hurt, like I just dropped the deuce in his Cheerios.

I shake my head and kick at the ground, spraying a cloud of dirt against the wall. "I can't wait to get a real job."

"What are you talking about? You've had one since you were eight."

Seven, actually. If I'd been a better striker, I might have gotten to play on a league team and travel with my dad instead of busing tables and refilling water glasses. "Working for my family doesn't count."

"You get paid, don't you?"

"It's kind of hard to make any tip money without customers. And besides, it's not a real job unless you get a pay-
check from someone who doesn't know anything about you. I
want bosses I've never met before so I can go home and bitch
about what assholes they are."

Zach nods like he knows exactly what I'm talking about.
"I always thought it would be cool to work in a video store."

"Yeah, right. For the porn."

"No doubt," he says, and we knock fists. "Laters, bro."

I toss my purple-stained toothpick into the bushes and
wipe my hands on the inside of my shirt. I hop on my bike and
leave him in his backyard. Zach chuckles to himself and slurps
up another grape ice cube, as if the very thought of free porn
dehydrates him.

three

THE TOWN OF BORGES is sandwiched between two Indian reservations about twenty miles north of Albuquerque and thirty miles south of Santa Fe. Both reservations, the San Felipe and the Santo Domingo, are proud owners of flashy casinos, or "Indian gaming palaces" as they're known out here. It's a classic magician's trick. Show everyone something shiny and clean in one hand, and they probably won't notice the dried piece of dog crap you're holding behind your back.

Just so you know, I can disrespect this place all I want; I live here. But don't you dare come at me with some lame-ass joke about how birds fly upside down over Borges because there's nothing worth shitting on, or how the speed bumps at town limits are designed to keep all the lowriders in.

The Rio Grande cuts through the center of Borges, and most of the land near the river is either rich people's houses or government-protected cottonwood bosque forest. The Daltons have over ten acres, and their house isn't even adobe—it's white stone, with pillars, like some Southern plantation. Those of us who live a bit farther away from the river have what I like to call ditchfront property. Dozens of irrigation ditches, filled only in the spring and early summer, carry water to little fields of green chile and big pastures of alfalfa. Our restaurant is closer to the center of town, so it takes me about twenty minutes to navigate the web of dried-up ditches and back roads.

I skid to a stop in the Los Torres parking lot and jump off my bike, leaning it against the side of the building without bothering to lock it up—nobody's going to steal that piece of crap anyway. I just realized how hungry I am, and the only good thing about working at the restaurant is that I get to eat before my shift. I yank open the door and the CLOSED sign clatters against the glass. A few little bells chime when the door hits them.

There's four booths and seven small tables. The booths are past their prime, with gold, clear-coated vinyl on the benches. All the tables are covered with light blue flowery oilcloth, and they also have little rice-filled vases of plastic flowers on them. The walls are dark wood paneling with a bunch of framed collages of old Mexican money that my dad found at a garage sale a couple years ago.

It's only a little bit after five, so nobody's here except my mom and dad, although that's recently been the case even during the "rush."

My dad handles the business side of things; he's always trying to figure out ways to, as he says, improve our market share. Sometimes we cater events and parties if people are sick of Tortilla Emporium food, but usually it's just opportunities to get our name out there, like when I was eight and my soccer team had *Los Torres* on the backs of our jerseys.

My parents are sitting in the booth closest to the kitchen, but when I walk inside, my mom jumps up and comes over to me. "Frankie!" she says, like one of those saleswomen in the mall—the ones next to all the makeup and perfumes—overly friendly and happy. "What a nice surprise."

My dad stands up straight and runs his fingers through his hair. He gathers his papers together and stacks them in his briefcase, then puts his left hand on the back of the chair as if he's waiting for the host to arrive before he sits down. They glance at each other and then back at me.

I feel like I just walked in on them having sex or something. They're trying so hard to act normal that they seem totally crazy. My mom smoothes out the wrinkles in the orange apron Steve gave her for her birthday last year.

Maybe I wasn't supposed to work today after all. "Isn't it my shift?"

Mom smiles and grabs me by the shoulders. "*¿Tienes hambre, no?* What would you like to eat?"

"Mom?"

"Stuffed sopaipilla, coming right up." She twirls around and pushes through the kitchen doors, her shiny black hair billowing behind her like a long scarf. After rounding the corner until she's visible again beneath the heat lamps, she opens the fridge and pulls out a bowl of dough, grabs a handful, and slaps it onto the counter.

My dad motions for me to sit down in his booth. "Why don't we have a little chat, son."

I love my dad, right? But it's like he learned how to be a father by reading self-help books. He tries hard, so you can't fault him for that, but any time he has to talk about something other than the restaurant menu or Steve's soccer games, he turns into a caricature of a concerned parent. Everything's so meaningful and special that nothing is meaningful or special anymore.

Once I'm settled in the booth, my dad eases in across from me. He leans his elbows on the table and clasps his hands in front of his chin. Then he gives me one of those real serious looks. "As you know, Frankie, it's a tremendous challenge for all of us as we struggle with the evolving economic climate."

See what I mean? He lost me already. "Okay," I say. The deep fryer sizzles to life when my mom drops in the dough for my sopaipilla.

From where I sit, I can see the Borges Ice-Cream Truck Depot next door. The only good thing about working here when I was a kid was sneaking into the Depot while the drivers restocked. It was crazy in the summer, buzzing with vans and converted trucks of all makes and models, every one of them white with all the tasty treats painted on the sides. Sometimes the drivers would be so distracted by the chaos that I could sneak a Bomb Pop or two.

Dad clears his throat. "I guess the best way to put it is that . . . it's essential for us to navigate these turbulent waters together."

It's official: I have no idea what he's talking about. He went straight from *evolving climate* to *turbulent waters*. I bet *discovering the oasis in the desert of our souls* is next. I just want something to eat before I start my shift, but he's working so hard that it would be cruel of me to ignore him. "I'm not really sure what waters you're talking about."

He plows ahead, obviously undaunted by the rumbling in my stomach and the bewildered look on my face. "You come to a point, Frankie, and I'm not saying you're there yet, but you will be, I promise. Someday. You come to a point when your life is suddenly right in front of you, like a mirror, staring you in the face. Do you understand what I'm getting at?"

Is he kidding? "Um. Sure. A mirror, right? So you can see your reflection?"

"Exactly!" he says, suddenly animated. "Your own reflection! Looking back at you as though it's waiting for you to say something, or make a decision."

I think it embarrasses my dad to admit that the restaurant isn't so busy these days. That's why he goes all "turbulent waters" whenever he asks me to work more because I'm cheaper than the other waiters.

"But you're not alone," Dad says. "You're united with those who care about you. And suddenly—"

My mom comes to my rescue with a heaping plate—stuffed sopaipilla, beans, rice—everything swimming in red and green chile. *"Aquí estás, mijo,"* she says.

I grab a fork and wolf down a massive bite. "Thanks, *Mamá,*" I say with my mouth full. I'm so grateful to have something to distract me from my dad that I spill a quarter-size drop of red chile on my chest.

"Your shirt is filthy, Francisco," she says.

"I'll wear my uniform over it," I say, wiping the spot deep into the once-white fabric. She's right, though. It's nasty. In addition to the chile, I also have stains from sweat, dirt, and grape ice cubes. Maybe even blood. "Nobody will be able to tell."

"You can't go around looking like a refugee, *mijo.*"

My mouth is so full that I have to cover it with a napkin in order to chew without showing her the food. "Sorry, *Mamá.*"

She crosses her arms and tilts her head to the side. "Your brother didn't come home last night. Did you know that?"

I need to stall for time to get my lying face on, so I slow down my chewing. Yes, I know that he didn't come home last night. He was probably off getting wasted on the mesa with his friends, but it's really none of my business. "Are you sure? I heard him come in."

My dad reaches across the table and pats me on the arm. "Is that true?"

"Yeah, it was late. Then he left early this morning to work out with the team," I say, anticipating the next question.

I feel like an ass, but they don't seem to have any choice but to take my word for it. In fact, I think they *want* to believe me. They'll buy anything to convince themselves that their perfect Stevie is still a little angel. Dad clears his throat again. "Well then, back to our conversation."

He kind of sizes me up, giving me a squint, like a little kid trying to get his X-ray vision to work. Unlike my mom, my dad is plain. Medium height, medium build, brown hair, eyes halfway between brown and green, big cheeks like mine. Don't get me wrong. Like I said, I love him and all, but he has the kind of face you could see every day for sixteen years, as I have, and still not know what it really looks like.

When I was about six or seven, I thought my dad was a magician. He convinced me that he could make traffic lights change to green whenever he wanted to. We'd be sitting at a red light, waiting, and he'd ask me if I wanted to go yet. Yes, yes! I'd say. He'd hold his hand up, middle finger and thumb together. One, two, three, he'd say. And then he'd snap and point to the light in one motion. Sure enough, it would turn green. It was the most amazing thing I'd ever seen, and I told him so every time. A few years later I found out that he was watching the cross-traffic lights, waiting for them to turn yellow.

"I'm sorry, Dad," I say. "Can we talk about it later?"

He opens his mouth as if to say something, but then he just breathes out. "Any time you want," he says. "You're probably hungry." And just like that, I'm free.

My mom makes the best stuffed sopaipillas in town. The chicken is shredded perfectly, so that it soaks up the juices from the beans. The chile flavors blend just right—green for the sharp instant pain and red for the deep slow burn—and the lettuce is nice and crisp to give every bite some texture. Unfortunately, I get only halfway through my dinner before the door chimes ring behind me.

"Excuse me?" The voice is soft and tentative. "Are you open yet?"

Yeah, *pendejo*, we're open. That's why the parking lot's empty and the sign says *CLOSED*. I turn around to see if the dude has a cane and a guide dog.

An older man holds the door open with his left forearm. Bald except for a ribbon of white hair wrapped above his ears, he wears a black fanny pack around front and wrinkle-free khakis pulled up near his nipples. Behind him, a woman peers over his shoulder. She's dressed in a flowing black dress and a knitted red serape, and her blond hair is gelled or moussed back tight against her scalp. Normally I'd have to go with Texas, but for some reason, I'm thinking Connecticut instead. There's something about the woman—she doesn't have enough turquoise on.

My mom almost leaps between me and the tourists,

shielding them from my nasty T-shirt, and orders me to change into my uniform.

"But we're not open until five thirty."

"Francisco . . . ?" she says. I can fill in the rest. We're not exactly in a position to turn people away.

As I grab my plate and shuffle into the kitchen, my mom seats them next to a window and tells them to make themselves comfortable. You may be surprised that any tourists come to Borges, right? But they don't exactly come *to* Borges, they come *through* Borges—either from or on the way to buying turquoise and silver jewelry from real live Native Americans at the plaza in Santa Fe.

Or maybe they're not tourists. They're old enough to be retiring, so maybe they're here to buy some land near the river and build a fake adobe house and spend their golden years enjoying the dry air and the breathtaking desert sunsets. My dad always tells me not to complain because more money in town, no matter where it comes from, is good for business.

I come out of the kitchen in my uniform—black pants, white shirt, black vest—holding a tray with chips, salsa, and waters. "This is our *salsa especial*," I say as I place the bowl between them. "The recipe has been in *nuestra familia* for generations."

They raise their eyebrows, and I know I made the right choice. If you want to milk a tip from tourists, you have two options. One is to speak entirely in English, with no accent at all, so that you give them the impression that even though you're from this crappy small town, you're still educated and want to make something of yourself. The other option is to embrace the culture, the language, and the accent—to acknowledge that they're here for an experience—and then to lay that experience on thick.

The woman selects a chip from the basket and dips only the very tip into the salsa. "Is it hot?"

It's like ketchup, actually. We would never serve tourists the real family recipe; they'd moan and complain and ask for more water, which I would have to bring, and they wouldn't even be able to taste their food. So we have a special, more pussy version we keep on hand for older white people with fanny packs.

"For me? *Sí*, it is," I say. "But you can probably handle it."

The husband immediately grabs a chip and scoops up a tremendous mound of salsa. He puts the whole thing in his mouth and chews, slowly at first—pretending to savor the taste—but soon his jaws are in overdrive, like he can't wait to get the salsa out of his mouth. After he swallows, he downs half his water and wipes his lips with his napkin. His forehead is sweating. "Not too bad," he says.

It's like a spectator sport, I'm telling you. "I'll give you a minute to—"

"We don't look at menus," she says. "What are your specialties?"

"I'm a big fan of the carne adovada. That's slow-roasted pork," I say, shrugging apologetically to let them know that I'm sure they already know that. "The stuffed sopaipilla is *fantasticio*, and the chile relleno is a local favorite, too."

The woman fiddles with a huge silver ring. "I don't know, what do you think, hon?"

Lines streak across her husband's forehead, and he growls like a confused puppy. He must be thinking real hard. "Tacos," he says finally. "One chicken and one beef."

The wife squeals. "Ooh! That sounds perfect. I'll have the same."

Unbelievable. They come to a New Mexican family restaurant and order goddamn Taco Bell. "Red or green?" I ask.

"I'm sorry?" she says.

I smile warmly. "For your tacos, *Señora*. Red or green chile? It's the state question. Passed the legislature and everything." Usually this wraps up the tip. It makes people laugh. Makes them marvel about how screwed up this state must be if it has an official *pregunta*.

When they're finished with their lame-ass order, I take their menus and shuffle away. There's an open area with a counter between the kitchen and the restaurant so whoever's cooking can see the customers. Behind me, I hear the woman screech to her husband, "It's a family restaurant, Henry. This place is so *authentic!*"

I promise I won't spit in their food.

When I get back to my mom, her eyebrows pretty much jump off her forehead. "Tacos?" she whispers.

I nod. And shrug. I tried my best. Gave them our specialties, threw in an accent, even spoke Spanish. With people like that, there's nothing you can do.

"With green on the side?" My mom shakes her head sadly and motions for me to come back into the kitchen. *"Ayúdame con los tomates."*

Mom keeps her knives sharp as hell, and the last time I prepped the tomatoes I sliced the crap out of my finger. It's healed now, but I was hoping five stitches would get me out of ever doing it again.

I glance at my dad for some help, but he's too busy with his paperwork, so I join my mom in the kitchen, which is about the size of a Chevy Suburban. On the side facing the restaurant there's a deep fryer and an old six-burner gas stove, and most of the food is prepared on the black ceramic tile countertop next to the stove.

I grab a few tomatoes and position myself at the butcher's table in the center so I can keep an eye on the tourists. I'm still pissed I didn't get to finish my dinner, and Mom must see it in my face.

"You can finish your sopaipilla later," she says, dishing scoops of Spanish rice and black beans onto identical orange plates.

"That's okay," I say. "I was full anyway."

Right now I'm almost positive she's going to ask me how my day was. I'll tell her it was fine. Then she'll try again. I don't mind talking to her if we ever get a real conversation going, but I don't know how to start one, and I get the sense that she doesn't know either, so we end up trying to talk about the weather.

"Did you have fun with Zach?"

That was good. Specific. I can answer specific. "I guess. We worked on algebra."

She smiles and tosses a few grains of rice my way. I dodge them no problem.

"Seriously," I say, working hard to keep a straight face. "Or at least we thought about working on algebra."

"How's his mother?"

She asks this almost every day even though they hardly know each other. I'm not saying I want them to have sleepovers or anything, but Zach and I have been best friends for years, and I can count on one hand the number of times our moms have hung out. I don't know if it's because Mrs. Mason lets us blow stuff up, because she has a kid with one eye, or because my mom feels uncomfortable that Zach's dad walked out.

"Fine, I guess." I point my knife toward the customers, accidentally flinging a piece of diced tomato to the floor. "What do you think? Connecticut? California? Arizona?"

This was my favorite game when I was growing up. My dad is amazing at it, like those guys at the state fair who can guess your weight just by glancing at you. He's also good at inventing life stories for people—what they do for a living, how many kids they have, what their favorite movies are. It's how he used to keep me from shooting myself in the head from boredom.

Mom lays out two taco shells on each of the plates. "Do they have accents?"

"Not really. Maybe the woman."

"Well," she says, leaning forward on the counter, "they ordered tacos, so—"

"Right, that's probably the only Mexican food they ever heard of. That rules out Texas, Colorado, and Arizona. California, too."

"Okay, *y ¿qué más?*"

"Jewelry," I say. "The woman has, like, three silver bracelets and a couple silver rings."

"Any turquoise?"

"A little, but I don't think—"

Before I can finish, the front door swings open so hard that I almost drop the knife. The chimes rattle back and forth like there's an earthquake, and the tourists whip their heads around just in time to see my brother in the doorway. Right behind him is his *carnal*, his homeboy Cheo Moya. The two of them strut past the tourists and all the way through the restaurant by the time the door even closes. They shake hands with my dad and then bust into the kitchen.

"Stevie, *mijo*," my mom says. "You can't scare the customers like that."

"Sorry," he says like he doesn't mean it. "I thought we were closed."

Here's everything you need to know about my brother. He's a ridiculous striker, he does pretty well in school, and he's good looking—tall, black hair, blue eyes. Chicks think he's the best thing that ever happened to them. Oh, and from the minute he started high school, he's never worked a day at the restaurant.

He's always playing soccer or chilling with his boys or going out with chicks. He's never had to bus tables or refill water glasses or put little scoops of homemade salsa into tiny bowls and arrange baskets of freshly fried tortilla chips around them like damned flowers. He's never had to do any of that.

It's cool, though. I don't resent him or anything. Sure, it pisses me off from time to time, but I can't get too mad, because it makes perfect sense. If I could finish like him, my parents probably wouldn't make me work, either. It's not like you can get a college scholarship busing tables for seven dollars an hour.

"How was the game?" my mom says.

Steve comes around and kisses her on the top of her head. He has to lean down because she's almost a foot shorter. "Good," he says. "Cheo played like crap."

I look over at Cheo, but he just rolls his eyes and smiles. "*Órale*, Frankie," he says with a slight nod.

I nod back. "*Órale*."

He may be kind of wiry, but Cheo's one of the strongest *vatos* you're ever going to run across. He's not huge—he wants to keep his quicks—but he's ripped, thanks to a weight bench in the garage behind his house, where he and his boys just lift and work on his car all day long. He's got a thin goatee and a haircut that I could never pull off but looks badass on him—bottom half buzzed, top and sides slicked into a ponytail. Basically, Cheo could kick your ass and steal your girlfriend without breaking a sweat at either.

Like I said, he's awesome, but if there's one person in the world that it would be best to keep away from impressionable younger kids, Cheo's the guy. When I was ten, he taught me how to break into cars with a coat hanger.

He's been in and out of school for the past few years. Not much of a student, but not really a dropout either; he shows up just enough to move on. His two true loves are his mom and his ride, a '65 Impala he's been working on with money he makes washing dishes at Los Torres or fixing trannies at a gas station near his house.

"Tacos?" Steve says. "Who the hell ordered tacos?"

Mom shushes him and points to the customers.

"Frankie didn't tell them the specials?"

"What, are you the waiter police or something?" I say.

"Ooh, waiter police. Good one." Steve helps himself to an extra taco shell and loads it with ground beef. Then he comes around to my tomatoes, grabs a handful, and sprinkles them on top.

"Damn it, Steve."

"What? I'm hungry, even if they are just tacos." Steve laughs and offers a shell to Cheo. "Want one? Frankie has plenty of tomatoes."

"Shut *up*," I say under my breath.

"Francisco," my mom says. She nods at the tourists, but they're busy gazing out the window at the sunset.

"*Buenas tardes, Tía,*" Cheo says. He calls my mom his aunt even though they're not related. I tried that with Mrs. Mason once, but she just looked at me like I was crazy. "You need anybody to wash this week?"

"Any day you want, *mijo.* Just call first so I know you're coming."

Washing dishes in a restaurant is totally different from doing it at home. You have the high-powered nozzle, so you can spray the hell out of everything. Except sauce cups and ladles—you have to be a little more careful with those, or the water shoots back up in your face. When I was little, I washed dishes all the time, and I loved it. It was like this great accomplishment every time I finished. Now I'd rather talk to customers than get my hands all sliced up from grabbing knives, so I'm glad Cheo needs the work.

Dad comes in with his folder of papers and leans against the kitchen door. "Well done today, gentlemen."

"Thank you, sir," Cheo says.

"Eldorado is up next."

"*Claro que sí,*" Cheo says. "They're going down."

"That's the spirit."

Borges High plays on Saturday against the defending state champs. They're also undefeated. And it's another home game for us, so yeah, it's a big deal.

"You get a date for Homecoming yet, Frankie?" Cheo says.

Oh my God, that sucks. I don't even know what to say to him. "I was . . . I didn't get the chance."

"You better hurry, that's all I know," Steve says.

A painful silence seeps into the kitchen. I don't need his advice on my love life. Not in front of Cheo. Or my parents, for that matter.

Steve fixes himself another taco, but I shield my tomatoes with the blade of my knife, so he doesn't even try this time. "We have to go."

"Already?" Mom says. "Why don't you sit down and have a real dinner?"

"Sorry, *Mamá*. Team meeting." He hugs her, then pretends to punch me. Of course I flinch.

"You boys should stay for a bit," my dad says. "Spend some time with us."

"Not tonight." Steve pats my dad on the shoulder. "See you, Pop. Frankie, thanks for the tomatoes."

"I guess we'll see you on Saturday, Cheo?" my dad says.

Cheo responds with a little fist pump. "Go Panthers."

"Go Panthers!" my dad says with a fist pump of his own. Steve rolls his eyes in my direction.

This is ridiculous. Either my parents are stupid or clueless or just in denial, because no way in hell is there a team meeting tonight, not on a game day. I wonder what they would do if they knew that Steve didn't actually come home last night. Part of me wants to tell them that he and Cheo were out drinking on the mesa, or cruising with Flaco, or whatever it was. Maybe then they'd make him work for once.

"Laters, *ese*," Cheo says to me.

And just like that, they're gone. The door swings closed, and the three of us stand in the kitchen, waiting for something to happen. I chop the tomatoes into smaller pieces. My dad clears his throat. Finally, my mom brings the plates over and sprinkles tomatoes inside the tacos. Dad steps aside, then follows her into the restaurant.

When the tourists are done with their food, they pay with a credit card. I ask to see a driver's license.

The husband reaches into his fanny pack, obviously annoyed that I made him pull out his wallet again. "I've never had a restaurant ask me that before."

"I think it's nice," the wife says, smiling at me. "I wish more businesses were so vigilant."

My Spanish has worked her over like a shot of tequila, just like I told you it would. *"Gracias, Señora."*

He hands me the driver's license.

"You're from Texas?" I'm so surprised that I actually ask the question out loud.

I was way off. It's not just the jewelry or the lack of accent or the fact that they both ordered tacos. It's that they were so quiet eating dinner.

"Not originally," she says. "We just moved from Connecticut a year ago." She reaches across for her husband's hand. "Now we get to shop in Santa Fe any time we want."

Oh, goodie.

four

BORGES HIGH SCHOOL sucks ass. I'm sure other high schools do, too, but Borges has to suck more ass than most. Originally, there was an administration building, a gym, a cafeteria, one big building with a bunch of classrooms, and a large quad area in the center. The campus was probably nice back when only fifteen thousand people lived here.

But Borges grew and grew, mostly with native New Mexicans who couldn't afford to live in Santa Fe or Albuquerque anymore, and instead of building a new school somewhere else that would fit all of us, they just added trailers from time to time. Now, with the dead grass, dirt athletic fields, and all the temporaries, it looks more like a shantytown than a school.

It's a few miles from my house, so I catch a ride with Steve if I miss the bus or don't want to ride my bike for a half hour each way. Because his schedule is so busy, that usually means I take the bus home, but sometimes Zach's mom can drop me off. Yes, I'm sixteen, and yes, I have a driver's license, but no, I don't have a car. Not yet, at least. I'm doing my best to save my tip money, and my dad said he'd help me buy one when Steve goes to college.

Steve's car, by the way, is legendary. Remember when I said he was the only one in town who could get away with kicking Dalton's ass? Well, he's also the only dude in town who can get away with driving the piece of crap he drives. A 1971 Dodge Demon Sizzler, which wouldn't be too bad except for the fact that the last time anyone worked on the body or interior was probably 1971. My dad gave it to him expecting that Steve would want to fix it up, or that maybe they could do it together, but Steve thought it was cooler to keep it crappy. I would tell you what color it is, but I'm not even sure there's a name for it. One day he went to Cheo's house and decided he wanted the car to be red, so they gathered all the spray paint they could find. Some glossy, some matte, all different shades of red and maroon. Now the damn thing looks like a melted scoop of rainbow sherbet, or a used tampon, depending on how the light hits it. Steve just calls it the Sizzler.

The rims don't even match. I'd be laughed out of town if I drove this car, but because it's Steve, everyone's all, "Gosh, that Steve Towers sure is a quirky guy." Cheo busts his balls about it, but I think that makes Steve like the bucket even more.

This morning, the Sizzler rolls into the lot five minutes late, as usual. Steve puts it into park and takes a deep breath. "Dude, Frankie," he says. "I'm only going to tell you this one more time, and then I'm going to leave it alone."

Last week he yelled at me for a full five minutes about the importance of the push-up. The week before, he warned me to ditch the nervous laugh I sometimes use to fill up dead space in a conversation. Back in the day, we used to have playful arguments about cars and sports and model rockets.

Steve turns, putting his right arm around the seat behind me, and points at my chest. "You need to get your shit together, *ese*."

I snort. "That's easy for you to say."

Steve's burned through so many girlfriends that I don't even try to remember their names anymore. It's like chicks flock to him. Even crazy *cholas* like Carmenita, apparently.

"Hell yeah, it's easy for me to say. It's easy for everybody to *say*. The hard part is actually doing it. But you have to."

"Don't worry about it, okay? It doesn't matter."

"My ass, it doesn't. You got to be a man. If you don't do it now, then you won't do it the next time, or the time after that. And then what? Nobody wants to be a pussy."

So that's what this is about. I'm embarrassing him. "Did Cheo tell you that?"

His eyes go cold in an instant. "You think I need Cheo to tell me how to be a man?"

"You think I'm a pussy."

"I didn't say that. I said you better take care of business now so you don't turn into a pussy down the road."

"Thanks for the tip," I say, grabbing the handle and opening the door.

Steve reaches all the way across my body and pulls the door shut. We sit for a few seconds, breathing into each other's faces. He's got a look in his eye like he wants to drill me in the head, but then he leans back and that look goes away.

"*Órale*, Frankie." His voice is much softer now. "I want you to be happy and everything, but you need to earn respect."

I think about his late nights, about the lies to our parents, the cuts and bruises; he's just been earning respect. I want to ask him if he respects me, but I'm afraid of his answer, so I nod a little bit to let him know I hear what he's saying. Then I get the hell out of the car.

I've never gone to another high school, but I imagine this one is pretty typical. It was an open campus at lunch for the seniors until last year, when they busted too many people leaving to smoke weed and drink. Now it's totally different. Now if you want to smoke or drink, you have to stay at school. They let us eat lunch outside, though, so it's not too bad.

As Zach and I weave through the quad, we can pretty much check out the whole scene. Dudes chilling, chicks trying to make the dudes pay attention to them without being too obvious. I don't want to be stereotypical about it, but yes, the popular kids all hang out together—at a group of picnic tables near the gym—and yes, Dalton is right in the middle of them, sitting on the table in his letter jacket while everyone stares and drools and hangs on his every word.

"What up, bitches?" Begay says, swooping in and putting each of us in a headlock. "Guess who has a Homecoming date?"

"Not Frankie," Zach says.

Begay releases us and cocks his head at me. Black hair falls over his eyes, and dark freckles dot his massive cheekbones. "Still?"

I wave him off. "I'm working on it."

"Well, I already worked it," he says. "Mandy Newmark style."

If they gave an award for most school spirit, Mandy would definitely win it. She sells Borges Panthers visors and T-shirts at every sporting event, even JV volleyball. She's on student council, and she's also the sophomore class representative for the Homecoming committee.

"She's hot," Zach says. "But aren't you supposed to only go out with other Indians?"

"Good one, kemo sabe. Did you get that from the History Channel?"

We reach the shade of a dying cottonwood on the edge of the quad, and I toss my lunch bag to the ground. It's not like we're the most popular dudes in school, but we don't pick our asses all day in the library either. "Thanks for the M-80's," I tell Begay, desperate to talk about something else.

"You going to the mesa party this weekend?" Zach says.

"Hell no," Begay says, shaking his head. "I have to hit the Rez again. My uncle needs help moving."

Begay's uncle is like something out of a movie. He doesn't care *what* you think. He came into the restaurant once and spent the entire meal telling dirty jokes. People were moving to tables across the room, but my mom couldn't kick him out because she was laughing so hard.

"I'll check you guys later?" Begay says, holding out his fist. I pound it. "Laters."

Zach and I lean against the tree and open our lunches. "Relax," he says, reading my expression. "Dude, you're not a pussy, okay?"

"I never said I was."

"But your brother—"

"He said I was on the way to becoming a pussy. Not that I already am one."

"Well, whatever. You're not on the way to becoming one, then."

"Damn, *ese*," I say, glaring at him. "Why are we even talking about this?"

His voice rises in disbelief. "It was the first thing you said when I saw you this morning."

"That doesn't mean I wanted a freaking counseling session."

You know that feeling when you get in a fight with your best friend? You feel stupid about fighting in the first place because you're friends, but you would never admit it to his face.

So there's two ways out of it. Either you start talking about something else, or you go home and give it time to blow over. Nobody's going home, though, so that means one of us will have to change the subject.

"Damn," Zach says finally. He points to Cheo, who's chilling with the other *cholos* in the center of the quad. Half the dudes are in beaters and baggy jean shorts, and the other half bust khakis with long-sleeved flannels despite the heat. If I were Cheo, I wouldn't be able to take my eyes off the *cholas*—no matter how skanky they are, it's hard to ignore that much exposed skin. The news of the day is that Cheo was suspended one game for excessive school absences. It's pretty shocking. Not that he ditched so many classes, but that the administration actually decided to do something about it. Now he's basking in his outlaw glory.

Zach bites on a peach. "That dude's a badass."

"Yeah. He's going to show me how to airbrush my bike."

"Dude, I totally want to come. Will you ask him?"

I take a swig of Mountain Dew, the hundreds of tiny bubbles pounding sugar and caffeine into my tongue. I've known Cheo forever, and we work together a lot at Los Torres, but for some reason I always have this feeling in the back of my mind that he doesn't really want anything to do with me. It's like I'm not cool enough or hard enough, and it's only a matter of time before he realizes that and ignores me completely. "Sure," I say. "I'll ask. But no promises."

"Sweet," Zach says.

My brother comes out of one of the temporary class-rooms and heads straight for Cheo. When he gets there, the group parts like the freaking Red Sea. Last year, Steve mostly hung out with the other soccer players, but now he walks right through these *cholos* like he belongs. Dudes with their heads shaved, with big-ass goatees, dudes with bandannas and silver chain necklaces, and my brother. Steve drops his backpack, and he and Cheo stand there, both shaking their heads. Finally, they clasp hands and pull close, doing the armless hug. That chick Carmenita walks up behind my brother and puts her arms around his waist.

"What do you think it would take for me to get with one those hot *cholas*?" Zach says.

Dew shoots through my nose like fire, instantly causing my eyes to fill with tears, and I cough for a good minute before I can breathe normally again. I look at Zach.

"What?" he says, his face deadpan.

"You and the *cholas*? You don't think they'd tear your Wonder Bread ass apart?"

"I could be a 'grolo,'" he says. It's a word he made up, a combination of *gringo* and *cholo*, to describe white people who front like *vatos*. "You don't think I could change from Wonder Bread to Flour Tortilla?"

I close my eyes for a moment and imagine Zach with a goatee, bandanna, and a beater; then I bust out laughing again.

"Whatever," he says. "At least your brother gets to

experience the full range of what Borges has to offer before he goes off to college."

"I guess I don't really blame him," I say, even though it feels to me like what he's doing is more than that. Part of it is that Steve has always fit in everywhere, even when we were little. Everyone likes him; he'd be a great waiter, and he'd get mad tips. And then you see him in Cheo's world—blending in perfectly with all the *cholos*. I don't know how he does it. Of course, maybe the blending is what's making him get up in my face all the time.

"Hey, check it out," Zach says, motioning across the quad.

You know those movies where the hot chick has a couple friends who are almost as hot but not quite? They always walk in slow motion with the hottest one in the lead, like a squadron of attack planes in V-formation? Rebecca could make that happen if she wanted to. But she doesn't need that kind of attention, and Katie seems to want it, so Katie's the one in front. The other chick is Andromeda Escalante, but she's not even in Katie's league, no matter how many upperclassmen she's yanked off already.

The three of them settle down on a concrete bench next to a patch of sage bushes about thirty feet away from us. Even from this far away, I can see Rebecca's face light up when she talks. She looks like she just won the lottery or something.

"You should go talk to her," Zach says.

"I don't feel like it."

"What are you thinking right now?"

"That I don't want to go over there," I say with a nervous laugh.

"See what I'm saying!" Zach says, slamming the ground with his open palm. "For five seconds, you're not thinking about your brother. See, she's good for you."

"That doesn't make any sense."

"I know. You should talk to her anyway."

I nod and take a deep breath. "Okay, I'll be right back."

"Remember, chicks like it when you take it slow."

"How the hell would you know?"

The walk over to Rebecca is a lot easier this time than it was at the game. Maybe that's because I'm proving my brother wrong with every step I take. I'm no pussy. I get this image in my head of me at home, all old and weak with a stack of crumpled porn on the table next to my rocking chair, watching cartoons on TV and waiting for the phone to ring. I'm not going out like that. Oh, hell no.

I shove my hands into my pockets and nod with my chin. "What's up?"

"Hey, Frankie," she says, looking surprised. Katie and Andromeda exchange a glance.

And my mind goes blank. I toe at the ground. "Um, you going to the game tomorrow?" I finally say. Yeah, yeah, it sucked, but at least I said something.

Andromeda laughs. Her ears are pierced like a couple of pincushions, and she's got these massive bangs like a wall straight up from her forehead. She could also lay off the flan, if you know what I'm saying. There's something about the way her eyes narrow at me, like I'm not worthy of seeing her entire pupils. I don't know why Rebecca hangs out with her.

"I'll see you there, right?" Rebecca says.

I blink a little longer than I probably need to. "Yeah . . ."

"Are you okay?"

"Yeah, *claro*. I was just wondering . . ." I'm ninety-five years old and I've only gone out with my hand. "Can I talk to you for a second?"

Before the words are even out of my mouth, I can sense it's a mistake. Her eyes fall, and she swallows and bites the inside of her bottom lip. Then her smile tightens—it's not even a smile anymore. More like she's bracing for a tetanus shot. Holy shit, I know what that means. Abort! Abort! Abort!

I try to slam on the brakes, but for the first time in my life, I can't stop talking. It's like that old man with the porn is pushing me along, and since he's deaf, he can't hear me screaming at him.

"Yesterday you said you didn't have a date to Homecoming?" I say.

About three years ago, my brother dared me to steal a two-liter bottle of Coke from one of the grocery stores. He said nobody had ever done it, and that I would be a legend if I pulled it off. The whole time, it felt like everyone was watching me, judging me. I knew it was wrong, but Steve was waiting for me. And when I came out with the Coke in my soccer bag, we ran around back and drank the whole thing together. He was proud of me. That's the part I always remember the most.

Maybe it's that feeling that makes me power through this time. Right off the damn cliff. "I thought we could go together?"

A lot of things happen right now. Andromeda and Katie actually turn away. Rebecca crosses her arms and takes a deep breath. She's talking—I can see her lips move—but my mind won't let me hear the words. She has this look of extraordinary pity on her face, and I actually hate her for it. Or maybe I hate myself for it, for the fact that I can make someone feel that way about me.

". . . asked me after the game yesterday."

I can't feel my body anymore. I want to get away from here so desperately that my soul is trying to leave. It's almost like I can see this whole thing from above—me stunned and immobile, Rebecca stepping slightly closer, Andromeda and Katie pretending not to listen.

"Frankie, are you okay?" Rebecca says. Her eyes, those deep blue eyes, stare me in the face, taunting me.

"Huh?" It's all I can do to meet her gaze. "Oh, yeah. Sorry. I was just thinking about something else. I have to work tonight, and—"

"I'm really sorry."

"Yeah, no problem. Cool. I mean. He's a good guy." Okay, so that's not even close to the truth.

"I hope we can still be friends."

"Totally," I say. "It's no big deal."

She cocks her head to the side, and I can't tell if she sees right through me or if she's disappointed that I'm not taking it harder. I see her blink. Her pupils adjust to the desert sunlight. A strand of black hair tumbles from behind her ear and bisects her flawless eyebrow.

I wish I could stop this from happening. I wish I could say something spectacular that would make her see what she's missing, that would make her change her mind. If I had any guts at all, I would wipe the smile off my face and tell her what I really think.

"Okay," she says.

I keep smiling. "See you at the game, I guess."

She nods one last time, then smiles and spins away. Katie and Andromeda turn to her as she resumes her place on the bench. The moment is gone, and I stagger back across the quad, speechless, breathless, and wondering what the hell just happened.

Zach is waiting for me, but he knows better than to ask. He can probably guess, anyway. I lean against the tree and slide down, scratching the hell out of my back. I don't really mind, though. At least I can feel my body again.

"Dalton," I say once I remember how to use my voice.

Zach winces. "When? Yesterday? After the game?"

"Can you believe this? I was there. I had it."

He shakes his head slowly. "I knew you had to get on that."

"Oh, you think?" It's like someone telling you to be careful *after* you trip. Yeah, real helpful, *pendejo.*

"Damn. Don't get all wounded."

"How am I not going to get all wounded?" Seriously, it's like I just had my nuts cut off. And thanks to Andromeda's big mouth, everyone's going to know all about it by the time school's over.

"Easy, bro. We'll figure something out."

"I don't want to figure something out."

Zach raises his voice for the first time. "Then invent a time machine. I don't know what else to tell you."

Suddenly, we're interrupted by the worst sound I could imagine. "Damn, it's like a fag fight," Dalton says, strutting by in his letter jacket. "You bitches sound like my parents."

It's so horrible that I throw up a little in my mouth. He just appeared out of nowhere, like a rattlesnake coiled up behind the tree, waiting for the perfect moment to strike. He was always full of himself, but when he got his letter jacket last year, his apelike wobble increased by at least two inches.

"What's up, Frankie-Spankie?"

I don't have the strength to do anything but lean my head against the tree and wait for him to lose interest in me.

"Hey, Cyclops," he says, turning his venom to Zach. "Here's a joke for you. What do you and my johnson have in common? You both have blond hair and one eye."

Unfazed, Zach smiles all pretty. "True, but I don't smell like your mom's ass."

Dalton flips him the bird. "How many fingers am I holding up?"

"I have an idea," Zach says. He takes out his eye and offers it. "How about you suck on this?"

"That's so nasty," Dalton says. Then he winks at me and cracks a little grin of his own. "So, Frankie-Spankie, you got a Homecoming date yet?"

I shouldn't even register on his radar, but he's such a *chingón*, he can't resist. I want to tell him to shove Homecoming up his ass. Or that I'm going to Frankie-spank that smile off his face. Instead, I just mumble, "Maybe."

"Huh?" Dalton says, cupping his hand to his ear. "I didn't catch that."

"He said your letter jacket smells like somebody wiped their balls with it," Zach says, coming to my defense. He pops his eye back into the socket and pinches his nose. "Damn, dude. Don't you ever take that thing off? Even *I* can see the sweat rings, and I'm half blind."

It's not true, of course. Dalton's jacket is immaculate as always: dark green with white leather sleeves. But he sniffs under his arms anyway, and whatever smell he finds there seems to cause him enough worry that he turns around and leaves us alone.

He walks toward Rebecca, and she sits up straight, chest out. But he's too into himself to notice anybody else right now, and he struts on by as though he's the only human being on the planet. Rebecca starts to give him a wave, but when it becomes clear that he doesn't see her, she converts the maneuver into a hair twirl and turns back to her friends. She laughs as if to excuse him, but her eyes aren't in it.

I shake my head. "What an asshole."

"Why didn't you say anything?"

"What's the point?" I say, but I'm asking myself the same question inside.

"God, don't be so Special Needs," Zach says, exasperated. "The *point* is to shove his stupid jock face in your verbal doodie."

I laugh. "My verbal doodie is constipated."

"Then we need to get you some Pepto or something."

Mr. Costas, our math teacher, spots us from across the quad and makes his way over. His entire wardrobe consists of nothing but khaki pants and short-sleeved collar shirts, all of which are some version of plaid. Not only that, but he has goofy-looking long brown hair that he keeps in a ridiculous ponytail. For years, students have been begging him to cut it off, but he just says that he wouldn't have the strength to deal with us punks without his flowing locks.

"Dude, I have to go," Zach says, gathering up his lunch and jumping to his feet.

"What the hell?"

"Mr. C.," Zach says. "I think he wants me to make up a quiz."

And he's gone—sprinting across the quad with his face shielded from our math teacher—before I can even answer. He passes Rebecca, who has recovered nicely. She's in the middle of a story, waving her arms above her head and laughing. Probably about me.

I'm pretty much trapped. Here comes another conversation with Mr. C. where he'll get in my face about making smart choices, and acting on my integrity, and shit like that. He likes to have meaningful conversations with his students, like he thinks he's in some movie of the week about a teacher who truly makes a difference. I could get out of it, I guess, if I go beg Rebecca to diss me again.

five

I'VE NEVER BEEN as happy to ride in the Sizzler as I am now. After what happened yesterday, my brother had to convince me to go out tonight, and I'm glad I listened. We're cruising toward the setting sun, with the windows down and old-school Delinquent Habits cranked high on the stereo. The one thing Steve spent money on is the system, so at least the bass is deep and the speakers don't rattle.

Zach and I exchange glances and a smile. We're on our way to the first mesa party of the year—our first mesa party ever. There's a sensation deep in the center of my stomach that I don't think I've ever felt before. It's like a combination of nervousness and excitement and happiness and fear. This is it.

Everyone's going to be here, and I have no idea what to expect. It feels like anything could happen tonight.

Calle Andrés becomes a dirt road a few miles west of Borges. The dust makes it hard to see the taillights of the truck in front of us as we snake up through the mesa for another twenty minutes. When we pull to a stop, shards of broken green and brown glass sparkle in the headlights like miniature constellations.

The moon is already out, almost full and casting huge shadows beneath the piñon trees. We walk up a dirt path toward an eroded drainage ditch, passing through little groups of people, all upperclassmen. Steve is totally at home here. He's like the conquering general returning to the home front. Eyes go wide in recognition, and then people either try to mask it, or they nod, or they turn away.

"Nice game," they say. "Sweet penalty."

He scored twice against Eldorado today, the last one on a penalty with less than five minutes left. The game was intense, but we won 3–2. "I should have had the hat trick," Steve says with a shrug.

The crowd gets thicker, and we lose my brother. Zach and I hang back. It's almost as loud here as it was in the car—everybody talking at the same time, flush with the sense of victory. I look down and notice that we're right in the center of a wash. "You know, this is the exact worst place to be in a flash flood," I yell to Zach.

"Huh?" he says.

What the hell am I talking about? Flash flood? Am I the biggest dork ever? "Never mind."

There are a few other sophomores here, but it's mostly juniors and seniors. Everyone seems to have people they're with, or some group they belong to. Even the dudes from the Science Olympiad—laughing and smoking around a case of hard cider—look a lot more comfortable than I feel.

"This is pretty sweet, huh?" I say.

"Yeah," Zach says, but I don't think he heard me. His head's on a swivel, just like mine.

"*Órale*, Frankie!"

I turn around just in time to see a can of Coors headed straight for my face. Luckily, I manage to knock it down with my hand. I don't want it to bust open on a rock, of course, and embarrass my brother in front of the whole school, so I kick my right toe out and stop the can from hitting the ground too hard.

"*Pelé!*" my brother says. He slides up to Zach and hands him another can. "You guys having fun?"

"Definitely," Zach says. He cracks open his beer, spraying tiny comets of white foam all over the ground. My own beer erupts when I open it, and I don't want to be seen wasting a drop, so I shove my face onto the can until it stops frothing.

"That's what I'm talking about!" Steve says, laughing.

He pulls his arm around my neck and gives it just enough of a squeeze that I cough a little. We've never really done this before—hung out like this. I'm always the little brother, the pain in the ass, begging for his attention. He's always annoyed with me, avoiding me, barely tolerating me. But not tonight. Tonight, we're almost equals, chilling on the mesa, having a beer together.

"Esteban Torres," comes a familiar voice behind us. *"¿Qué te pasa, chingón?"*

"Cheo," my brother says, raising his beer.

"Órale, vato," Cheo says, "where'd you get that?"

"Over there." Steve nods toward the massive crowd next to a gnarled piñon. "Have this one." He pulls another can from his back pocket.

"What's up, Cheo?" I say, all calm.

"Órale, Frankie." Cheo extends a fist, and I pound it. *"Oye,* your brother told me what happened with that chick Rebecca. That *pinche* Dalton was running his mouth about it all practice, *ese."*

Great. Whatever self-confidence I had a second ago just evaporated. I stare at my brother, who shrugs. He takes a sip of his beer while I try to come up with something to say.

"I was going t—"

"She should go with you, *carnal,"* Cheo says, stepping closer and clapping a rock-solid hand on my shoulder.

It feels like my mouth is full of sand. I take a sip of my beer, but I tilt too fast, and it gets all fizzy and goes down the wrong pipe. It takes everything I have to keep from coughing, but even though I manage not to spit it back up all over everyone, my eyes start to water. They probably think I'm crying.

Cheo turns from me and looks over at Zach. I know they've seen each other around, but I'm not sure if Cheo even knows his name. It feels like that should change, now that we're hanging out at the same party and everything. I think about introducing him, but I might burp.

"You're that dude with one eye, right?" Cheo says.

Zach nods, getting quiet all of the sudden. Maybe he isn't as sure of himself as I thought. He's got this reservoir of self-confidence, and it's deep enough for him to pretend not to care about what most people think, but I guess Zach's tank isn't big enough for Cheo.

"Shit, you really got a glass eye?" Cheo says. "I can't even hardly tell."

Zach nods again. He points to his left eye.

"I heard someone shot you in the face."

Zach clears his throat. "It was a knife."

"Damn." Cheo frowns in appreciation. "In the eye. That shit must have stung."

"This is Zach," I finally say.

But it's too late. Cheo has already turned back to Steve. "How you gonna make me ask?" he says.

My brother smiles and unbuttons his shirt. He pulls down one of the sleeves to reveal a large bandage on his left shoulder. Zach looks at me, but I shake my head. I have no idea what's going on.

Cheo scoffs. "You needed first aid?"

"Flaco said it would heal faster."

"He go with you?" For an instant, I think I see irritation flash across Cheo's face, but then he shakes it off, and when it's gone, he laughs again. "I bet you cried like a little *puta*."

Steve takes a swig of his beer and flips Cheo off with the same hand. Then he reaches over and peels away one side of the Band-Aid. Underneath is a tattoo. It's about two inches, a red zia, like on the New Mexican flag, but the circle inside is a soccer ball. Above the zia, written in script: *El Matador*.

I don't mean to say it, but I can't help it. It just pops out. "Mom's going to freak."

Cheo glances over at me and raises his eyebrows. He grins at Steve and whistles through his teeth. "Yeah, bro. You better watch out for Moms."

This is exactly what I was trying not to do tonight. I should tape my mouth shut from now on. Steve already thinks I'm a pussy, and now Cheo thinks I'm a momma's boy. "I just meant—"

"*Tranquilo*, Francisco," my brother says. "I can handle it." He replaces the Band-Aid and buttons up his shirt.

Suddenly Carmenita comes up from behind, reaches between my brother's legs, and grabs his package. He jumps in surprise, and when he drops his beer on the ground, she squeals in delight and comes around to the front, as though none of us are even here, and kisses him hard. She puts his hand on her ass. The whole thing lasts way too long. Cheo nods to Carmenita's friends before heading off toward the beer.

Zach and I look at each other, and he gestures for us to

get the hell away from there. "Laters, Steve," I say as we back away. There is no response.

"Damn," Zach says. "Did you see that? She just flat out grabbed his junk!"

"If you were really a 'grolo,' the Flour Tortilla would have put a move on her friends."

I glance around, scanning the crowd for friendly faces but not finding many. Over by a cluster of sage bushes, a bunch of people are buying hits of nitrous from Willy Stinchcomb. I know Dalton's going to be here. He played like crap again today—his man burned his ass all day long and scored both of Eldorado's goals—but he'll still show. I don't know about Rebecca, though. My guess is that she'll come. Hot chicks are welcome anywhere.

I'm glad to have a beer in my hand, and not because I want to get drunk. I don't even like the taste that much, but if I didn't have anything in my hands, I'd have to jam them in my pockets, or cross my arms, or pick my ass.

Zach has a little smile on his face. "Cheo knew who I was."

"Name another one-eyed loser in Borges." I laugh, maybe a little exaggerated because I feel the need to show everybody I'm having a good time. "You want to go up to the house?"

Zach nods, so we follow a dirt trail up through one of the drainage washes. It snakes around a little collection of yucca plants—our state flower, by the way. Other states have roses and columbines and daisies; we have clusters of pale green daggers.

"*Matador* means *killer*, right?" he says. Soon, the trail becomes a stone path about four feet wide. The shards of glass on the ground are more plentiful here, and they glow under the moonlight.

"Yeah," I say. "It's Steve's soccer nickname."

Up ahead, a stone wall about three feet high encircles a small abandoned house. Sage and piñon and different types of cactus jockey for space inside the patio wall. The house itself is solidly built, but the roof is just a skeleton. Nobody knows how long it's been here. There's no plumbing, no sink, no floors. It's all dirt inside. The walls are about a foot thick, made of the same stone as the small patio wall. There's no insulation or drywall or fixtures. Electricity was never even an option. There are no windows, no doors. It's basically a shell.

Moonbeams pierce the roof. Some rooms are full of people hanging out. Others are a little more vacant, with a few couples hooking up in the corners. Zach and I creep through the house to the far end, where the stench of piss is so strong that it makes me want to throw up.

"You waiting for the bathroom, bro?" someone says behind me. It's Will Burrage, one of Dalton's friends, and he's wasted.

"Huh?"

"Let me cut, okay?" He pushes past us and stumbles into the nasty room. He faces a corner and takes a leak right there. He has the entire mesa to piss on, and he does it inside?

Zach and I get away from the "bathroom" as fast as we can. I slide through a crowd at the opposite end of the house, and suddenly—surprise!—I'm face-to-face with Rebecca. I don't see Dalton anywhere, but Andromeda and Katie, as always, are right by her side.

My next move is critical. I told Rebecca we could definitely be just friends, but now I have to prove it. I feel like everything in the entire room slows down in anticipation of me opening my mouth for the first time.

"What's up?" I say. I consider it a major victory that I didn't crap myself.

"Hey, Frankie," she says. She looks at the beer in my hand, and when her eyes are back at mine, they're a little wider. Maybe she's impressed.

"Hey, Rebecca," Zach says behind me. He waves like a dork. "Hey, Andromeda. Hi, Katie."

Andromeda puts one hand on her hip and uses the nail of her other index finger to scratch the corner of her mouth. Her fingernails are so long that they curve like talons. She's sizing me up, and given that she was three feet away yesterday when I had my manhood handed to me, I can only imagine what a *maricón* she must think I am. I take another swig of beer to wash her attitude away.

She turns to Zach and shows her teeth. "You got a date to Homecoming yet, Cyclops?"

Rebecca glances away. "Andromeda," she says under her breath.

"What?" she says, plucking something off the shoulder of her skanky see-through shirt.

"Why, you want to go with me?" Zach says, taking Rebecca off the hook. "A little beauty and the beast action?"

That was a good one. I think everyone here knows who the beast would be.

Andromeda narrows her eyes. "I got a date."

"I bet you got twenty," Zach says. He nods, pretending to recognize someone behind the girls.

You may think he's handling it pretty well, but I can tell he's upset. He gets this twitch on the eyelid of his good eye when he's pissed at me and wants to kick my ass, and right now that eyelid's twitching like a bitch. I should stand up for him, but I don't know what to say.

Maybe I should change the subject. "Did you guys see the game?"

I know Rebecca did; I saw her there. I want to make a joke about how bad Dalton got burned today, something with white toast in it, but I can't think of anything that won't make me sound jealous.

"Your brother played great," Rebecca says.

The lights of Borges twinkle in the distance through the window behind her. I wish I could get her out here alone sometime. The stars, the lights, the moonlit mesa. Then we could actually have a freaking conversation, like normal people, without having to worry about what everyone else thinks of us.

"Frankie?" she says.

"Huh?" It would be bad form for me to look anywhere but her eyes, but I can tell that she's wearing jeans and a tight black T-shirt. It's like she's *trying* to get me to look down.

"Are you okay? You were totally zoned out."

For some reason, Zach seems to have dematerialized, and Andromeda and Katie are in the other corner, draped all over a couple senior guys. I'm alone with her. It's exactly what I wanted, so why do I feel trapped? I have to make this work.

"So . . ." I smile and look around again. Zach is definitely gone. Acting normal is torture.

She squints a little, like she's in pain. "Sorry again about Homecoming," she says.

Now is the perfect time for me to show her what she's missing by going with Dalton. We're talking; there's nobody else around. Maybe Cheo was right. Maybe I need to tell her that she doesn't really want to go with him, that I'm the one she should be with.

I open my mouth to tell her exactly how I feel, and this is what comes out: "Dude, Rebecca, it's totally cool. Seriously."

Huh? Totally cool? Seriously?

"I just don't want things to get all weird between us."

"What," I say with a chuckle, "like after the Loma Vieja pool?"

After a split second of confusion, her face goes white. She blinks a few times in stunned disbelief. I just fucked up big-time.

The Loma Vieja pool is where most kids in Borges learned to swim. One year, when I was about five, the pool was closed for over two weeks because of rain. When we finally showed up to swim, we saw a crowd of people standing around the pool, just staring at the water.

There must have been hundreds of tiny frogs—thousands of them. Hopping on the concrete, jumping in and out of the bushes, diving into the murky water. Most of the girls were squealing; the adults stood around with their hands on their hips trying to decide how to clean up the mess. Because swimming was definitely out of the question, a few of the older kids got out a soccer ball and played barefoot in the dirt parking lot. Others were called to help their parents with the cleanup: holding trash bags, scraping frogs off the plastic mesh of the leaf skimmer, or unclogging the pool vacuum.

Somehow I found myself behind the pool house with a group of kids my own age. There were probably about seven of us, and though I don't remember everyone, I know one of the girls was Rebecca. We all took off our clothes. We looked and pointed but didn't touch. I think the whole thing lasted only five minutes.

I've never mentioned this to anybody, not even my brother, and the fact that I do so now, in the middle of my first mesa party, is worse than humiliating. Rebecca has this strange look on her face, like she's trying to figure out if I really said what I just said, or if it was all just a bad dream.

"I can't believe you just brought that up," she says, more to herself than to me.

"Yeah," I manage. I take a long swig of my beer. Maybe that will cool my cheeks down. "Me neither."

She looks around, but now her friends are gone, too. There's nowhere for her to go.

I want to talk about something else, something less painful, like the Holocaust or something. "Does your dad know about this place?"

"My dad?"

Like I said before, he's the chief of police, and I really am curious about whether he knows about the mesa. But it occurs to me, too late, that mentioning her father at an illegal party probably isn't the smoothest thing to do. "Never mind."

"Are you trying to check off the most awkward things you can think of?"

"How am I doing?"

She smiles, and it's a real, genuine smile. "Pretty good. Now you just have to ask if I'm pregnant."

I stare at her.

"God, Frankie," she says, slapping my shoulder. "I'm not."

"What? I didn't think you were."

"You are *such* a bad liar."

"Okay, so maybe I thought that was going to be your way of telling me—"

"Jesus, Frankie."

We're both laughing now. This is how it could be. Whenever she laughs hard, she gets a dimple on her left cheek. Not a huge one, and it only happens when she's really laughing, like now. She turns away and tucks some hair behind her ear, then glances back at me, all coy. She thinks I'm hilarious. I love this.

"I figured maybe that's why you'd rather go with Dalton," I say. "Maybe he's your baby's daddy."

She stops laughing. The smile is still on her face, but it's gone from her eyes. She looks at me with a hint of pity. Like I'm a three-legged dog. "I thought you said we could still be friends."

"Dude, Rebecca," I say, "I was totally kidding."

"If you're really mad about it, you should just tell me instead of making jokes like that. It's so, like, passive aggressive."

"I thought we were . . . laughing." I sound pathetic, I know, trying to explain everything to her. Steve was right about me.

Suddenly, Zach busts into the house. "Frankie, you have to get out here."

"What's wrong?"

"Just follow me. It's your brother." He glances at Rebecca. "And Dalton."

We jostle our way out of the house and follow Zach down the path to the drainage gulch. A small crowd has gathered, and from our position overlooking the gulch, I can see Steve and Dalton in the middle, standing chest to chest, right up in each other's faces. Headlights pierce the branches of a juniper tree, sending bony shadows across the makeshift ring.

As we scramble down the path, Zach explains what happened. Steve busted Dalton's balls about his weak defensive skills, and Dalton responded by calling Steve a "pussy wetback bitch" and offering our mother a job scrubbing dishes at the Tortilla Emporium. What a fucker.

I look behind me, but unfortunately Rebecca is too far away to hear—her flimsy sandals don't do well on the rocky path.

Zach and I reach the crowd and push our way through to the front. Part of me wants to see them throw down. It would be a pretty fair fight—my brother is quicker and tougher, but Dalton is probably a little stronger.

Rebecca comes up behind me and puts her hand on my shoulder. "Frankie, do something."

"Like what?" If I tried to do anything to stop this, Steve might beat me down, too.

"He's your brother. Can't you talk to him? Get him to back down or something."

If there's one thing I know, it's that Steve is not going to back down. It doesn't matter who I am. And after what Dalton said, I'm not sure I blame him.

Cheo stands—calm as hell—across the circle next to a couple of Dalton's friends. His lips move as he holds his arms out to keep them from jumping in. They're staring at Dalton and my brother, but they're not going anywhere, with Cheo where he is. I can't find Carmenita and the other *cholas*; they must have taken off already.

Dalton glances over and makes eye contact with Rebecca.

Then he looks back at my brother and pushes him in the chest with both hands. My brother takes a step back, but he's got good balance so he's able to absorb most of Dalton's weak-ass push.

There's a little shoving at the edge of the circle over to my left, and then that dude Burrage, from the "bathroom," explodes into the open space. He lowers his shoulder and heads for my brother's blind side.

And now it's like things go in slow motion. The wind rustles the juniper tree. I see a tiny dust devil at Steve's feet. The blood gushes through my veins. I can feel my pulse in the tips of my fingers. I know exactly what I have to do. Cheo can't make it there fast enough—besides, he's too busy with the other dudes.

I feel the pebbles crunching under the soles of my shoes as I push off.

Rebecca's voice rings out. "Frankie, no!"

Burrage doesn't see me coming, so I manage to wrap my arms around his waist and divert him from my brother. I've got the element of surprise on my side, but that's where my advantage ends. He recovers in no time and knocks me back. I stumble and fall onto a small yucca plant. The spines shoot up like needles, right into my side. I scream in pain and jump up, but suddenly I'm surrounded by chaos. Jostling, pushing, yelling.

The circle collapses on us. Cheo grabs my brother's arms and holds him back. Dalton's friends hold Dalton back, and

I'm in the middle of this whole thing. Someone is in front of me, but it's not like I'm trying to get away. I'm just thankful I don't have to get my ass pummeled by Will Burrage.

"Fuck you, Towers," Dalton shouts.

"Oh, you don't want to fuck with me," Steve says. "Me and my boys will rip your heart out."

Cheo throws a glance my way as my brother wrestles his arms free. "Easy, *compadre.*"

Dalton scoffs. "You think you're so bad?"

"I'm right here. You can bring it any time." Steve points at him, and spittle flies from his mouth.

"*Cálmate,*" Cheo says, pulling my brother back farther.

Dalton's friends lead him away. "This is bullshit," Dalton says. He stomps a dying juniper branch and snaps it clean.

People mill around for a while, talking about how crazy that was and how they wish the fight hadn't been broken up. Things are tense, but the dust settles eventually, as it usually does after a scuffle. Tempers cool just enough for everyone to go their separate ways. Dalton bitches to his friends about what an asshole my brother is, my brother does the same about Dalton, and Rebecca disappears.

When it's time to go home, Zach and I pace in front of the Sizzler. My blood feels like it's made of lighter fluid. My fingers are still shaking, and my breath comes in short spurts unless I concentrate on breathing deeply. I'm halfway through another beer, but I'm hardly aware of drinking it. My mind is all over the place. That was the closest I've ever come to being in a real fight, and it was actually kind of fun—once it became clear that I wasn't going to die.

Cheo comes up and puts his arm around my neck. "*Órale*, Frankie," he says, "since when do you got those quicks?"

My brother laughs. "Like a missile, bro. Burrage didn't even know what hit him."

"You got to work on your second move, though," Cheo says.

I shrug. "Must have tripped."

"Right onto a yucca," Zach says.

"That shit hurts." I lift up my shirt and try to see my back. "Dude, Zach, am I bleeding?"

"Shh," Steve says. "Check it out."

Rebecca walks slowly toward us, alone. I quickly pull my shirt back down. Cheo and Steve lean against the Sizzler, watching.

"Hey, Frankie." She comes to about three feet from me and stops. She raises her eyebrows. "You okay?"

Hell yes, I'm okay. I'm fantastic. I had my brother's back. And I didn't even get my ass kicked. "Yeah," I say. "Fine."

There is a long pause. I don't know what to say, and if I've proven anything tonight, it's that I should keep my mouth shut.

"I just wanted to make sure." Rebecca nibbles on her bottom lip. "Because it was me who asked you to do something and all."

"Cool," I say. "Thanks."

"Okay," she says. "See you on Monday?"

I nod. "Definitely."

As soon as Rebecca is out of earshot, my brother and Cheo double over laughing. "That's the way you work, player," my brother says.

Cheo leans back and nods. "Definitely." They both laugh again.

Zach smiles. We pound fists. "Damn. That's all I have to say, Frankie. Damn."

I could get used to this feeling.

six

THE VINYL SEATS of my *mama's* truck are peeling enough to expose the foam cushion and the springs beneath it. The dashboard surrendered to the sun a long time ago, and now it's cracked and misshapen. The truck used to be light blue, but now the right front fender is black, and the hood is orange. Wire and chipped yellow plywood replaced the rear gate a year ago. Basically, it looks like something I could have thrown together from a handful of mismatched Lego sets. Normally, the thought of being seen in my mom's piece of crap is enough to get me out of bed in time for the bus, but I was a little distracted this morning.

By now, I'm sure everybody knows what happened at the

mesa on Saturday, but I don't really know what to expect. It's not like I went on the offensive against Burrage—I had my brother's back, that's all. Maybe now that's what people are going to think about when they see me, and not that some *pinche* tortilla millionaire stole my date right out from under me.

I'm halfway out the door when my mom lays a hand on my back. *"¿Cómo estás?"*

"Good, *Mamá*. Ready to learn." I wonder if she knows what the smile on my face means.

"Do you have a date for Homecoming yet, *mijito?*" she says.

How am I supposed to respond to that? If I tell her the truth, she'll try to set me up with some random daughter of one of her friends. I could thank her for her concern, but then she'll see that I don't want her help. I could even tell her all about that look Rebecca gave me after the fight at the mesa party, but she'll just ground my sorry ass.

"I won't miss the bus on the way home," I say instead, and climb out of the truck.

Her hand goes back to the wheel, and I ease the door shut behind me. The truck lurches forward—she forgot to take it out of second gear again—before it gains momentum and rolls through the parking lot and out onto the street.

Zach's waiting for me at my locker, wearing an absurdly clean and wrinkle-free blue shirt. "How's that bus working out for you?" he says.

"Where the hell was my wake-up call, smart-ass?"

"At least you got dressed up."

And suddenly I understand why his shirt has a collar. I look at my own white T-shirt and shake my head. "It's picture day, isn't it?"

"We have a winner!" he says, throwing his arms in the air like I just scored a touchdown.

"Freaks." The sneering voice belongs to one of the kids across the hall in the doorway to Mr. Morrill's room—either Jeffrey Johnson or Rubén Gutierrez, my best friends through fourth grade. For the first few years of elementary school, the three of us were inseparable, but we had a little falling-out when I kicked Rubén's ass during recess. A new kid had transferred from a school in Albuquerque, and everyone was giving him a hard time. Rubén and Jeffrey dished it out more than anyone. Once people found out that the new kid had a glass eye, Rubén kicked his taunting into overdrive.

That's when the new kid became "Cyclops." Rubén covered his eye whenever the Cyclops was nearby, saluting him with cries of "Ahoy, matey!" He perfected a maneuver he called "the blind mummy," which was basically him staggering like a drunk, his arms outstretched, groping clumsily around with one eye winked.

The day Naranja Elementary competed in the Junior Ironkid Triathlon, every student was on the playground, moving through the stations: the shuttle run, the half-mile, the cone slalom. Suddenly Rubén, with the loyal Jeffrey Johnson at his side, dropped to his hands and knees, screaming, "I lost a contact! I lost a contact!" The playground quieted down as everyone turned to see what the commotion was all about. "I can't see! I lost a contact! Wait, wait . . ." Then he stood up and shouted. "I lost my EYE!"

Most of the kids laughed a little bit, but for some reason I walked over and punched Rubén in the stomach as hard as I could. I can't remember why. Maybe I just wanted him to shut up; I don't think it was out of any sense of moral obligation to the new kid. I served a week's suspension, returned to the fourth grade as an outcast, and Zach and I became inseparable. It didn't earn me any respect, but at least I got a best friend out of it.

Now, as they've done since the fourth grade, Jeffrey and Rubén smirk, as if to convince me what a bad choice I made. And, as I've done since the fourth grade, I smirk back. As if to remind them that Rubén fell to the ground like a little *puta*. They shake their heads and continue into Mr. Morrill's room for first period history.

"Dude," Zach says as I slam my locker shut, "that was the best mesa party ever. Everybody says so. I still can't believe what you did."

"Not to bring you down," I say, "but how come you didn't jump in with me? That fight goes five seconds longer, and Burrage kicks my ass."

"My eye, bro."

"Your eye."

"Seriously, once you left my blind spot, you were already halfway there," he says with a shrug. "There was nothing I could do."

"Right."

Zach smiles and elbows my shoulder. "I'll get your back next time, though."

"Next time, my ass." The bell rings, and I sling my backpack over my shoulder. "Won't be a next time."

No sooner are the words out of my mouth than John-freaking-Dalton rounds the corner. "Cyclops," he says as he struts by. "Spankie."

Zach shakes his head, and I know what he's thinking.

I'm sick and tired of just thinking it, though. My heart quickens a bit, and I narrow my eyes. "I got your Spankie right here, you *pinche güero.*"

Dalton whirls around and steps to me with a look of complete shock. "What did you say?"

I glance over at Zach, whose expression tells me he's wondering the same thing, considering this is my first time actually standing up for myself. Maybe it's the leftover adrenaline from what happened this weekend. It feels good to be crazy sometimes. I move closer to Dalton so that we're less than a foot away from each other. At this distance, I have to look up at him. He could kick my ass in his sleep. "What, are you stupid *and* deaf? I said any time you want a little Spankie, feel free to come and get it."

"Well, well, well," he says. "It can talk after all." I feel his warm breath on my eyebrows. He didn't brush this morning.

I make a show of sniffing the air. "Damn, Dalton. When was the last time you brushed your teeth?" And then I open my mouth wide and breathe right in his face. I had a breakfast burrito on the way to school, and I know for a fact that my breath is . . . less than minty fresh.

Dalton staggers back and covers his face. It takes him a moment to regroup, but when he opens his eyes, there's murder in them. "You're a little pussy, Frankie-Spankie. Just like your *cholo* brother."

"Gentlemen," Mr. C. says, ambling up to us with an armful of textbooks, "I bet there's a class out there with your names on it."

Dalton shakes his head violently, like a dog drying off, and I can only assume that my stank breath has set up camp somewhere within the thicket of his nose hair. "Whatever," he says, turning away and heading down the hall.

Mr. C. raises an eyebrow, and I respond with a shrug.

Zach and I jog away from Dalton, leaving Mr. C. in the doorway of his classroom with a bemused look on his face.

"You want to get your ass kicked?" Zach says.

"He's not going to do anything," I say. "Besides, I think he was more surprised than pissed."

"I don't know, dude, your breath can get pretty nasty."

"Yours smells like roses?"

"Fair enough. Like I said, though, I got your back. Even if it's just us against the whole soccer team." We reach Miss

Reyna's classroom, and Zach puts his hand in front of me before I go inside. "Behind you. Don't turn quick, but you've got to check this out."

Rebecca is outrageously hot today, dressed in white jeans and a skintight red shirt. She's the only girl in school who never gets camel toe; she must put cardboard down there or something. With each step she takes, her shirt rises just enough for me to steal a glimpse of her olive stomach. How am I supposed to keep my wits about me if she's going to come to school like this?

As she walks by, she glances my way and gives me a little wave with the pinky and ring finger of her left hand. It's a small motion, like the way my dad greets people in the pickup trucks we pass on the back roads. Because the whole hand isn't involved, not to mention the wrist and forearm, there's no real commitment. It could be interpreted any number of ways. I take it as an invitation.

"What's up, Rebecca," I say with a confident backward nod. What the hell, right?

"Hi, Frankie," she says, her eyes just peeking over the armful of books she has cradled underneath her rack. And just like that, she's past me, her hips rocking back and forth like a hypnotist's watch. I make no effort to mask where I'm looking.

Zach snaps his fingers in front of my face. "Hello?"

"Sorry. I'm back."

"I'm Zach Mason," he says, offering to shake my hand. "And you are?"

"Going to be late." I push past him and drop my backpack next to one of the desks in the back row just as the second bell rings.

Zach plops down next to me, as always, and starts arranging his supplies on his desk. Our homework was to finish the third act of *Julius Caesar*, but I didn't really feel like reading much past the part where all his friends gang up on him. I'll get to it.

"Frankie," Zach whispers, "what's up with you today?"

I shrug. "So I forgot it was picture day. I'll just borrow your shirt like last year."

"Yeah, I give a crap about picture day." He shakes his head in a kind of wonderment. "Telling off Dalton like that, being all cool with Rebecca?"

Begay rushes in and drops his books on the desk in front of me. "What's up, Homo sapiens?"

"Frankie lost his mind," Zach says.

"I knew it," Begay says. "Is that why you picked a fight with Burrage?"

I glance up at him and burst out laughing. "Is that what people are saying?"

"Gentlemen," Miss Reyna says as she stands up from behind her desk. "Care to share with the class? I could use a good laugh this morning."

She's easily my hottest teacher. Short black hair, huge green eyes, big jugs. Reyna's smooth and relaxed, and she seems even better looking than she really is—even though she's hot to start with—because she couldn't care less what we think of her.

Today she's wearing black pants and a white shirt, which is no big deal, but she's also got on a kind of black half-vest that comes around and lifts up her *chichotas*. Not only that, but for some reason she's wearing a black bow tie. She said she could use a good laugh this morning? She's about to get it.

"Sorry, Miss Reyna," Zach says, and he opens his book even though she hasn't told him to.

She claps her hands twice to wake us up. "Okay, everybody. Please turn to page seventy-three in the text and—yes, Michael?"

She points to Mike Pine, who's raising his hand in the front. Basketball player. His parents own the Dairy Queen downtown. Nice enough kid, I guess. I went to his third-grade birthday party at the Chuck E. Cheese's in Albuquerque. "Miss Reyna" he says, "I'd like a table for four, please."

I told you. It's like freaking clockwork. Everyone starts laughing, even Miss Reyna. She blushes and straightens out her bow tie. And it's on.

"I didn't know we had penguins in New Mexico," Willy Stinchcomb says, looking up from tagging his desk. I can't help noticing that he has a new gold chain around his neck. I bet he sold over two hundred bucks worth of nitrous at the party.

"Hit me," Zach says. "Blackjack!"

And here comes Begay. "Were you the groom or the best man?"

We're rolling now; it's mostly boys talking, but the girls

seem to be getting into it too, if only to hide smiles behind their hands and look at each other with those I-can't-believe-this-is-happening-I'd-die-if-it-ever-happened-to-me looks. Thirty-one kids all shouting "compliments" at the same time. She looks around, her face bright red by now, and raises her hands, almost pleading for quiet.

"Okay, okay. Ha, ha, ha, people," she says, and we finally mellow out enough for her to continue the class. "Let's talk about your homework."

She looks right at me. She does this a lot. I try to hide in the back when I haven't done my work, but my grades are good enough that nobody bothers me about them. Maybe she has a crush on me. I've heard about that, about teachers secretly wanting to get with their favorite students. I know I'm not her favorite student . . . but maybe I could be.

I give her my brother's patented look of self-confidence: the head tilts back slightly, the mouth forms a half-frown, and the eyelids close about halfway. And finally, a wink. The look is a classic. It says: I'm the man . . . Want to find out why? As soon as I lower my eyelid, I know I've made a ridiculous mistake. Nobody winks at a teacher.

I know a wink back is probably a long shot, but she looks like she just watched someone shoot her dog. Complete shock. Worry, even. Deep creases separate her eyebrows, which form tiny peaks over her wide eyes.

Zach leans in. "Did you just do what I think you did?"

Somebody please put out the fire on my cheeks. I open

my annotated *Julius Caesar* to page seventy-three and wait.

"Frankie," she says pleasantly, "can you tell me what justification Brutus gives for Caesar's assassination?"

Um, actually, no. I was too busy basking in the glory of defending my brother. "I . . . I remember when Brutus killed him and everything. . . ." It's useless. Just give up. "I . . . guess I didn't get to that part yet." Somebody *please* put out this fucking fire on my cheeks.

I drop my head on the desk as hands shoot up all around the room, and I hate everybody. Not so much because I didn't know the answer—it's not like this is the first time—but because she gave me a chance. She gave me the opportunity to show her what I was made of, and I blew it. She moves on, and I'm forgotten just like that.

"Yes, Zachary," she says. "Why don't you give it a try?"

I peel my forehead from the pages of my text and stare at my friend. *Et tu*, motherfucker?

"Brutus says that Caesar was ambitious, and that's why they had to kill him."

Even though I'm completely humiliated right now, I have room in my heart to feel sorry for Zach. I may not have answered the question, but at least I didn't say something stupid, like that Caesar was ambitious. First of all, of course he's ambitious; he's freaking Caesar. Second, people don't get killed for being ambitious; they get killed for slacking off and not making something of themselves—or so my dad keeps warning me. Ambition doesn't get you assasinated; it gets you respect. This country was built on ambition. American dream and all that. It can't be ambition.

"Very good," Miss Reyna says.

I pull myself together and raise my hand. "Miss Reyna?"

Now she looks confused. "You have something to add?"

"Just a question, I guess." Everybody's staring at me. I clear my throat. "So, Brutus says it's all about ambition, right? But what's so bad about that? I mean, like, it's okay to be ambitious and everything, isn't it? Isn't that why we're supposed to do our homework every day? So we can go to college and get good jobs and have people respect us and all that?" I sound like an idiot, I know. I can't help myself.

Miss Reyna considers me for a while. She motions to the rest of the class. "Other thoughts? Is ambition a bad thing?"

As the hands go up around the room, Miss Reyna rewards me with a nod *and* a smile. Maybe a wink back isn't out of the question, after all.

SEVEN

IT SHOULD HAVE been obvious, with my burrito breath having singed Dalton's nose hairs earlier, but my mind is wandering, and I'm thinking about the little pinky-wave I got from Rebecca and imagining my smooth lines for our next meeting, when Dalton leaps out from around the corner and annihilates my nose with his right fist.

It's no use calling for help—school's over, and there's nobody around. Zach went home already, and I missed the bus even though I promised my mom I wouldn't, so I get a two-hour walk instead. I'm stepping across a field of dirt and patchy yellow tufts of dry native grass behind the gym, not even off campus yet, when it happens.

My face explodes blood everywhere, like a water balloon against a brick wall, and just before my vision becomes so blurry that I can't see, I take some small satisfaction in the red splotches raining all over the white leather sleeves of Dalton's pristine letter jacket. My backpack falls to the ground, and the rusted zipper busts open, ejecting secondhand textbooks and sheets of wrinkled, folded notebook paper.

I take a fist to the kidneys, and a few drops of piss come squirting out. I glimpse extra fists and feet, but it really doesn't matter who they belong to. Me against Dalton wouldn't be a fair fight anyway, but three on one is just plain ridiculous. I'm on the ground now, rolling in the dirt, trying as hard as I can to stay in the fetal position.

"Who's stupid and deaf now, you punk-ass bitch?" Dalton screams. "You said I could come and get me a little Spankie whenever I wanted, right?" He kicks me in the chest, hard—no wonder he made varsity as a freshman—and for a second I can't breathe. I hear them panting like dogs around me.

Dalton leans in, close enough that I can feel his words on my ear. "I'll be taking that Spankie now." He kicks me again, but I hardly feel it this time. Like at the dentist, when you can feel him working around in your mouth but there's no pain.

I imagine Steve coming to my rescue. He wields a crowbar with both hands like a broadsword, denting foreheads and cracking shins. I smile as my brother buries the crowbar in Dalton's stomach. Dalton doubles over in pain, and Steve's elbow lands hard on the back of his head. When Dalton crumples to the ground, I laugh.

"Oh, I think he likes it." Dalton says, and I'm back to the real world. "Here's some more."

Naturally, the one person I don't want to see right now is the one who finds me here—alone and beaten, leaning against the gym wall, surrounded by dusty puddles of my own blood. Yep, it's Rebecca. And now my humiliation is complete.

"Oh my God, Frankie!" she says. She puts her hand on my shoulder, and I grit my teeth to keep from squealing in pain. "Are you okay? Want me to call a doctor?"

"I'm fine." It hurts to talk, so I nod. It hurts to nod, too, so I slump against the wall behind the gym.

"You don't look fine."

I have never put so much effort into not throwing up. "You should see the wall I ran into."

"I'll be right back," she says. She hops to her feet and jogs around the corner toward the gym entrance.

I want to yell for her to stop, that I don't want her to call anybody, but I can't make my voice much louder than a whisper, so I ease back against the wall and wait for the nurse, or someone from the athletic department, or whoever. I look at my bloodstained shirt and shorts, the splotches of dusty maroon like spilled red chile and I can't help thinking of my brother's lame excuses to our parents. I have no idea how I'm going to explain this.

A few minutes later, Rebecca comes back with a small paper cup. "Here," she says, offering me the water. "Wash out your mouth."

I mumble a thanks and gingerly lift the cup to my lips. The water is cool, and the sensation as it spreads through my mouth is unlike anything I've ever felt before. Like the Pepto commercial where the pink wave oozes instant relief across the dude's stomach.

Rebecca leans down, resting her hands on her knees, her wondrous cleavage staring me in the face. Through some miracle, the scent of her perfume finds its way past the clotted blood and through my nostrils. Some kind of sweet berry, I think.

"You okay?" she says, sounding worried.

I smile, and a trickle of blood runs down the back of my throat. I take another sip of water to wash it away, and hand Rebecca the empty cup.

"You sure you don't want to go inside and get cleaned up?"

I'm dying to, but my face is caked with blood, and I don't want anybody else to see that I've just had my ass kicked. "Not really."

"Yeah, okay." She rummages through her little purse and comes up with a packet of Kleenex. There's a spigot and hose coming out of the wall, and she uses it to wet the tissues. "Here, stay still."

I wince, but her touch is worth it. She settles in front of me, the combination of her white jeans, light brown stomach, and red shirt like the flag of some country where I can seek asylum, where there's no Dalton extradition treaty. She gently rubs the dried blood and dirt from my cheeks with the corner of a wet tissue. Three times she has to return to the hose to moisten a new tissue, and each time, she sits back down, crosses her legs, scoots a little closer, and tucks her hair behind her ears. I should've had the shit beat out of me years ago.

"I think I got most of it," she says, gazing at my face like a painter unhappy with her canvas. "There's still some on your upper lip, but that's probably going to hurt too much."

"Might as well get it over with."

"Whatever you say. But remember—I warned you." My eyes begin to water the instant she puts the Kleenex to my lip, and she pulls her hand away.

"Just stings a little," I say, trying as hard as I can to keep from passing out. My ears throb and I can see two of her and it feels like someone's taking a jackhammer to my skull. "I'll be fine."

Rebecca must realize how full of it I am, because she passes the tissue over my lip even more gently this time. "Are you going to tell me what happened?"

"Your jeans are going to get dirty," I say.

"We have a washing machine." She keeps her eyes on mine.

I chuckle, and my ribs scream. "Can I borrow it?"

"What is this, a code of silence?"

I'm guessing she doesn't think fighting is cool. I want to

tell her everything. But I can't; it would be too obvious—like I was telling on Dalton. If only she could see for herself what an asshole he is, I wouldn't have to say a thing.

Instead, I look away. "It was just guy stuff."

"Guy stuff."

"Yeah, guy stuff."

A slight roll of her eyes tells me she doesn't buy it. Not that I blame her.

A gust of wind blows her hair into her face, and I notice a dried piece of grass sticking out just behind her ear. I reach up and pluck it away as if it's the most natural thing in the world. We must look like a couple of chimpanzees, grooming each other. I like being this close to her. I'm about to do something even more idiotic than getting up in Dalton's face.

"What are you doing Friday?" I feel like the Hunchback of Notre Dame asking that hot chick out, or like any of those Disney movies where true love conquers all, even though in real life the hot girl is scared to death of the monster—if she even notices him.

"I don't know . . ." She trails off and looks down at the tissue—it's all bloody. "Time for a new one."

When she sits back down, after she's completed the ritual hair tuck, I open my mouth and start talking. "I like movies." What a retard. Of course I like movies. Everybody likes movies.

She pulls the tissue away and tosses it behind a scraggly sage bush. "That's good." She stands up and brushes the dirt off her jeans. "I have to go. Are you going to be okay?"

"Yeah," I say. "Thanks and all."

Rebecca puts her hands on her hips. "You sure?" The afternoon sun is right behind her, and her silhouette doesn't quite block it out.

You should go to the movies with me, I want to say. But I close my eyes instead. I'm such a pussy. "Yeah. I'll just rest here for a while."

"Okay, then. I'll see you tomorrow maybe."

I nod. I'm screwed: I want to spend more time with her, but at this point I don't think I could take her saying no again. Insult to injury, or whatever they say.

Her footsteps get softer and softer as she walks away.

And then it strikes me, as I slouch here in the dirt, that I have absolutely nothing to lose. "Hey, Rebecca?"

"Yeah?" She turns around and walks back. I hold up my hand to shield my eyes from the sun.

"I was thinking . . . if you want to see a movie . . . I'll go with you."

Someone please tell me what my problem is. Here I am with blood running down the back of my throat, with a nose the size of an orange, and all I can think about is what it would feel like to put my arm around Rebecca in the middle of a movie, to know that she wanted to be there with me. This is the same chick who broke my heart not even a week ago, and I'm crawling back to her. I might as well go running after Dalton and beg him to kick my ass again.

"Frankie," she says, "you're so cute."

And here it comes: John Dalton is my boyfriend, and that's the way it's supposed to be. Besides, your eyebrows are too thick, and you should lose a little weight. You're not very smart, you don't work hard in school, and your best friend is a one-eyed freak. I didn't clean you up today because I like you, but because I feel sorry for you.

She squats down next to me. "Just as friends, right?"

I'll go however she wants me to, just as long as we go. "Will Dalton be okay with that?"

"It's not like I'm married to him or anything," she says. "We're just going to Homecoming."

Somewhere in the back of my mind, I know it's not as simple as that. "Are you sure—"

She grabs my hand and gives it a gentle squeeze. "What do you want to see?"

Screw it, I'm in! I'm the man! *Of course* she wants to go out with me. Chicks dig the quiet guys.

Due to the beating I took, I'm a little slow getting home, and it's pitch dark by the time I shuffle into the driveway. Even the Sizzler is here before I am, which almost never happens. I guess the *cholos* aren't cruising tonight.

My mom greets me at the door with a look that is equal parts worry and rage. I'm not even fully inside the house before she starts yelling. And I know I'm really in trouble, because it's not in English.

"Francisco! *¿Porqué me haces esto? ¡Tu papá no está y hace tres horas que te espero aquí! ¡No debes preocuparme tanto!*" She stops.

I slouch in the doorway and look up at her. My eyes are almost swollen shut, I can't breathe through my nose, and I've resorted to dragging my backpack because it hurts too much to sling it over my shoulder.

She covers her mouth with the tips of her fingers. "*¿Qué te pasó a la cara?*"

"I'm sorry, *Mamá.*" I say. Sounds more like "I'b sorry, *Babá.*"

"I said, what happened to your face, Francisco?"

I collapse on the faded brown couch in the living room. She did laundry today, and as usual she's put the clean clothes on the couch in order to fold them all at once. I push a pile of shirts away with my elbow so I don't get blood on them.

She kneels down, putting her hands on my thighs, and tries to make eye contact with me. Her voice is almost out of control. "Francisco, *por favor*. What happened to you?"

I know she's just trying to help, but this is the last thing I need right now. "I fell."

"You fell? *¿Te caíste?* You expect me to believe that?" As she stands up, she pushes against my thighs for leverage. Ouch. "I'm calling the police," she says, grabbing the phone.

Steve rushes into the room. "What's wrong?"

"*Mira,*" she says, pointing at me.

The speed at which rage overtakes my brother is shocking. His shoulders tense up, his eyes narrow, and his chest begins to heave. It's nice to know he cares.

He can only manage one word. "Who?"

My legs hurt too much to stand up, so I just hold my palms out to him. "Don't worry about it."

"Who?" he says again, his voice a gravelly whisper.

Mom still has the phone in her hands, but now she's looking at my brother. She's probably as worried about the change in his attitude as I am.

Steve and I just stare at each other. After a few seconds, he takes a deep breath and nods to himself. "Give me the phone, *Mamá*."

I wave him off. "Steve, don't—"

"Just one phone call, Frankie. That's all I need."

"Who?" my mom says. "Who was it?"

"Let me handle it," I say. The last thing I want is for my brother to go all Scarface on everybody, even though he's probably looking for any excuse to bust Dalton's kneecaps.

Steve grits his teeth. "It's my fault anyway."

"It's not your fault." Maybe it is, a little, but he wasn't the one who busted stank breath in Dalton's face.

"Francisco," Mom says, "what are you talking about?" She's trying her best to control herself, but I know it's only a matter of time before she freaks out completely.

Steve pounds his chest with a closed fist. "That was between me and him, and now he takes it out on my brother because he's too much of a pussy to come to me?"

Classic Steve, right? He has to be at the center of everything. "How do you know it's about you?"

Not having received an answer from either one of us, Mom waves the phone over her head like it's a road flare. "I'm calling your father."

Steve turns as if to stomp out the door. "He's going to pay, that's all I know."

"Steve!" I yell. My ribs throb, but finally there is silence. "This is my thing."

Mom glances at me, and at Steve, and back at me as though she's watching tennis. Steve contemplates things for a moment and then takes a step toward me. "You sure?"

"Just let me handle it."

"If that's what you want—"

"*¡Alguien me tiene que decir algo!*" Mom's voice finally cracks, halfway through the last word. "Someone attacked my baby and my husband's at work and my boys won't talk to me for some reason *pero no se porque no me hablan*—"

"Mom." She's panicking now. Talking to herself. Making no sense.

"—both coming home with bruises all over, and I don't know what's happening to my family—"

"Mom!" What the hell am I supposed to do with this? I come home after getting my ass totally beat, and my mom goes off the deep end. How does that help anything? "MOM!"

"Frankie's right, Mom. It's just school stuff. He can handle it." Steve's voice is measured and gentle. Apparently the sight of our mom having a breakdown is enough to quench his anger.

She looks at the phone. It's insane that after all the crap he's put her through, *he's* the one talking her down.

"I promise, Mom," I say. "I'm going to be okay."

And now she bursts into tears so suddenly, and with such force, that I almost forget to breathe. She drops the phone and the battery cover crashes across the brick floor, the rechargeable battery pops out, and the phone itself bounces twice before coming to a stop against the thick wooden leg of our coffee table. My mom collapses onto the heap of clothes next to me.

Though it hurts my whole body to do it, I put my arm around her and pull her head onto my shoulder. She sobs uncontrollably and uses one of my clean white T-shirts as a handkerchief.

Steve and I make eye contact, and he shrugs as though he doesn't know what to do. He comes up to our mother and puts his hand on her shoulder. She whimpers at his touch. He shakes his head and turns away.

"What's happening to my boys?" she says. Her chin jerks up and down as she tries to regain control.

"It's okay, *Mamá*. I'll be okay."

She falls asleep like this, curled up on the couch, having pushed all the clean clothes onto the floor. I don't have the heart to wake her, or the energy to move, so I stare at the ceiling, listening to her breathe, and wonder how many times my parents soothed my fears with bluffs and empty consolations. Just as I drift off, I hear the front door slam, and moments later the roar of the Sizzler's engine.

eight

THE WORST PART about getting the crap kicked out of you is the shame. Not so much right as it's happening—although there's plenty of shame in not being able to protect yourself—but it's afterward, when the blood has clotted, when the bruises are showing. When other people start looking at you. That's when your heart shrinks to nothing, when the tension in your chest is so strong that it feels like a fat man is sitting on you. That's where the saying "He's got no heart" comes from. Shame makes your heart disappear, and once your heart's gone, the rest of you is bound to collapse on top of it like a hot air balloon with a gash in the side.

In exchange for my mom and dad not calling the police, I

agree to a full day of rest. Zach calls Tuesday afternoon and wants to hang out, but I can barely get out of bed, and I'm not in the mood to talk anyway. The extra day away from school does two things. First, it gives my face plenty of time to swell up and my eyes to turn black, so that I look like an overstuffed raccoon. Second, it gives the shame a chance to develop. Instead of fading, it multiplies like some sort of nasty virus that grows exponentially, while the helpless scientists look on in horror.

On Wednesday morning the Sizzler eases into a parking spot, but Steve makes no move to turn off the engine. Yesterday he was all protective and everything—hanging out at home after school, even offering to get me food—but he hasn't really said much today. Mostly he looks pissed off whenever he sees my face.

"What?" I say.

"I was just thinking."

"Don't hurt yourself." I try to force a laugh, try to keep it light, but my face is so swollen that when I smile, it feels like I'm taking a sledgehammer to the nose, so what comes out sounds more like a weak cough.

Steve does not laugh. Instead, he narrows his eyes at me. "You ready for this?"

"Ready?"

"If you're going to come back today, you have to come all the way back. No hiding, no avoiding nothing—"

"I'm fine."

"You only get one chance at this. Dudes have to see you

in control. People have to know that the motherfucker didn't get to you."

"Did you read that in your gangster manual?" I say under my breath.

He sticks his chin out. "What was that?"

"I'm not a pussy," I say, opening the door.

"I know you're not—"

"I'll catch you later." And with that, I get out of the car and don't look back. When I slam the door, my side hurts so much I almost scream, but that wouldn't do much for my case, so I grit my teeth and handle it.

I tell people I was hit with a soccer ball, or fell off my bike, or that if they think *I* look bad, they should see the tree I ran into. I'm sure most of them know what really happened, but I try my best to have a sense of humor about the whole thing—at least outwardly. Unfortunately, there's nothing I can do about the sideways glances, the sudden whispers when I walk by the lockers, the pointing they think I don't notice from across the hall.

I try to avoid Dalton the best I can. Not that I think he's going to pound on me again, although I wouldn't put it past him. I just don't think I could handle the smirk on his face—the blue eyes closed halfway, the lips pressed together in a flat smile, the corners of his mouth turned slightly down. I know what his smirk looks like; it taunts me every time I close my eyes.

Most teachers have no idea what to say. They pretend nothing's wrong with my face, and they seem content to let me endure their classes in silence. But, as I think I've told you before, most teachers aren't Mr. Costas. He calls on me at least seven times during class, even though I start giving fake answers. If x is an acute angle of a right triangle, $sin\ x$ equals Budweiser.

When the bell finally rings, he points at me. "Hey, Frankie, would you mind sticking around?"

The obligatory collective "Ooooh" rises from my classmates as they pack up. I notice Rubén out of the corner of my eye. He leans toward Maya Bechtel and nods in my direction, and a giggle escapes before she can cover her mouth. She shakes her head and her eyebrows reach for the sky, and Rubén nods again. His parents have both worked for the Tortilla Emporium since the beginning, so it's no surprise whose side he's taking.

Normally I would laugh it off, but I don't have the energy today. A full minute later everyone is gone, and I'm still in my seat, arms crossed. Mr. C. leans against the corner of his desk, waiting. From outside come the sounds of lockers slamming, kids shouting. Lunchtime, and I'm stuck in here.

I look up at him. There's something depressing about his room. Maybe it's the lingering scent of twenty-five students, somehow more disgusting now that the room is empty. Or maybe it's the dry erase–marker stains on Mr. C.'s fingertips. The half-erased whiteboard. The box of tissues on his desk. I feel sorry for him. First of all, what kind of a man dedicates himself to math? And then he deludes himself into thinking that any of us actually give a crap about his stupid subject.

"Well?" he says.

You know that moment right before you lie to someone? It's the split second between when your brain gives you the go-ahead and when your breath strums your vocal cords. You think of all the times people have told you that lying is wrong, that it's better to be honest, that a person of integrity tells the truth no matter what. And then you go ahead with your lie anyway.

"I fell."

"On whom?"

I roll my eyes and give him the most exaggerated fake smile my pain will allow. "I can't remember."

He crosses his arms and shakes his head. "Right. Well. If you do remember, you'll be sure to let me know?"

"Mr. Costas, I'm really touched that you care and every-thing, but can't you just let me eat my lunch?"

"The door's right there," he says with a gesture, and though he's trying to hide it, I can tell I've hurt his feelings. "You're free to go any time you want."

"*Thank* you." I sit up and throw my math books into my backpack. He doesn't move from the desk as I walk out of the room.

Zach is waiting for me outside. "What was that all about?"

"Costas wanted to know who did it."

"Did you tell him?"

"What the hell do you think? I may be a punching bag, but I'm not stupid."

"Ease up, dude. I was just asking."

"Yeah, asking a stupid question," I say. He looks down with a shrug. I'm such an asshole. I hit his chest with the back of my hand. "Sorry."

"You want to grab your lunch?" he says. We walk outside, toward the cafeteria, but I'm in no hurry to get to any densely populated parts of school.

"Nah, that's okay. I'm not sure if I could open my mouth wide enough to eat anything."

He stops under a cottonwood tree that's begun to lose its leaves. It's a perfect fall day. The air is crisp but still warm enough that you don't need anything other than a T-shirt. "Frankie, I . . ."

"Dude, you weren't even there, okay?" We're not looking at each other, but I can sense that, like me, Zach has his hands in his pockets and is kicking at the ground.

"Yeah, but I said I'd have your back."

"You wouldn't have been able to do anything except get your own ass beat." Still not looking at him, I scoot over and kick his shin with the outside of my foot. "Let it go."

Zach takes a deep breath. "Your eyes look good, though. If I had known you were going to dress up as Zorro, I would have worn my patch."

Pain spreads across my face. "Damn it, dude, don't make me laugh."

"You Lone Ranger, me Tonto." He shakes his head and tries to keep himself from smiling. "Hi-ho, Silver . . . away!"

While Zach entertains himself at my expense, I scan the campus for any sign of Rebecca. She's the one person I haven't seen yet today, and I'm worried.

When I was in seventh grade, I went out to a movie with Erin Lucas. She was hotter back then than she is now, by the way—she didn't have braces yet, and she wasn't all anorexic. Anyway, it wasn't really a *date* date, because we went with other people, but it gets dark in those theaters, if you know what I mean. I don't remember what the movie was, and I don't think she would either, because we spent the whole time making out in the back. One guy in front of us even got up and moved to another seat—it was awesome. I went home all proud of myself, thinking I was in, thinking I had a girlfriend, already planning the next weekend's action. But when Monday rolled around and I walked up to her, she dissed me so hard that I still can't believe it. Right there in front of everybody, she rolled her eyes at me and turned away.

That's how school is, man. Especially with the ladies. You have absolutely no idea where you stand. One second everything is all good, and the next you're alone in the hallway, trying to figure out what you did wrong, your self-confidence in little shards around your feet.

"Don't you think Dalton's going to be pissed?" Zach says. "You going out with his girlfriend and all?"

"She said she wasn't his girlfriend," I say. But yes, I am a little worried. That's why I'm hanging out all the way over here, where I can see people coming.

Suddenly, two hands grab my shoulders from behind. In the split second before my instincts take over, a river of absolute terror comes gushing into the pit of my stomach. Then I recover. I duck and whirl around, ignoring the stabbing in my ribs, and cock my fist. There's no way I'm getting wrecked again.

But instead of John Dalton, I'm about to hit the smiling, somewhat astonished face of Cheo Moya. "*Órale*, Frankie!"

Zach is at my side, ready to do battle. He looks at me, waiting for me to make some sort of a move. I lower my fist. "What the hell?"

Steve comes up behind Cheo. "Chill, bro, it's just us."

And now all the pain I should have felt when I whirled around comes back. I can hardly breathe. I double over and stagger to the cottonwood trunk. Cheo and Steve bust out laughing.

"*Chingao*, Frankie," Steve says. "I thought you were going to take Cheo's head off."

"Like spidey sense and shit," Cheo says. "You were on my ass before I could blink."

"I think I pissed my pants," I say. The pain in my ribs spreads to my entire chest, and I can only take short breaths.

"Your boy was right there with you," Cheo says. "Ready to throw down. I like that shit."

Zach chuckles awkwardly. I think he's just glad he didn't have to get into a fight today. I know I am.

"What's up, Zach?" Steve says.

Zach nods. "What's up."

"Sit down, Frankie." My brother motions to the base of the tree. Only now do I notice that Steve is holding something behind his back. "We got a surprise for you."

"Is it Dalton's nuts on a stick?" Zach says.

They all laugh again, and this time I let myself join them. The pain is worth it.

"Damn, *cieguito*," Cheo says. Little blind kid. "That was some funny shit."

I settle into a position that doesn't make me want to throw up, and Steve hands me a paper plate covered with aluminum foil. I don't need a nose to tell what's underneath: a Los Torres stuffed sopaipilla plate to go. I'd recognize that wrapping job anywhere.

"So much for the closed campus," I say.

"I know people," Steve says with a shrug. He pulls a plastic knife and fork from his back pocket and hands them to me. "Turns out Cheo has a lot of experience ditching class. He's a bad influence."

"Suspended for one game. It's not like you missed me."

Zach nods at the sopaipilla. "You think you can eat it?"

"Please. I'd figure out a way even if my jaw was wired shut." Only now do I notice that everyone is standing but me. "You guys want to sit down?"

Steve waves me off. "Nah. We can't stay long."

"Are you back on the team?" Zach says, also standing.

"Back running circles around this *maricón*." Cheo takes a swipe at my brother, but Steve dodges it with little effort.

"My ass."

"Frankie," Cheo says, "you should be proud of this moth-erfucker."

The stuffed sopaipilla is just what I needed. Except for one small problem: I still have a few open cuts in my mouth. Let's just say the red chile burns a little more than normal. "Oh yeah? Why?"

"That *pinche güero* Dalton's still alive."

"You should have seen practice yesterday," Steve says.

"Your brother took him down hard," Cheo says. "First thing, too, like five minutes in."

"It was clean."

"Hell yeah, but it was hard."

"Every time I came near him after that, he freaked out. He couldn't trap the ball, couldn't pass." Now Steve does a high-pitched impersonation. "'Oh shit, here comes a cleat, what do I do? I'm just a little pussy! I want my daddy!'"

I love the sound of my brother making fun of Dalton. I could listen to it all day long. "I guess you got in his head, huh?"

"*Chingao,*" Cheo says. "Built a brick house up there."

Steve nods. "It was pathetic."

Part of me wonders whether I should actually worry about what's going to happen between them now, if it won't stay limited to a few hard tackles at soccer practice. But that's overruled by the other part of me: the part that can't stop smiling about Dalton flailing around to the sound track of Steve's voice.

"So anyway, Frankie," Cheo says. "You still want to airbrush that piece of shit bike you got?"

"Piece of shit?" Steve says with mock indignation. "That was my bike."

Cheo points at him. "And that's why it's a piece of shit."

"Whatever."

"You up for it?" Cheo says.

"That would be sweet." I glance over at Zach, and his eye goes wide. "Can Zach come, too?"

"*Claro,*" he says. "Tomorrow good?"

Tomorrow is perfect. I don't have to work at all. "After school?"

"Hell yeah, after school. I can't miss no more classes or I get kicked off the team."

"Dude," Zach says, "there's Rebecca. Four o'clock, over by the gym. I think she's coming this way."

I look up so fast that I feel dizzy. She hugs her books against her chest, like always. Hips swaying back and forth. Today she's wearing a black skirt that goes all the way down to her knees, but the way she moves her legs makes it seem a lot shorter.

Zach rubs his hands together in anticipation. "What's the plan? Want me to wave at her?"

"Hell no, you don't wave," Cheo says.

"I was just—"

"Don't worry about it, Zach," I say. "Let's just wait and see what she does. Maybe she won't notice us."

My brother scoffs. "Wait and see? What the hell is wait and see?"

"I look like a busted piñata."

"*Órale, vato,*" Cheo says. "Ain't no 'wait and see' when it comes to *chicas* like her."

Suddenly, Rebecca hands her books to Katie and peels off in our direction. I take a deep breath and stand up. Here it comes.

"Hey," she says.

"Hi, Rebecca," Zach and I both say. God, we sound like morons.

Steve and Cheo both wince a little. There is an awkward silence while we all look at each other.

"Hey, Steve," she says.

He nods, and then suddenly he pats his stomach. "Damn, am I hungry. You guys want to get something to eat?"

Cheo whistles and looks at his wrist. He's not wearing a watch. "It's lunch already?"

"Yeah, um . . ." Zach says. "Laters." He follows my brother and Cheo toward the cafeteria.

Rebecca smiles when everyone is gone. "You okay?"

"Yeah." Jesus, it's hard to act cool when your head's the size of a balloon.

"I missed you yesterday."

By now she has to know who did this to me, but I wonder if Dalton has her so fooled that she's convinced the other two guys started it—whoever they were. "You did?"

"Why is that so weird? I was worried."

"I guess I've been trying to keep a low profile, you know?"

She reaches out toward my face but then seems to think better of it and runs her hand back through her own hair instead. "Does it hurt?"

I shake my head a little. "Nah. It feels great. Very relaxing. I think more people should have this work done."

Her eyes light up, and her perfect face beams back at me. What have I done to deserve this?

"You're funny," she says, leaning in and hugging me. I'm so surprised when it happens that I don't react in time, and the moment passes before I can hug her back. "I have to go, but I just wanted to make sure we were still on for Friday."

Are we still on for Friday? Is she freaking kidding me?

"Sure," I say.

"Good. I was worried you wouldn't want to." She looks down, no doubt waiting for me to come up with something clever and manly. "Okay," she says, "I told Katie I would be right back."

I can only manage three words. "See you later."

"Bye, Frankie. I really hope you feel better." She turns around and does the girlie jog over to the cafeteria. You know the jog I'm talking about. It's the one where they keep their arms straight down, pressed against their bodies, while they kind of bounce along. I've always hated that jog, always wished girls would just learn to run normal. But as I stand here under the partial shade of the cottonwood, I have to admit the girlie jog looks pretty freaking hot when Rebecca does it.

nine

"FRANKIE, BRO, you got to move your arm back and forth," Cheo says, his voice muffled by a paper dust mask as we huddle over the frame of my bike.

I hold the airbrush like a pencil, with the blue compressed air hose dangling over my wrist. A little canister below feeds Testors burgundy-red metallic paint into the cylinder. "Easier said than done."

My arm is about to fall off, and my ribs still hurt like a bitch. Before we even got to this part, I spent forever rubbing the frame with an emery cloth, trying to get rid of all the rust and scratches. After that, we put on two layers of white primer from a spray can. Now we're on the second coat with the airbrush.

"Well, you better do it anyway," he says, hovering over my shoulder. "Or else the paint's going to bead up on you."

You'd never know it to look at him, but Cheo is a neat freak. His garage is spotless. The entire back wall is covered with shelves holding different types of spray paint: cans of primer and polyurethane clear coat, plus every color you can imagine. There are also drawers and drawers of acrylic paints kind of like what Zach uses on his plastic model cars. I can't think of a better place to spend my day off.

I can tell my lack of skill is driving Cheo crazy. He keeps reaching out to grab the airbrush from me and then pulling his hands back at the last minute. The compressor hums as I concentrate on the tube in front of me. *"Así,"* he says. "There you go."

Zach and Steve watch from a safe distance, without masks. A few exposed lightbulbs dangle from the ceiling. Pictures of *Lowrider Magazine* models dot the walls. The floor is cracked concrete, covered with oil stains but swept clean. There's an old weight bench in the corner, but most of the space is taken up by Cheo's prized possession: a 1965 Impala convertible.

He bought it off some dude in Española two years ago, but even though the engine was good, a nice 327 V-8, the rest of the car was a piece of crap. Mismatched fenders, rotted out floorboards, busted windshield. The steering wheel was missing. When Steve first saw it, he bet Cheo ten bucks that he'd be dead by the time Cheo got it done.

It's almost fully restored now. The interior and engine are finished, and he recently hit the exterior with metallic Desert Gold and tricked it out with chrome everywhere.

My bike, on the other hand, is still a piece of crap. At least so far. It's not as dark a red as I want it to be, so we'll probably need a few more coats.

Just as I'm finishing the second one, I'm startled by a loud, deep voice behind me. *"Oye, pendejos!"*

I flinch just enough to send a red spray up against the wooden wall. It looks like blood spatter, like someone blew his brains out. "Shit, I'm sorry."

"No te preocupes," Cheo says. "We were done with that coat anyway."

He flicks the switch on the compressor, and the room goes silent. I take off my mask and glance over my shoulder to see who's responsible for me almost painting a red stripe across my handlebars.

Flaco leans against the garage door smoking a cigarette, wearing baggy jean shorts and a white beater, his arms covered with intricate tattoos. When he walks into the garage, the whole atmosphere changes. I can see it in my brother's eyes, and I can even see it in Cheo. His shoulders tense up just a little bit, as though he's steeling himself against something.

"Órale," Cheo says, his voice thick, almost wary.

Flaco is the tallest *cholo* I've ever seen—well over six feet—but he probably weighs less than I do. And there's no way a voice as low as his should come from someone that skinny. "*¿Qué pasa?*"

Steve and Cheo go over to shake his hand. "Just doing a little work on my brother's bike," Steve says.

"*Vale,*" Flaco says. He comes over to where I'm standing and inspects my work. As he walks under the light, I see his tattoos more clearly. One arm is on fire from wrist to shoulder, and the other has a complicated weave of tire tread and skulls and lightning and the Virgen de Guadalupe. "First time?"

Is it that obvious?

"We still got two more coats to go," Cheo says.

Flaco pats me on the shoulder. He may be skinny, but his hand feels like a rock. "*Que bien el color.*"

"Thanks," I mumble. "I like red." God, I'm a dork.

Flaco notices Zach, who hasn't moved from his spot near the wall. "*Órale,* you're that dude Cyclops."

Zach shrugs and nods at the same time.

"It's Zach," my brother says.

"Zach, right," Flaco says. "I heard you can take your eye out."

"Yeah."

"Well?"

After a slight hesitation, Zach pops his eye out and holds it in the palm of his hand.

"Let me check it out." Flaco says, mesmerized.

Zach glances at me as though he wants me to intervene. "I guess," he says. "Be careful?"

Flaco grabs it between his thumb and index finger and holds it in front of his own eye like a monocle. "Check it out, *ese*, I got one blue eye."

"*Que bueno*," Cheo says. "Better to pick up chicks." He and Steve start laughing.

"Um," Zach says nervously. "It's really expensive."

"Yeah, here you go," Flaco says, extending the eye back. "Oh shit!"

Suddenly, Flaco drops it. Zach leaps forward to catch it, but before the eye falls to the ground, Flaco snatches it with his other hand and stands up, laughing. "I'm just kidding, *ese*."

Zach swallows hard and takes the eye with both hands and pops it into his mouth for a thorough cleaning. When he's done, he puts it back into the socket and leans against the wall, scooting farther away from Flaco. I feel like shit, but I don't know what I could have done.

"Damn, *ese*," Steve says.

"What? I said I was just playing." He turns to Zach and offers out his palms. "We cool, right, *güero*?"

Zach nods and forces a smile. "Yeah, we're cool."

Cheo takes the airbrush from me. He disconnects it from the compression hose and places the brush back on the shelf. Then he opens up a cracked Styrofoam cooler and comes out with a sixer of Coors. "Who's thirsty?"

Steve and Flaco help themselves. Cheo offers me one, but the garage suddenly seems less friendly with Flaco here, and I don't feel like a beer. "No," I say. "Thanks, though."

Cheo looks surprised. "You sure? You earned it."

"I'm good. Trying to cut down." Damn, peer pressure's a bitch.

"More for me," Cheo says when Zach also refuses.

Flaco raises his can, winking at my brother. *"A las cholas."* I think of Carmenita clutching Steve's package at the mesa party and quickly shake the image out of my head.

"What's up tomorrow, Frankie?" Steve says after a sip. "You got to have a plan."

"I don't know. Maybe a movie."

Flaco wraps his arm around my neck and leans down. *"Ese,* I heard about what happened with that *tortillero* the other day."

"Yeah," I say to the ground. Dalton's beatdown is the gift that keeps on giving. Every time I think I can't feel worse about it, something like this happens. My raccoon eyes start to pulse. I can't even imagine how much of a punk Flaco must think I am.

"You going to do something about that?"

"Don't worry about Frankie," Cheo says. "He can handle his shit." He punches me lightly on the arm.

"I'm just saying," Flaco says. "Everybody knows where he lives. All you got to do is say the word and maybe the next morning he wakes up tied to his bed and all his shit's in my house."

Zach's face goes even whiter than normal, and I know what he's thinking. Nicole Lawrence hiding in her closet, scared out of her mind. I glance up at Flaco as Zach tries to push his body into the back wall.

"To revenge," Steve says.

"Ain't nothing sweeter." Flaco raises his beer, and they toast.

Cheo tilts his head to the side so slightly that I almost don't notice. He contemplates my brother for a second and then drains the rest of his beer. The garage is silent as he goes for another.

"Just be careful, Frankie," Zach says. "I don't think you want to piss off Dalton."

"I'm not scared." Of Dalton, that is. I can't help thinking, as Flaco and my brother toast each other, that the worst place in the world to be is on Flaco's bad side.

Zach is quieter this time. "I'm just saying, don't rub it in or anything. It's unnecessary."

"Unnecessary?" Flaco says, his voice tinged with disdain. "Who brought the dictionary?"

Zach stares at the concrete floor.

Steve chugs his beer and tosses the can outside. He leans back as a massive burp echoes throughout the garage. "He tries anything else? I'll get wicked on his ass."

"That's what I'm talking about," Flaco says, exchanging a handshake with Steve.

"You better check yourself," Cheo says dismissively.

"Bullshit, *ese*," Steve says. He opens another beer and glances up, still chuckling. "You know you'd be right there with me."

Cheo glances at Flaco before turning back to my brother. "Shit like that ain't playtime."

Now Steve isn't smiling anymore. His eyes narrow, and he takes a step toward Cheo. "Some tortilla fucking millionaire thinks he can beat down my family, and I'm going to do nothing? Like I'm some kind of bitch?"

I've never seen the two of them go at it like this. "Stop talking about me like I'm not standing right here," I say. "I can handle it myself."

Steve whirls to me, pointing. "Like you handled it last time?"

Humiliation nearly knocks me down. My adrenaline spikes, and I can barely keep my fingers from shaking. "Fuck you," I say. My voice cracks.

"Fuck *me*? I'm talking about helping you."

"Everybody *cálmense!*" Cheo says, and immediately there is silence. He walks outside the garage, taking a long sip from his beer. He makes a fist, crunching the can in his hand, and throws it onto a pile of rotting scrap wood.

Nobody says a word. We just watch him. Flaco lights another cigarette and takes a drag. When Cheo turns around and comes back into the garage, his voice is mellow and patient, almost like a parent talking to a small child. "I ain't calling you out. *Soy tu amigo, compa.*"

"You don't think I'm real?" Steve turns to Flaco in disbelief. "You hear this shit?"

Flaco shrugs and takes another sip of his beer.

Cheo leans against the hood of his car and takes out his ponytail. He looks exhausted all of a sudden, running his fingers through his hair. "*Te respeto, ese,* but you can't go being no vigilante motherfucker."

"This is bullshit," Steve says. He throws his beer against the garage wall, splashing a foamy arc across the wood.

"Steve—" I try to stop him, but he brushes past me and over to the Sizzler. He climbs in and slams the door shut. Twin clouds of dust spray from his rear wheels as he guns it down the driveway.

We all listen as the rumble disappears into the night. Flaco finishes his beer and goes for another. The sound of him popping the top is like the crack of a whip.

I turn to Cheo. "What the hell was that all about?"

He raises his eyebrows and whistles through his teeth. "Your brother's got a temper, huh?"

Steve and I used to fight a lot when we were younger. Usually it was no big deal, but once in a while, he'd get a look in his eyes that scared me for real. Times like that, I went running to our parents because I honestly thought he was going to kill me.

"You want to be real about it," Flaco says, leaning against the doorjamb, "you did disrespect him."

"*Chingao,*" Cheo says. "I don't even want to talk about it."

Flaco takes a long drag and exhales a thin cloud of smoke up toward the light. "I don't know what you expect." They consider each other for a few seconds, and then Flaco pushes away from the door. "Laters," he says with a backward nod, and then he steps out, the burning ember of his cigarette bouncing like a firefly as he disappears into the darkness.

A silence fills the garage as the sensation of Flaco dissipates. Zach stays immobile against the back wall. I scrape my foot across the dusty concrete floor. I'd never considered that *Cheo* would be as worried about Steve as I am. Cheo moves to the cooler for another beer, and I get the sense that I should be more afraid for my brother than pissed.

"Damn, Zach," I say finally, unable to handle the quiet any longer. "Steve was our ride home."

Cheo waves me off. "He'll be back."

"How do you know?"

"Just needs to cool off a little, that's all."

I find myself wondering if this happens a lot, but before I can ask Cheo about it, he puts his hair back in the ponytail and moves to the airbrush. He hooks up the hose and flicks on the compressor. Then he holds out the brush and a mask. "Ready for another coat?"

If he's done talking about my brother, I might as well try to finish my bike. It's even harder to keep steady now, and at first I have to use both hands. It's good, though, to have something to concentrate on. Soon I'm focused enough to use just one hand.

"*Oye*, Zach," Cheo says when I'm almost through the next coat. "*Ven.*"

Zach, hands deep in his pockets, walks around the Impala and stands next to Cheo, who reaches into the cooler again.

"You sure you don't want one?"

"It's okay," Zach says. He looks a little shell-shocked, and I don't blame him.

About ten minutes later, just as Cheo predicted, the Sizzler comes rolling back into the driveway, but Steve doesn't get out of the car. I can see him behind the wheel, waiting, looking at us.

Cheo reaches for the airbrush. "*Dámelo*, Frankie."

I hand it over. "Don't we need another coat?"

"I'll do it. Just don't let that fucker go *loco* on us." He's trying to crack a joke, but he can't make eye contact with me.

Without another word, Zach and I climb into the car. It's probably good that we're going—we said we'd be home by nine, and we're already fifteen minutes late—but it feels wrong, leaving like this.

The ride to Zach's house is completely silent. No talking, no music, barely even any breathing. After we drop Zach off, though, I decide I can't take the silence anymore.

"Steve, you know it was just a fight." I'm searching for the right words, but I don't feel like I'm anywhere close to them. "I'm going to be okay."

"That wasn't about you," he says, his eyes still on the road.

"Then what was it about?" I don't understand it at all; he's Steve Towers, captain of the soccer team. What can he possibly have to prove? Especially to Flaco?

For a second, I think he's going to tell me, but instead he exhales slowly through his nose and forces a flat smile.

"Nothing. Don't worry about it."

I remember when I found out Santa wasn't real. I'd suspected for a while, but I held out hope, and when Steve showed me our parents stuffing the stockings, my world was different. There was less hope, less optimism, because, let's face it: who the hell wants to live in a world where Santa doesn't exist?

Now I have no idea what to make of my brother, and that scares me. It's not that he and Flaco were *talking* about messing Dalton's shit up—it's that I recognized the look in Steve's eyes. If Flaco had made the move tonight, I can't say that Steve wouldn't have gone with him.

ten

THERE'S A DIFFERENCE between the houses closer to downtown Borges, like Rebecca's, and those more on the outskirts, like mine. It's mainly lawns—we don't have them. Plus, their houses are closer together, they all look the same, and they're all fake adobe. It's easy to tell the difference if you know what to look for. Even though they're stucco, the edges are way too sharp. I think if you're going to build a house out of wood, build it out of wood. Don't just stucco it and try to pull a fast one on people who've been living in adobe houses for five hundred years.

That said, the houses here are much nicer than ours, even though they don't really seem to belong in New Mexico.

Rebecca's, for example, has green bushes lining a flagstone walkway that leads to the front door. There's a small sign, MI CASA ES SU CASA, sticking out of a rosebush under one of the front windows. The lawn is actually green, and the driveway is paved.

I tried to convince my parents to lend me Dad's truck tonight, but my mom insisted on being chauffeur. At least she parks way down the block so it doesn't seem like we're picking up Rebecca for carpool.

Rebecca's door has one of those brass knockers on it, and while under normal circumstances I probably wouldn't mention this, the fact that it's in the shape of a skull and crossbones worries me. There seems to be a fresh coat of red paint on the door, and there is no doorbell in sight. I hesitate. Do I grab the skull and rap away at this newly painted door? Do I knock with my hands? I'm reaching for a brass skull the size of my fist when the door swings open to reveal Rebecca's dad. We stare at each other for a second, me with my hand half raised, him with one hand on the door and the other on his waist.

Mr. Sanchez, Mr. Chief of the Borges Police Department, is about three inches taller than I am, although without his combat boots, he and I might be the same height. His black hair is cut military style: almost completely shaved on the sides and only a bit longer on top. I guess there's some Rebecca in him, but it's hard to find. His face is more round, his skin more leathery, his eyes more piercing and much less kind.

Everything about him pales in comparison to the sight of

his cop arms. Big, beefy, cop arms, as if he's decided the only way to keep the streets safe for his daughter is by having the thickest arms in the state. His biceps stretch against the fabric of his T-shirt like two water balloons about to burst. Thank you, Rebecca, for leaving me out here with this carnival sideshow.

"You going to stand there all night?" he says, his eyes narrowing.

Somehow, I tear my gaze away from his enormous pipes. "Uh. No, sir."

He breaks into a sudden smile and motions me inside. "Well, get inside then. Becka's just about ready."

Dr. Jekyll and Mr. Sanchez.

Their house is nice, like what you see on sitcoms. Light brown carpet everywhere, even in the hallway. As someone who grew up without it, carpet has always seemed like such a luxury to me. I hate walking barefoot at my house—no matter how much we sweep and mop, the bricks get dirty fast, and I can't even go the ten steps from my room to the bathroom without getting grainy dust between my toes. Plus, brick gets really cold in the winter. But Rebecca's house is amazing—I could walk barefoot here all day long.

In the living room, there's a fireplace with a bunch of family pictures on the mantel. A big-screen TV takes up almost the entire wall, with a well-worn recliner pushed to the side. Opposite the television sits a long couch with plaid upholstery, and in front of it a coffee table covered with old issues of

People, Newsweek, and, it warms my heart to see, *Shotgun News* and *Guns and Weapons for Law Enforcement.*

"Want to take a seat," he says, not asking.

I nod and arrange myself at the end of the couch, close to the door, beside a small needlepointed pillow. A Siamese cat with a halo and white wings hovers over a perfect representation of the house I'm now sitting in. Under the house it says, "Bless this mess." How . . . cute.

Mr. Sanchez takes a seat in his recliner and clasps his hands together, resting his chin on top of them. Somewhere within the depths of his house, I hear the jet-engine whirr of a blow-dryer, and for the first time I see a negative side to Rebecca's beautiful long hair. With shorter hair, she'd be out here already. He narrows his eyes again, as if he can't quite figure out what to make of me. What is he thinking?

"That's an interesting door knocker," I offer.

"I hear your brother has a scholarship."

Thank God. I can make small talk about my brother all day long. I have practice. "Yes, sir. At least one, from UNM, but he might get other offers."

He leans forward, resting his elbows on his knees, and stares at me for a few seconds. "Your parents must be proud."

I glance away. There's something uncomfortable about the way he said that. Like he doesn't really think they must be proud. Like he just switched from good cop to bad cop.

"Yes, sir," I say. A roof-mounted laser-sight bazooka points up at me from the cover of *Guns and Weapons for Law*

Enforcement. Rebecca's hair dryer drones down the hallway.

"Tell me . . . what happened to your face?"

I clear my throat and try to make light of it. "It's a funny story—"

"You're not in any gang trouble?"

Where the hell did that come from? "No, sir—"

"Why are you so nervous?"

I clear my throat. What does he mean, why am I so nervous? Maybe because I'm getting the freaking third degree over here. I try to compose myself. "If I were in a gang, my mom would kill me." I laugh just a little. "I'm not in a gang, sir."

"You'd better not be," he says. His face looks like it's about to explode, but I know he's trying to keep quiet so Rebecca doesn't hear him. "Because if you think I raised my daughter to go out with gangbangers . . ." He leans in closer. "You. Are. Mistaken."

"Yes, sir—"

Just then, Rebecca hops into the room, and her father's face lights up. "There you are, sweetheart," he says, standing up and taking her hand. "You look nice."

She smiles. "Thanks, *Papi.*"

Mr. Sanchez looks at me and motions to his daughter. "Doesn't she look nice?"

Is this some sort of a trick? I'm smart enough keep my eyes above her neck, but my peripheral vision is 20/15 around Rebecca. She doesn't just look nice. Her jeans are so tight it must have taken her two hours and a jar of Vaseline to get them on. And still no camel toe. Her hair is pulled back into a ponytail, and she's wearing a blue tank top as close to the color of her eyes as I've ever seen. She looks great. So great, in fact, that my first instinct is to wonder what she's doing going out with me tonight.

"Yes, sir," I say, peeling my eyes from Rebecca's and looking at her father. "Yes, she looks very nice."

"You ready, Frankie?" she says.

Mr. Sanchez hasn't stopped smiling since his daughter came into the room. He puts one of his meaty hands in the small of my back and steers me toward the door. "Of course he is."

We're out on the walkway before I know it. The door slams behind us, and the bronze skull raps twice. I have the strangest feeling that if I turn back toward the house I'll see his narrow eyes peering at me through the blinds.

"Wow," I say, wiping my forehead. I just realized I've been sweating.

"What? My dad?"

"No." I shake my head. "You look great."

"You're the worst liar ever. What did he say?"

"Normal dad stuff. Have a good time, don't be late, take care of my daughter or I'll kill you."

"That's all just an act, you know. He's really sweet when you get to know him."

"I'm sure."

Cheo told me about one time he was speeding and a cop

pulled him over, threw him to the ground, and almost broke his thumb. That was just for speeding. Imagine what they do to you if you bring their daughters home late.

"He kept looking at me all funny."

Rebecca laughs and takes my hand in hers. It's so soft. "No offense, but you don't look like yourself right now."

I can't help but smile back. "I guess."

My mom sees us and starts the truck. I open the rear passenger-side door, like a gentleman, and help Rebecca up and inside.

"Hello, Mrs. Towers," she says in her most polite voice, extending a hand for my mom to shake.

"It's so wonderful to see you again, Rebecca. It seems like just yesterday you and Frankie were in the fourth grade."

Oh God, she'd better not go there. I hop in, and we drive away. After staring at Rebecca in the rearview mirror for at least ten extremely awkward seconds, my mom turns around and smiles at me. "She's beautiful, Francisco."

You have got to be kidding. As if she's not sitting right here. "Yeah, I know." I look over, ready to apologize for my mother, but Rebecca cuts me off.

"Thank you, Mrs. Towers." She winks at me, and I know everything is going to be okay.

eleven

IF YOU WANT to go out on a date in Borges, you pretty much have three options: movies, bowling, or minigolf. You'd have more choices if you hit the mesa or drove all the way to Albuquerque, but if you don't have a car of your own, that's a long time to spend with your mom. So, until people get cars, they're limited to the big three.

There are pluses and minuses to each. Normally, movies are the best bet, especially for a first date. They're low pressure, relatively cheap, and I don't need to tell you what the darkness leads to. Unfortunately, Rebecca and I couldn't agree on what to see, so we decided not to see anything at all.

Bowling should always be ruled out on the first date

because of the shoes. Used, stanky, dork shoes are absolutely no way to get on base. Not to mention the fact that I suck at bowling. One time Zach and I went on his birthday, and even the people next to us were calling me a wino because I spent so much time in the gutter.

That leaves us minigolf, which is fun but also a little dangerous. The parking lot at Golf n' Goof is one of the biggest in town. That means cars, and tons of them. Chicks get all dressed up, *cholos* cruise by in their freshly waxed rides, hitting switches on the hydraulics and blasting music. Everyone thinks they're the shit. It's intimidating even before you try to putt the ball through a castle, a spaceship, and a clown's nose all in the same hole.

To get to Golf n' Goof from Rebecca's house, we have to drive over Arroyo del Águila and past downtown. I can't take my eyes off the Tortilla Emporium, lit up as it is against the deep red evening sky. Instinctively, my hand goes up to the bruises on my face.

I glance over at Rebecca—staring out the window at something—and I can't help but feel a twinge of uncertainty. Is she really going out with me tonight? Or is this some sort of complicated practical joke she's pulling with Dalton? He'll meet us there, pound my face some more, and take her away from me again. She's leading me straight into a trap, and I'm only too happy to go along like a lamb to the slaughter. This is a huge mistake. I need to tell my mom to turn the truck around right now.

Rebecca catches me staring. "What are you thinking about?"

I shake my head. "Nothing."

Golf n' Goof is *the* multipurpose entertainment establishment for the town of Borges. It says so right there on the big neon sign at the entrance. There's golf, of course, but the goof consists of an arcade, an indoor basketball court, and batting cages. It's only seven thirty, but there's already action in the corner of the huge parking lot between a black '67 El Camino and a bright orange '84 Coupe de Ville. The El Camino goes first—the left side bounces at least a foot off the ground—and then the '84 answers with a sick pancake: all four wheels off the ground at the same time.

My mom pulls in front of the main building, and suddenly the only thing going through my mind is: please don't embarrass me, please don't embarrass me, please don't embarrass me.

"I'll pick you up at ten thirty," she says.

I unlock my door and open it. "Okay, Mom."

"Out here, Francisco. Don't make me park and have to come inside to look for you."

"Okay."

"What does your watch say, *mijo*? I want to make sure you're out exactly on time."

"Mom, I said I'd be out at ten thirty."

She turns to Rebecca, pointing to me as a lawyer would indicate incriminating evidence. "I bet you don't talk to your *mamá* that way, do you, *princesa*?"

Rebecca forces a smile but says nothing. Her parents divorced a few years ago. This is getting worse by the second, and there's only one way for me to get out of the truck in one piece. "I'm sorry, *Mamá*," I say, leaning over the seat and kissing her on the cheek. "I didn't mean to be rude. We'll be out here at ten thirty on the dot."

We hop onto the sidewalk and I slam the door. After a few seconds, my mom drives away. I watch until she's turned out of the parking lot and back onto the street. It's not like this is my first date, but given the current condition of my face, it was all I could do to convince her to let me leave the house tonight. "Sorry about that."

"That's okay. I thought it was cute. She called me *princesa*."

"She's been a little overprotective . . ." I trail off. I hadn't meant to bring that up.

"Can you blame her? I mean, I don't know what I would do if something like that happened to my kid. I'm amazed she's even letting you out of her sight for the next twenty years."

That surprises me. Most people have no idea how to handle this, but she actually said something—something honest. Great. Now I feel like an ass for being embarrassed.

I lead her inside, opening the door like the gentleman I've just been reminded I'm not. The wanna-be *cholo* at the club rental counter is trying to grow a mustache, but he's got the fuzzy caterpillar thing going instead. He leans over an old issue of

Street Customs magazine, and when we walk up to the counter, he gets all annoyed, as if we just barged in on him taking a dump.

"Two putters, please," I say, reaching for my wallet. I may be a social idiot tonight, but because I work in the restaurant, I have spending money. I'm not the only one, of course—lots of people my age have jobs in some of the fast-food joints or even in Albuquerque and Santa Fe—but the point is that I have cash in my pocket. Enough to lavish upon my date an entire evening of Ski Ball, minigolf, Whac-A-Mole, and Slush Puppies.

"You want to play Enchanted Forest, Alien Attack, or Circus Spectacular?" He recites the names as if he's reading the phone book. Would we please just make a goddamn decision and let him get back to his magazine.

"What would the lady prefer?" I say with an exaggerated bow. The club guy stares at me, and Rebecca raises her eyebrows in shock. Oops, that was freaking lame. Lesson learned. I give Rebecca a shrug and point to my black eyes. "Sorry, I still have a concussion."

As soon as we get out to Alien Attack, it becomes clear that I'm no better at minigolf than I am at bowling. I have no control over how hard I hit the ball; sometimes I smash it so it bounces off the railings and onto another hole, and other times I need to hit it four feet but barely tap it. Rebecca, on the other hand, is phenomenal. On our fourth hole she threads the ball through a damaged alien spacecraft, around a corner, over some wreckage and debris, and into the cup for a hole in one.

She drops her club, and when she throws her arms up in celebration, her shirt rides up a little. "Who's your *princesa?*" she says with a squeal.

"You come here a lot?"

"What's the matter, Frankie, can't handle losing?"

Oh, I can handle it. As long as I'm losing to her. "All right, all right. Don't rub it in." I roll my shoulders like a boxer and gently place my ball on the little rubber mat. "Watch this."

It's a funny thing about being bad at something that your date is good at. The pressure is off the charts. There is nothing I want more than to put this ball in the hole. Everything rests on it: my honor, my standing in Rebecca's eyes, my own sense of self-worth. I say a silent prayer and remind myself to hit it nice and easy. I clear my throat, bring the club back . . . and absolutely crush it.

The ball hits a little rip in the Astro Turf and veers sharply to the right. It bounces off the side of the UFO, over the guardrail, and onto the concrete pathway between the holes. Rebecca and I watch it bounce, bounce, bounce down the concrete, over one of the holes in the Enchanted Forest, and through the fence into the parking lot. Good thing I got a yellow ball. Otherwise I wouldn't have been able to see it roll all the way down the street.

Rebecca leans her elbow on my shoulder and shakes her head. "Wow, Frankie. I've never seen anybody hit a golf ball that far."

God, I suck. "I'm going pro next year."

We look at each other and smile. She lets out a snort and quickly covers her mouth, doubling over laughing. It's safe to say that the ice has been broken.

When I get back with a new ball—after paying for the one I lost—things are much more relaxed. Secure in the knowledge that there is nothing I can do to become better at putting, I don't try too hard. Funny thing is, not only do I enjoy myself more, but I even start playing better.

We're standing over the disemboweled carcass of a three-legged Martian when I ask her one of the world's most important questions. "What's your favorite New Mexican food?"

Rebecca shrugs. "Umm. I don't really have one."

"Come on," I say, "you have to have a favorite. Carne adovada, stuffed sopaipillas, chile rellenos?"

"I'm not really into New Mexican food."

I stare at her as if she's turned into one of the aliens on the twelfth hole. "You're kidding."

My shock seems to catch her by surprise, and she gets all defensive. "No, I'm not kidding. I don't like hot food."

Who is this person standing in front of me? Doesn't like hot food? Her grandmother used to run a restaurant. We're in north central New Mexico and her last name's Sanchez, for Christ's sake. I know that's a bit stereotypical of me. But damn, even still. "You don't like hot food?"

"Sorry. Don't take it so personal."

"Maybe you just haven't had the right kind." That would explain it, right? I mean, if nobody's ever taken the time to prepare her an authentic plate of stuffed sopaipillas, she can hardly be blamed.

"I have my mom's taste buds."

I *knew* there was a good reason. Rebecca's white mom has robbed her of the ability to appreciate the best food on the planet. Maybe taste buds are like being Jewish—you get them from your mother's side. If that's the case, thank God my mom's the Torres. "Where's she from?"

"California." She expertly putts the ball through a papier-mâché black hole. "That's where she went back to, and that's where I want to go as soon as I get out of this place."

"What do you mean?"

"Out of Borges. Out of New Mexico." She shivers and gestures to the parking lot with her putter. The scene is starting to fill out now, competing bass lines rumble from the open car doors. A souped-up Honda Civic peels out of the parking lot, followed by some shouting and laughing. A Chevy truck roars to life and chases the Honda.

"I didn't know you hated it so much."

"It's not that I hate it. I just know there's more for me than cruising the Golf n' Goof and hanging out with a bunch of *cholos*. No offense."

"None taken," I say. But I wonder if it has anything to do with the whole Tortilla Emporium thing. If it were my family's recipes putting money in Dalton's pocket, I probably wouldn't be able to think about anything else. Maybe that's why she wants to leave. Just to get out of here and put it all behind her.

"What about you?" she says as I line up my putt.

I've actually been thinking about it a lot lately. Steve has his scholarship, so he's definitely going to college, but I don't know about me. My parents want me to go for sure, but we still have to figure out a way to afford it. "I don't know," I say. "Maybe go to UNM. That seems like such a long time from now."

"But it's not," she says. She shivers again, and this time she rubs her arms.

"Are you cold?"

"Yeah. It's, like, sixty degrees out."

I'm such an idiot—I should have noticed that earlier. But it's really her fault, right? I mean, she wore a tank top even though she had to know it would get cold later. I accidentally glance down at her chest and see that she's smuggling raisins. Though I look back up almost instantly, it's too late. She catches me—I'm busted. Damn.

Wait, maybe she *knew* it was going to be cold, and she didn't wear a jacket as some sort of a test. Chicks are sneaky like that. I take off my jacket and hold it open for her. "Here."

She drapes the jacket over her shoulders like a cape. "Thanks a lot. I should have worn a sweater." She pulls the collar up close to her chin and kind of snuggles into it. "You sure you don't need it?"

"Nah, that's okay."

"That's so sweet of you, Frankie." She leans in and wraps both of her arms around one of mine, pulling me closer to her.

I am the man. I'm so thoughtful and caring. My mom did a great job raising me.

We move on to the next hole, which is a narrow double-decker approach to an alien's head, followed by a tiny pathway over a river of green "blood." If you miss the head, your ball rolls back to you covered in slime. I might as well mark myself down for fifteen strokes.

"I want to live in a city. And Albuquerque doesn't count." She hits her ball hard and true; it stops less than three feet from the hole. "When I was little, I couldn't imagine living anywhere else. Now, it's like, I just want to get as far away as possible."

Maybe it's because her dad's the chief of police. That would explain everything. I mean, how much would it suck to have your dad be the freaking cops. "You have to admit, we get to do things in Borges that you could never do in a city."

"Like what?"

I close my eyes and strike the ball. Miraculously, I manage to avoid the alien slime blood. "You could never set off bottle rockets in Albuquerque. It's illegal."

"Didn't you and Zach almost burn down somebody's house one time?"

"That was more than three years ago."

"My dad was all pissed off. He said everyone in the department was talking about how stupid you were."

"That's a little unfair, don't you think? They weren't even there."

I'm trying to defend myself here, but she's right: we were stupid. It was before the Fourth of July, the hottest—and driest, as it turned out—part of the summer, and Zach and I had just gotten a couple packs of bottle rockets: about four gross. When I found some old three-foot sections of PVC from back behind my house, we got the brilliant idea of strapping the half-inch pipes to our forearms. We covered the bottom with some duct tape to keep the rockets from falling all the way through, and then we each used our free hands to light the fuses and drop the rockets into our arm-mounted silos.

We started out shooting them straight up, but there were three red-breasted robins just chilling on the telephone wire. We had noticed early on that the pipes increased our accuracy, so you can hardly blame us for what happened next. Once we lowered our trajectories to aim at the robins, my neighbor's sage bushes came into range.

It wasn't pretty. A fire truck showed up at the neighbor's house and put out the burning sage. I still don't think the fire would have spread to the house, but like I said, it was a dry summer. The two cops who came to my house soon afterward made sure we knew exactly how much danger we had put everybody in. We promised it would never happen again, so the cops let us off with a long lecture and fifty hours of community service each. I must have pulled weeds for half the families in Borges.

"Okay," I say. "Maybe just a bit stupid."

Here comes the dreaded long pause. We're officially in

one of those really awkward moments in a conversation where all that needs to be said has been said, and to add anything else would be overkill. You would think that these moments would be kind of satisfying, like proof that we actually got somewhere. But right about now is when I freak out because I have no idea how I'm going to get another conversation started. It's like, Oh shit, what if we don't say another word to each other this whole night?

There's nobody behind us, so we're just hanging out in the middle of the sixteenth hole. I'm about to mumble something really stupid, like "yeah" or "hmmm." Luckily, Rebecca interrupts me.

"You know what my dad and I were talking about before you picked me up? That time—was it third or fourth grade? When you punched Rubén in the gut."

"You remember that?"

"Of course. Rubén was such a jerk, and I wanted to do the same thing. I went home right after school and told my dad how cool you were."

"You did?" Damn, I wish I'd known about this earlier—like eight years ago! Who knows how I would have acted around her. "He didn't want to come arrest me?"

She laughs. "He said that even though violence is not the answer, he was impressed that you'd stood up for the new kid."

I look away and nod, but I'm afraid that if I make eye contact with her, she's going to notice how much it means to me. "Yeah, Zach's a good guy."

"Anyway, I'm glad you're not totally mad about Dalton and Homecoming and all that. I'm glad we can still be friends."

Damn. Friends. I thought I was making headway, what with the tight jeans and skimpy tank top and the little snuggle. I'm such a punk. I feel sick to my stomach.

I don't know whether I should play nice and try to enjoy what's left of our "date," or if I should bust out of here and save what's left of my dignity. I'm just about to give the second option a try when a low rumble fills the parking lot.

I know that sound. That's the sound of a 1969 Pontiac GTO convertible, one of the most beautiful cars ever made: 370 horsepower, 400 cubic-inch V8 Ram Air IV engine. Zero to sixty in 6.2 seconds. I love that car.

The only problem is, I know who that car belongs to, and I hate the driver.

Rebecca turns her head at the sound, just in time to catch John Dalton pulling into a parking space with the top down and a couple of goons along for the ride with him. The GTO's immaculate midnight blue paint glistens under the lights of the parking lot. As if it wasn't enough that he kicked my face in, he has to go out and drive my dream car?

Not that I have a car yet, I know. But when I get one, that's the car I want. If it were mine, though, I'd throw some Chassis Tech compressed-air suspension on that bad boy and drop it a good five inches.

Part of me can't shake the thought that Rebecca planned this, that she told Dalton we'd be here so that he could finish the job. It's ridiculous, I know, but it gnaws at the back of my mind, and I suddenly want to get the hell out of here. But if I told her that, I would never stand a chance again.

So here's what I need to do: I need to be gracious but honest, and I need to let her know that I value her friendship as well. "A lot of girls would've been all weird with this," I say, summoning all my energy to my poker face as I try to come up with something she might want to hear. "I think it's cool that you have guy friends. Makes you seem older. Like more mature, or something."

For a second, I think I might have pushed it too far, but then she sticks out her bottom lip, giving me the puppy-dog face. "That's so sweet."

Chicks love it when we talk about our feelings. For my understanding, I am rewarded with a kiss. I think she even lingers a bit longer than she needs to, and she's still got her lips firmly planted on my cheek when Dalton struts onto the minigolf course, waving a putter like some psychotic baton twirler.

"What . . . the . . . fuck?" he says, and Rebecca backs away from me. Dalton has his hair all slicked back tonight, like a used car salesman. Naturally, he's wearing his letter jacket, although it's cleaner now than it was the last time I saw it. His daddy must have hired someone to scrub my blood off the sleeves.

Standing right behind him, also flaunting their rented putters, are Will Burrage and Matt Austin, two soccer players who I can only assume were the coward motherfuckers who helped Dalton kick my ass.

"Hey, Spankie," Dalton says. He dropped the "Frankie," so I guess we're buddies now. "What are you doing here?"

"Playing minigolf, you dipshit *pendejo*, what does it look like I'm doing?"

I don't think he was expecting me to tell him off, because he squints at me and can't quite seem to think of what to say next. What a Neanderthal. He finally points his club at me. "Are you any good?"

"John," Rebecca says, "don't."

"Don't what? I'm just wondering if he's any good at getting it in the hole."

"Are you kidding me?" she says, shaking her head. Maybe this time she'll finally see him for who he is. "Don't be such an ass!"

Dalton steps forward and pokes me in the chest with the end of his putter. Instinctively, I knock it away with my own club like a sword.

"I don't want trouble," I say, taking a step back.

"Of course you don't want trouble, Francisco." He spits my name out, one syllable at a time. Fran-cis-co. "You don't want to get your ass kicked again is what you don't want. How are you feeling, by the way? I should have sent a card, but I was busy. You know how school gets."

He's trying to provoke me, but I'm not going to fall for it. They smoked me easily enough last time, and they didn't even need golf clubs to do it. Will and Matt seem to be enjoying this whole thing, and why shouldn't they? Stupid *chingones* don't know what to think until Dalton tells them.

"Can you even putt with your eyes like that?" Dalton says, stepping toward me. "You look like a freaking animal, you know? Like a baboon."

"Damn it, John!" Rebecca says. "Just get out of here and leave us alone."

"What about it, Spankie? You need a girl for protection?"

"I don't want to fight you," I say as evenly as I can. I'm stalling. A crowd has started to gather, and it's only a matter of time before the Golf n' Goof manager comes out with one of his rent-a-cops to break it up. If I can just last that long, I should be able to get out of here alive.

Dalton smiles. "I know you don't want to fight me— you'd just get your ass Frankie-Spanked again. But I don't want to fight you either," he says. "Last time was so boring. You didn't even put up a struggle."

"That was you?" Rebecca says, her voice filled with disgust. "That was really you?"

"I'd do your brother, too," Dalton says, ignoring her and taking a step toward me. "But I bet he's as much of a pussy as you are. A whole family of pussies."

What am I supposed to say to that? I squeeze the handle of the club in my right hand, trying to regain control of my temper. I can feel my heart beating in my ears and the crisp breeze on the back of my neck. The putter's rubber handle is smooth and worn, and the fingerprints of previous users meld with my own. Somewhere, one of the onlookers is smacking her gum, but I don't see her. Dalton's smirk is the only thing I see—everything else has fallen away. I'm going to kill him.

"Frankie Torres!" Suddenly, a deep, accented voice breaks through the silence.

Like some *cholo* in shining armor, Flaco emerges from the arcade building and heads directly for me. He pushes through the crowd and gives Dalton a little nudge with his shoulder as he struts by. Before I know it, Flaco's standing right in front of me, between me and Dalton, and he's giving me a hug and a strong fist pat on the back. Because he's almost a foot taller than I am, he has to bend way down to do it.

"What's up, *carnal?*" he says, as if we're the only two people around; as if a rich, white, golf-club wielding lunatic wasn't just a few feet away, a crowd of onlookers surrounding us. He looks extra fierce tonight—the khakis, the wallet chain, the flannel buttoned at the top over the white beater, the mesh trucker hat pulled low over his eyes, the shiny ponytail halfway down his back. I've never been happier to see anybody in my life.

I drop my club and shake his hand. "*Órale,* Flaco. Good to see you, *ese.*" Understatement of the freaking year.

"You having a good time?"

This is so surreal, our private conversation. I shrug. "Not bad. Except I suck at golf."

Dalton can't deal with it. He makes a big show of clearing his throat. "Um. Excuse me?"

Flaco turns around and pretends to notice Dalton for the first time. "Can I help you?" It comes out more like *calp-yoo*.

"Hell yeah, you can help me," Dalton says, stepping forward. Will and Matt keep pace behind him. "You can start by getting the fuck out of here and breaking back into prison. Me and Frankie-Spankie here were in the middle of a conversation."

Oh, this is too good. For some reason, Dalton isn't nearly as afraid of Flaco as he should be. I know they've seen each other around, but whether it's that Rebecca's watching or that he and his two gorillas still have a majority, it doesn't seem to occur to him that Flaco couldn't possibly be here alone. If Dalton's eyes weren't so clouded with testosterone, even he would be able to see what's about to happen.

But he can't stop himself. "So, what do you say? Can you help me or not?"

I almost feel sorry for him when Flaco's friends start coming through the door, one after the other, like they're hopping out of a clown car. Dalton knows he's screwed when the first one stands behind Flaco and me with his arms crossed, but it doesn't stop there; they just keep coming. One by one they walk past, each one more badass than the last, bumping into him on their way by. We don't really have gangs here in Borges—not as bad as Albuquerque, anyway—but if we did, this is what they'd look like. These dudes are so hard they make Flaco seem like a teddy bear, and by the time all seven of them take up position behind me, a hush has fallen over the crowd. It's electric.

A bunch of *cholas* are here, too, smacking gum and

whispering to each other and waiting. If looks could crap their pants, Dalton would have skid marks right now. Ladies and gentlemen, the tables have officially turned.

"*Órale, gringo,*" Flaco says, holding his hands out in an exaggerated gesture of apology. "I had no idea you were in the middle of a conversation. *Ándale,* go right ahead."

Dalton clears his throat. If you listen real hard, you can hear the sound of his heart shrinking. "That's okay," he manages to say. "We were finished."

"I don't think so. I didn't hear no 'I'm sorry.'" Flaco takes a step toward him, and the seven *cholos* behind me uncross their arms at the same time. Damn, this is awesome.

"Hey," Dalton says, glancing around at the crowd, "I don't want trouble."

"I said, I didn't hear no 'I'm sorry' from your disrespecting ass."

Matt and Will look at each other, no doubt wondering how their putters are going to feel shoved two feet up their *culos.* Flaco shakes his head like a disappointed parent. "I heard what you said before, you *pinche güerito.* Steve Towers is a pussy?"

And now is when it gets really good. My brother's voice cuts through the night air. "Holy shit," he says, sniffling and faking tears as he pushes through the crowd. "I'm a pussy?" Carmenita is right behind him, the rose tattoo on her chest glistening in the harsh white light.

"*Simón,*" Flaco says. "This *puta* said it, so it must be true."

Steve takes position next to Flaco and crosses his arms.

Remember that look I told you about? The one I used to think meant he was going to kill me? He's giving it to Dalton right now, but it's worse than anything he ever gave me. "Hello, John," my brother says.

"I . . . I didn't mean . . ." Dalton stammers. "What I said—"

Flaco turns to my brother. "You a big pussy?"

"About this big, I think." Steve holds his hands a foot apart.

"No," Flaco says. He spreads his arms wide. *"Así."*

Steve turns to Dalton, his voice thick with sarcasm. "We can't seem to agree on how big a pussy I am. Want to help us find out?" And with that, he takes a little step forward.

The situation is hopeless for Dalton now, and he knows it. He tosses his putter to the side, and it bounces a few times before coming to a stop next to the eighteenth hole. "Let's go, Rebecca," he says.

She doesn't move. This whole time, she's been looking back and forth from me to Dalton. It's like she's watching one of those animal shows on TV, like she's not quite sure if the hyenas can really take down the elephant, and she can't tear her eyes away.

"Rebecca, let's go." Dalton storms over and grabs for her hand, but she pulls it away. As she does, my jacket falls to the ground. There is a moment when I think he could do anything; he's the wounded animal right now. His pride is gone, and he might decide he has nothing to lose by going psycho on us.

Finally, Rebecca breaks the silence. "I came here with Frankie."

"And you're leaving with me," he says. On the outside he looks defiant, but there's too much effort going into his posture, and his voice rises a little bit at the end. He won't accept it. Pitiful, really, when you think about it.

"No, John," she says evenly, "I'm leaving with him." She walks over to me and wraps her arm around mine.

Don't you love the way life works? Five minutes ago I had an appointment with another ass-kicking, and now I've got Rebecca on one side and Flaco and my brother on the other. Talk about a roller coaster.

Dalton clears his throat and tries to stand up a little straighter. He's about to turn around when Rebecca stops him with her voice.

"By the way. Frankie just asked me to go to Homecoming with him, and I said yes. I just thought you might want to know."

In front of everybody! Now, *that's* hardcore.

A visible jolt shoots up Dalton's spine. He stands in front of me, a little vein popping out the side of his neck, and stares.

If we weren't still in a crowd of people, I'd . . . Oh, hell, I'll do it anyway. I give Dalton a little wink and then wrap my arm around Rebecca's waist. Dalton nods so slightly I almost don't pick up on it. I should probably wonder what that means, but right now I'm having too much fun to worry about it. Just before he turns to go, he spits in our direction.

Not a good idea. Flaco takes two quick steps, cutting him off before he can escape to the inside. It looks for a second like he's going to kick Dalton's ass, but instead he just leans in close. "Don't you ever fuck with one of my boys again."

Matt and Will are trying to get to the door, but the crowd has blocked their way. Not aggressively, but just enough to let them know what would happen if shit really went down. Dalton glances at his friends before raising his chin at Flaco. I want a poster of this moment hanging up in my room.

"Whatever," Dalton says.

You have to hand it to him. Even with the odds so stacked against him, he's still putting on a brave face. He probably figures that whatever Flaco wants to do, he won't do it here.

"You'll never know where I'm coming from, tortilla boy," Flaco says with a cocky smile. "You got lots of money, you got yourself a fancy-ass GTO, your daddy may own half the town, but you know what, little *güero*?" He steps forward, pointing to himself, and his voice gets real low. If I weren't so close, I probably wouldn't be able to hear it. "He don't own me, so I got nothing to lose."

There is a moment of silence as they stare each other down, and then Dalton slowly backs away, before turning around and leading his lackeys through the door. This time, the crowd parts to let them through.

Seconds later, the arcade door opens again, and out comes the manager. He's a little man. Mr. Gonzales, I think. He looks the same as when I first came here—still has the salt-and-pepper pencil-thin mustache, still wears Wrangler jeans, old boots, and a tight-fitting cowboy shirt with pearl snaps. He's pissed, and his greasy comb-over is all disheveled. Sure enough, a rent-a-cop is right on his heels.

"What's going on out here?" the manager says with his hands on his hips. The rent-a-cop adjusts his hat and tries to make eye contact with the crowd so he can stare somebody down.

"Just a celebration, sir," Flaco says.

Mr. Gonzales isn't buying it. "A celebration?" he says, gesturing to the crowd, which for some reason is still gathered around. We're a train wreck; they can't take their eyes off us. "What, may I ask, is the occasion?"

To my surprise, Flaco points to me. "My boy just hit a hole in one."

Huh?

The manager looks around suspiciously, grabbing the front of his belt and readjusting it over his hanging belly. "Is that right?"

"Hell yeah, that's right," Flaco says. He winks at me and raises his arms.

As if on cue, the crowd begins to applaud. Slowly at first, a golf clap, like they think Alien Attack is the U.S. Open or something. But soon, prodded along by Flaco and my brother, the tentative claps turn into actual cheers, and I find myself in the center of a massive standing ovation.

For the first time, I really look at the people around us.

They're mostly like me—just here to have a good time. I know some of them and recognize others. They're couples out on dates, groups of friends, even some families. But here's the thing: they're scared. They see a badass teenager and his crew. They're clapping because they think they have to.

I look over at Rebecca, who seems as unprepared as I am. She bows her head. I can see John Dalton out in the parking lot, standing at the open door of his GTO and looking my way. His thugs are in the car already, but Dalton waits, watching me.

The manager, apparently convinced by all the cheering, comes up to me with his hand outstretched. "Congratulations," he says. "When you're done with your round, come on inside for a free Slush Puppie."

As the GTO roars out of the parking lot, Mr. Gonzales turns around and motions for the security guard to follow him. Only then does the crowd's applause begin to die out. People pick up their clubs and go back to their own conversations, their own competitions, their own dates. Seconds later, the course is silent once again.

Steve bends over and snatches my jean jacket off the ground. "I think your lady dropped something," he says, handing it to me.

My lady. Maybe not yet, but Homecoming is a start. I put the jacket back on her shoulders.

"Thanks," she says, and pulls it tight.

"Where's Cheo?" I say.

"Washing dishes," Steve says quickly.

"On a Friday night?"

Steve shrugs.

"So, Frankie, ¿estás bien?" Flaco says.

"Yeah," I say, "I'm good. *Gracias.*"

"Anytime, *carnal,*" he says.

"*Órale,* Flaco," Steve says. "Let's get out of here."

"You don't want to play no more?"

Rebecca chuckles, her eyes shifting nervously from my brother to Carmenita and the *cholas.* "I think Frankie broke the first three holes anyway."

Flaco laughs and playfully socks me in the shoulder. "*Órale, vato.* She's busting you." He gives me a backward nod and pats me on the shoulder. "Laters, Frankie. We got some shit to take care of. Rebecca, you be nice to my homeboy."

On his way back inside, my brother glances over his shoulder and smiles at me, and I wonder what it means. Soon, we're all alone again. In the parking lot, Steve and Flaco and the rest of them pile into the *ranflas,* the engines growl to life, and the Sizzler leads a fleet of lowriders out of the parking lot.

As the rumble fades, I can understand why my brother hangs out with guys like Flaco. I feel invincible right now. I feel safe and protected, like I belong here. And this feeling is almost like a drug.

"Since when is Steve so tight with those guys?" Rebecca asks warily.

Considering what just went down, I feel an overwhelming

urge to defend my brother. "It's no big deal," I say. "He's just getting his *cholo* on."

"You can see what I mean about California, though, right? There's too much drama here."

Rebecca and I don't talk much for the rest of the night, but we don't have to. For the first time ever, I'm comfortable around her. It could be that I know she chose me over Dalton. Or it could just be that there's already been way too much excitement for one night, and we're both in the mood to chill. Whatever the reason, we play golf together, quiet and stress-free, until I hear the unwelcome sound of my mother's horn.

twelve

THERE'S SOMETHING about the way school looks, even on Monday, when a girlfriend is on the horizon. Suddenly it doesn't matter if someone bumps into you, or makes fun of your hair, or cuts you off on the way to class. You know there's only so much effort to go around, and wasting it on getting angry means there's less energy to devote to the fact that Rebecca Sanchez is going to come out of her history class any minute now, and you have to be ready when she does.

With only two weeks until Homecoming, the banners and publicity and reminders are popping up everywhere. Or maybe they were up last week, too, and I was trying not to notice. But now, after what happened at the Golf n' Goof, I can allow myself to read them. Campaign posters for Homecoming king and queen line the walls between classrooms. Green-and-white banners above the lockers remind the Panthers to GET ON THE PROWL for the Homecoming soccer game against Albuquerque High.

The theme of this year's dance is "Land of Enchantment," which, judging by all the posters for ticket sales, has less to do with the state motto than it does with forests and fairy tales and magical evenings. One of the posters shows a sparkling white unicorn jumping over a pile of dance tickets with the caption underneath: BUY YOURS BEFORE THEY VANISH INTO LEGEND.

I'm wearing a red polo shirt—untucked over baggy cargo shorts, yes—but at least it has a collar. Even though I haven't run into Rebecca yet today, I can't allow myself to be seen waiting for her. I'm about to give up and head toward Mr. C.'s classroom when Begay swoops in and pulls me aside, looking over both shoulders before slipping me an envelope about the size of a deck of cards. Whatever's in it bulges a little.

"Put it in your pocket," he says so softly I can hardly hear him above the bustle of the hallway. "Now."

"What—"

He shushes me and leans in closer. "Dude, you could totally get kicked out of school if anybody caught you with this on campus, but I figured you deserved it."

I quickly jam the envelope into the side pocket of my shorts. "Are you freaking kidding—"

"Just be cool, my brother." He steps back and pats the sides of my shoulders with both hands. "Look at you, all preppy."

And then he's gone, down the hallway, blending almost instantly into the crowd. I swallow hard, and I imagine my pocket bulging grotesquely as I continue on to Mr. C.'s room. There's no way I can make it through the day without one of the teachers asking me what's in my pocket.

I get only two steps before someone taps me on the shoulder, and my stomach practically leaps out of my mouth. I peek out of the corner of my eye, expecting to see Señora Fernandez wagging her finger at me, but instead I find Rebecca.

"Jeez, Frankie," she says with a smile, "I thought you'd be glad to see me."

Glad to see her doesn't even come close. What I want to do right now is drop my books on the ground and pull her chin toward mine and give her the fattest kiss she's ever had. I want to hold her tight against me and tell her how much fun we're going to have at Homecoming. But I can't do any of that. After all, it's only a dance. It's not like we're going out. Yet.

"I thought you were someone else," I say, instead of making an ass out of myself.

"I'm late." She pinches me on the side of the arm, and I instinctively flex my bicep. We happen to have stopped just under a "Vote John Dalton for Homecoming Court" sign. I don't know if she notices, but I love it. "See you at lunch?" she says.

I nod. And I smile. And I keep my hands right where they

are: one at my side and the other on the strap of my backpack.

"Nice shirt, by the way." She spins to her left and darts into the Spanish classroom.

I'm not about to go into Mr. C.'s room with whatever Begay gave me, so I duck into the bathroom and lock myself in a stall. I reach into my pocket for the envelope, expecting to pull out weed or maybe some peyote from Begay's uncle, but instead I find a small Ziploc Baggie of dark gray dust. I almost laugh out loud—it's gunpowder. From the looks of it, at least three or four M-80s' worth.

There's plenty of things I could do with it—stuff it into a racquetball, trail it along the ground and use it as a fuse, toss a match on the Baggie itself—but I can't do any of those things at school. Given that I'm still on probation from the homemade smoke bomb in Mr. Montgomery's chemistry lab last year, I would *definitely* have some issues with the administration if anyone caught me with this stuff, so I'm forced to make a difficult decision. As I pour the contents of the Baggie into the toilet, I can't help but think of the starving children in Africa who don't have access to high explosives.

The bell rings as I flush the toilet, the shrill buzz echoing off the concrete walls. When I open the stall door, the bathroom is totally empty except for Will Burrage, who's leaning over one of the porcelain sinks, popping a chin zit. He looks at me in the mirror, moving only his eyes, and smirks before returning his attention to the whitehead below the corner of his mouth.

"You think you're all bad now?" he says.

I want to get the hell out of there, but I just came from the stall, and even though I didn't actually drop the deuce, Burrage doesn't know that. And the last thing I need right now is for him to go outside and tell everyone that I don't wash my hands after taking a crap.

I adjust the backpack on my shoulder. I turn on the water and soap my hands up. I stare straight ahead. I felt a lot more comfortable with Flaco and my brother by my side, and I bet Burrage knows it.

The only thing I can think to say is, "What's up?" And then I wipe my hands on my shorts and head to class. I'm not sure, but I think I can hear him laughing as the door closes behind me.

When I slink into the classroom, Mr. Costas marks something in the open grade book on his desk. Luckily, I didn't interrupt him teaching, and I feel a little better about coming in late when I see that Mandy Newmark is wrapping up announcements in the front of the room.

"We really, really need everyone to participate," she says as I take my seat. I can see why Begay likes her. Big green eyes, blond hair to her shoulders. She's wearing glasses again, which makes her look kind of like the secretary in some porn movie. "We're working hard to make this the best Homecoming ever!"

As soon as she says that one word, I don't care about anything else. I'm going to Homecoming. Screw Burrage.

"Yo, Frankie," a whisper comes from over my right

shoulder. A guy named Justin sits behind me every day—his last name is Morrison, but everyone calls him Case—and this is the first time all semester that he's said anything to me.

"Dude, I heard about the Golf n' Goof. I wish I could have been there to see it." His parents used to own a food supply business downtown. Back before the Tortilla Emporium closed them down, they supplied Los Torres with all our vegetables.

Rubén leans across the aisle and sneers. "You think Frankie had anything to do with it?"

Case doesn't even look at him. "I heard Dalton pissed his pants. Is that true?"

Mr. C. suddenly appears, towering right over us. "Gentlemen, may we please get started?"

Rubén sits back in his chair, and Case looks up at the teacher. "You betcha, Mr. Costas, sir," he says. I can hardly keep the smile off my face.

At lunch, Rebecca and I sit across from each other at one of the picnic tables. The wood is faded and warped and carved into—I want to add our initials to the collection, but that's not really how you play hard to get. Zach sits down at my side, but I can't take my attention off Rebecca. She's wearing the berry perfume again. When I breathe it in, I can feel some kind of warmth spread down through my lungs, like a healing power—aromatherapy or something. Maybe those hippies selling incense in Santa Fe know what they're talking about after all.

And I'm not even looking over my shoulder for Dalton. By now, I'm sure everybody knows what happened at the Golf n' Goof. And even if Flaco's protection was only good for that night, there's no way Dalton would try anything, especially right here in the middle of the quad.

"This is where we're sitting?" Andromeda says, coming up to us and plopping down next to Rebecca. There is a look of resignation on her face.

Rebecca smiles at me. "I think it's nice out here."

"Right," Andromeda says with a roll of her eyes. "It's a beautiful day in the neighborhood."

Nothing brings you down like Andromeda Escalante. Here I was, enjoying myself, lost in the fog of Rebecca's blue eyes, and now *that* sits across from me? No matter how much I try to employ tunnel vision, I can't seem to get all of her piercings—twelve in her ears and one in her nose—out of my sight. At least I know where not to stand during a lightning storm.

"Hi, Andromeda," Zach says.

She gives him a tight-lipped, eyeless smile. I hate that she's here right now. Given that she was a witness when Rebecca declined my first invitation the other day, it's a bit awkward to be hanging out with her.

Not that I blame her too much. Last week her best friend was going out with the popular rich white kid—she thought she was playing with the big boys. Now it's like she's been demoted to the JV. Andromeda wheezes a sigh and pushes her

Sloppy José around the tray with a plastic fork.

After a few minutes of silence, Zach takes his eye out and washes it off in his mouth.

"Real nice," Andromeda says, shaking her head.

Rebecca gives me a look, and for the first time, I can see where people are coming from when they complain about Zach's eye tricks. It is kind of nasty when you think about it. I mean, it's in his eye socket, and then he puts it in his mouth. Not exactly the most sanitary thing in the world.

"Come on, dude," I say under my breath. "Put that back in."

"Like I haven't ever done this before?"

"Have a little class. I mean, we're eating lunch." I feel bad about saying so, but for people who aren't used to it, I can see how the sight of his empty socket could be a little gross.

He contemplates me for a second. Then he opens his mouth, the eye looking up at me accusingly from the center of his tongue. He gently plucks it out with this thumb and index finger and replaces it in its socket.

"Bon appetit," he says.

Andromeda chuckles as if victorious. "*Thank* you."

"So, what's up with Nicole?" Zach says, turning to Rebecca. "When's she coming back?"

"Why, is there something you want to ask her?" Rebecca says playfully.

"I was just wondering," he says, looking away. "You know, if she's all better or not."

"She'll be back soon. I'll tell her you said hello."

He shakes his head. "You don't have to, you know, I mean . . . not if you don't want to."

Just now Steve sees me and strolls all the way across campus for a visit. His tattoo is all healed now, and I have to say, it does look good. He wears a beater at school to show it off, but I don't think *Mamá* knows about it yet.

He nods at Zach, who returns it like a pro. Andromeda scoots toward him, pushing out her chest like an offering. It warms my heart to see that he hardly gives her a glance.

"You guys have a good time the other night?" he says.

Rebecca laughs. "It was hilarious. Frankie is so bad at golf."

Steve winks at me and points to his head. "It's all up here," he says. "Dalton give you crap today?"

"Haven't seen him."

I can feel people's eyes on me—it's almost as if I'm being filmed—making my arm hair stand on end. Steve rarely acknowledged me at school before. It was like he thought I was social kryptonite or something. But now here we are, chilling at lunch. I bet a lot of people wish they were me right now.

"Practice is going to be intense," he says. "Coach has no idea."

"Your tattoo is tight," Andromeda says. What a chickenhead.

Steve takes this as an opportunity to flex his bicep. "Thanks," he says. "Got to represent Borges."

Represent Borges, I love it. "Do you and your arm want to get a room?"

Steve pats me on the back. "I'm out. But Flaco and me were going to chill tonight—you working?"

What an ass. I know he knows I'm working. There's no need for him to rub it in. Of course, he could be inviting me in front of Rebecca in order to make me seem cool, like he and his friends would want to hang out with me.

"All week," I say, deciding on the second possibility. "Tell him I said what's up."

"*Vale.*" He shakes Zach's hand and then mine, and he gives a little bow to Rebecca. "Ladies."

We watch him walk away, the four of us still basking in his presence. I can't shake the feeling that my own presence is a little more significant than it was five minutes ago.

"Isn't his tat awesome?" Andromeda says. "I think it's sweet."

I bet you do, you little skank.

"You have to work all week?" Rebecca says, sounding disappointed.

No matter how she might feel, it's nowhere close to how bummed I am. I would rather hang out with her than do anything else in the world, but one of the waitresses is taking the week off, and I told my mom that I would help out. "Someone has to," I say.

Begay comes running up with a look of panic on his face. Sweat dribbles down his temples. "Holy crap, you guys. I need help."

"What's wrong?" Rebecca says.

"Freaking disaster is all I know." He walks in small circles with his hands behind his head, trying to catch his breath. "Mandy was all worried that we didn't have enough posters. . . . I told her to relax, and that's when she said I didn't care about . . . what was important to her. . . ." Now that he's breathing normally again, he actually looks embarrassed. "I can't believe I'm asking you to do this."

Five minutes later, we're sitting in the student council office around a table covered with ribbons and glue and paper and markers and a whole lot more. Rebecca had a quiz to study for, and Andromeda had some seniors to bone, so it's just me, Zach, and Begay. The walls are covered with posters and flyers from previous dances and events, and there are three other tables spread out around the room. The energy is manic—people yelling at each other, asking if their posters look good, demanding more silver ribbon braids, stressing that the enchantment level must be heightened at all costs—meanwhile Begay has this look on his face like his mom just caught him yanking it.

Mandy stands behind Begay's chair, smiling brightly, as though fifteen minutes ago she hadn't made him run, run, run for help. "Thank you *so* much! You guys are awesome. Just do whatever you want. Publicity or decorations; it's up to you."

When she turns away, Begay holds up his hands like he's stopping traffic. "Your jokes are very funny, I can tell. Ha-ha, you kill me. Can we just move on and make some damn decorations?"

Zach and I exchange a glance, stifling our smiles. Begay is right; it would be too easy, so I quietly select a yellow marker and get to work. Zach grabs some silver ribbons and attempts to braid them. Begay looks warily from me to Zach and back to me, then grabs a sheet of poster board and a wide black marker.

"So, Frankie," he says, taking control of the conversation. "What did you think? El gift-o. Not bad, huh?"

I don't know how to tell him the truth, and he must pick up on that, because his face falls. "You didn't."

"At school? Are you kidding me? I'm on probation!"

"I'm on probation," he says, mocking me.

"I had Costas the next period!"

"You're killing me, dude." He drops his marker and looks up at me in surprise. "It's Rebecca, isn't it? I can't believe she's already gotten to you."

"Me?" I grab the knotted silver ribbon braid from Zach's hands and wave it in Begay's face. "Pretty soon you're going to be knitting pink-and-yellow pot holders. Besides, it's not like we're dating. It's just Homecoming."

Zach scoffs and snatches back his ribbon. "Dude, she likes you, okay?"

"Besides," Begay says, "it's not like some other guy is going to make a move on her. After what that dude Flaco said? The way I heard it, he practically dared anyone to mess with you."

"It wasn't that bad," I say. My poster is going nowhere, so I replace the cap but keep pretending to draw just in case someone's watching. "You should have seen the look on Dalton's face, though."

"Since when is your brother hanging out with Flaco? I heard that dude—"

"You heard, you heard, you heard. Can we talk about something else? Like the fact that you're so whipped that the three of us are sitting here doing arts and crafts?"

Mandy appears at Begay's shoulder and leans in conspiratorially. "What are you guys whispering about?"

Begay glares at me, and I quickly remove the cap to my marker. Zach holds up his mangled silver ribbon braid. "We were just wondering how the braiding thing went," he says. "Is it left over right, or what?"

"That's a square knot, idiot," Begay says.

"Thank you, scoutmaster."

He hands Zach a pair of scissors. "Here, use these."

"And do what?"

"Slice off the crappy part and start over. Or poke out your other eye, I don't care."

Mandy covers her mouth. "Josh!"

"I was kidding," he says, but she's already scandalized that her beloved would even *think* of making fun of a kid with only one eye. "Okay, fine. I'll take the scissors back."

"Indian giver," Zach says, handing them over.

Begay slaps his knee. "Ha, ha, ha. I get it. That's a funny joke, 'cause I'm an Indian. But did you ever think that expression might have come from all the broken promises you white people made? Here, have some land . . . Just kidding! There'll be plenty of jobs on the reservation . . . Psych! Oh, don't worry, that's just a harmless rash . . . Oops, smallpox, my bad!"

Zach breaks into a grin. "What is this, civics class? Did I miss a work sheet?"

"This one's for you, kemo sabe." Begay holds up the poster he's been working on. Huge black letters, white background: DON'T BE AN ASSHAT. GO TO HOMECOMING.

"Nice, Josh," Mandy says. "Very subtle." She shakes her head at us and turns away.

When she's out of earshot, we all bust out laughing. Begay flashes a victorious smile. "Just one more crappy poster and she'll never ask for my help again."

"So, Frankie," Zach says. "Has Carmenita met the family yet?"

"Hell no. My mom would have a heart attack."

Begay pulls out a fresh poster board and selects a red marker. "His old girlfriend Annabelle was hot, but Carmenita is spicy, if you know what I mean."

"She grabs junk," Zach says. "In public."

"That's what I'm talking about." Begay glances over his shoulder at Mandy, who's wrapping strands of silver ribbon gently around a large spool while having a deep conversation with a senior committee member. "You think she'd give my lady some lessons?"

While Zach and Begay pretend to work, I try to imagine what would happen if Carmenita came over for dinner. My mom would probably be stricken speechless, staring at the hair and the cleavage, imagining her future grandkids with tattoos and black eyeliner, while my dad would blab on and on, trying to make a connection with her. Steve would sit back and watch, and Carmenita would probably have her hand in his lap the whole time. It would be like my parents' worst nightmare. Come to think of it, I'd pay money to see that.

thirteen

IF YOU'VE EVER worked in a restaurant, you know what the back of a kitchen smells like. It's not the way it is in the movies, where the delicious aroma of herbs and spices wafts through the entire room like a cloud from heaven. In real life, the dishwashing area takes over like a scented plague. Water mixes with sauces and half-eaten plates of food, and then splashes onto the floor and collects, festering, into the holes of the rubber mats. No matter how quickly or thoroughly you clean, you can't avoid the moldy scent of decay.

At least as a waiter I can walk around and get some different air circulating in my lungs. Plus, it's the dishwasher's responsibility to take the trash outside. And you don't even want to know what the New Mexico summer can do to a Dumpster filled with black plastic garbage bags of food scraps.

But like I said before, Cheo manages it without complaining. He works his ass off—he's much faster than I ever was—and he's usually smiling. He gives the waitresses a hard time when it's busy and chats with my mom in Spanish. He probably keeps the image of a fully restored '65 Impala in his head to get him through the shifts.

Tonight is different, though. It's well past eight o'clock, and Cheo has hardly even said a word to me. When I saw that he was working tonight, I was psyched. I was looking forward to talking about Rebecca and what happened at the Golf n' Goof. But he's just kept to himself all night. Even my mom notices.

"*¿Estás bien, mijo?*" she says to him as she scoops a heaping spoonful of carne adovada from the pot in the oven. There aren't many customers tonight, so she's spent most of her time in the kitchen.

Cheo turns around and leans against the sink, wiping his hands on his dirty white apron. "*Sí, Tía,*" he says, always polite with her.

"You seem a little *preocupado*. Doesn't he, Frankie?"

I shrug and lean against the counter, near the heat lamps. It's one thing for my mom to say something, but it feels weird for me to check up on my brother's best friend. "A little, I guess."

"Don't worry about me, *Tía*. I'll be fine."

She gives him one of her maternal smile-and-nod combinations and then asks me and Cheo to unpack the new boxes from the Tortilla Emporium. I usually hate doing this, but tonight I feel a sense of victory; my smile gets bigger with every stack of Dalton's tortillas I load into the fridge. He has nothing on me now.

"You okay?" Cheo says.

"Yeah, just thinking. How was soccer practice today?"

Cheo shrugs. "*Órale*, Frankie. You got to come by my house and pick up your bike soon."

"Sorry. I meant to do it on Sunday, but I forgot."

"Yeah, I heard about what happened at the Golf n' Goof. Wish I could have been there, *ese*."

We finish unloading, and I break down the boxes while Cheo leans against the wooden prep table. "I didn't think you liked to work on Friday nights," I say.

Cheo gives me an expression like he's trying to figure out if I'm serious. "Yeah, well. When you got to work, you got to work."

"Friday?" Mom says. "He didn't work Friday."

Cheo turns back to the sink. He seems annoyed, but it's hard to get pissed at her for eavesdropping when the kitchen is so small.

The door chimes ring, and my dad walks through with his briefcase. He looks exhausted—his hair falls flat on his forehead and his tie is loosened. He makes his way to a corner booth. The cushion sounds like a squeaky fart when he plops down.

"Francisco," Mom says, "*dame un plato de frijoles.*"

I scoop out some beans and hand her the plate, and she quickly wraps up a chicken burrito. Without another word, she unties her apron and leaves it on the counter. Then she takes my dad some silverware and his food and sits across the table from him.

"Your brother told you I was here on Friday?" Cheo says when we're alone.

I can see my parents through the heat lamp counter. They lean forward, whispering to each other. Dad scoops up the beans with a piece of tortilla.

"*Órale*, Frankie?" Cheo says.

"Huh? Oh yeah, sorry. He did."

My dad frowns and leans back. He wipes his mouth with a paper napkin and takes a deep breath.

"He say anything else?" Cheo's trying hard not to let his anger show, but I can tell he's really pissed right now, and it's enough to get my attention away from my parents.

"You weren't here?"

"Hell no. I was working on the six-five. Fucking Steve was going to come by with the Sizzler. He said the tranny felt a little sticky."

It takes me a little while to understand. "Is this about what happened in your garage the other day?"

Cheo's mouth forms a tight smile as he breathes in

through his nose. Then he exhales without looking at me. "Flaco's my cousin, right? So I'm not trying to disrespect—"

"*Mijo*, can we talk to you?" Mom says, poking her head into the kitchen.

"Yeah," I say. "Just a second—"

"Now."

I want to finish my conversation with Cheo, but what choice do I have? I rack my brain, trying to figure out what I did wrong, but I can't come up with anything. The walk to their booth feels like the plank. My stomach is suddenly churning. Maybe they found out about those beers I had at the mesa party last week. Rebecca's dad must have had a cop tail her there and hide in the bushes.

I sit on the plastic and scoot over to the wall. My mom climbs in on my side of the booth, and I'm now trapped. I put my hands together on the table, waiting. The fan rattles overhead. My parents stare at each other. The longer none of us moves, the more a sense of dread begins to creep around the table. Just as I think I might get sick, my mom finally nods to my dad. Here it comes.

"I can't tell you how difficult this is for us to bring up with you. . . ." he says.

Jesus Christ! I wish they'd just tell me what I did and get it over with.

My mom puts her hand on mine. "Your brother didn't come home again on Saturday."

"Huh?" I can barely process her words. This is about Steve?

"He didn't tell us where he was, and we thought maybe you could help."

"What do you want *me* to do?"

"It's just so hard for us to know what he's involved in," Dad says.

They want me to rat on my brother? "Ask him."

My parents glance at each other again, and my mom leans back against the cushion. I just noticed that they're probably way more nervous than I am. *Mamá*'s voice is filled with urgency. "Should we be worried about him?"

The chimes ring again, and a group of older women I don't recognize comes through the door. We have plenty of tables available, but they seem happy to wait for someone to tell them where to sit.

"I'll take care of them," I say, but my mom gets up and motions for me to stay where I am.

Once she's gone, Dad pushes his half-eaten burrito aside and leans his elbows on the table. "You have to understand, Francisco, we don't want him to jeopardize his scholarship."

Right, his scholarship. How could I forget? "Take away his car," I say.

And here comes more dad-speak. This is my role model. "You have to weigh the benefits of certain courses of action. We don't want to push him away."

Sometimes I catch my dad staring at me. I'll just be going

through my day—eating breakfast, or walking through the house, or picking up an order at the restaurant—and I'll turn around and he'll be watching me. As soon as we make eye contact, he'll break out into a smile, or he'll wave, or sometimes even look away quickly, like he's hoping I didn't notice. But I do notice.

The chimes ring again, and I'm just about to make some excuse about how Mom needs my help when my dad's face goes completely white. I turn around to see Steve standing in the open doorway with Carmenita. He's even holding her hand. My mom's arm is frozen, a menu half extended; she looks down at the women and back to her son before finally placing the last menu on the table.

The reaction is exactly how I imagined it would be, and I kid you not: the only thing that would make it better is if Carmenita grabbed his junk.

My mom glances back at my father, her eyes searching for a clue about how to proceed. The surprise of this is bad enough, but coming as it did, only minutes after they basically admitted that they had no idea how to deal with Steve, I wonder if they'll be able to function at all.

"To what do we owe this surprise?" my dad says from the booth. His voice is awkwardly loud, like he's talking to someone across the street.

Steve shrugs as if Carmenita's fishnet ass weren't practically hanging out of her skirt. It looks like she wrapped a black leather hand towel around her waist. Black makeup rings her eyes like a mask, and her eyebrows are drawn on her forehead in an expression of perpetual desire.

"We were hungry," he says, "and Carmenita has never been here before."

Mom pulls herself together and reaches out her hand. "Carmenita, is it?"

"Uh-huh," she says, smacking her gum. She clutches my mom's hand and shakes it once, clumsily; then she looks around the restaurant, taking it all in.

"Well. It's certainly good to have you." My mom gestures to a table on the opposite side of the room from the four women. "Please, have a seat."

Steve waves her off. "Nah, I was just going to grab something from the kitchen, if that's okay."

"Hey, baby," Carmenita says, waving at me. I wave back— a slight fingertip motion—and my mom's eyes nearly roll across the floor.

I steal a peek back into the kitchen, where Cheo leans against the sink, arms crossed, watching everything from behind the heat lamps.

There's a moment of silence as the shock of it all sets in, like that brief pause between when the fuse enters an M-80 and the explosion itself, and then a bunch of stuff happens at once.

"Ma'am?" one of the women says. "We're ready to order."

My dad stands up and goes over to his wife. He puts a hand on her shoulder, steering her to the women at the table, and whispers something into her ear.

"You should really stay," he says to Steve.

"No can do, Pop. Gotta be somewhere." He pats my dad on the back and then heads toward the kitchen. "What's up, Frankie?"

I'm completely torn; I can't decide whether to watch the disaster that is my dad's attempt at conversation with Carmenita or whatever's about to happen in the kitchen between Steve and Cheo.

My dad introduces himself to Carmenita, who has spent the last few minutes checking her reflection in one of the old mirrors and chomping her gum like she needs to keep her jaw in shape. She smiles at him.

"I like your hair," he says, pointing to the wall of bangs. "Is that mousse?"

Cheo and my brother hardly get a chance to talk, because Cheo emerges from the kitchen seconds later. He unties his stained white apron. "*Lo siento, Tia.* I got to get going. My mom needs me." He doesn't look at Carmenita, nor does he wait for a response from my mom. He yanks the door open—ringing the chimes violently—and he's out.

My mom still hasn't made it all the way to the customers. She has her pad and pen out, ready to take their orders, but she hasn't been able to make her feet move close enough; she seems to have her attention divided between the dishwasher who just stormed out the door, her hooligan son in the kitchen, and her husband's tortured conversation with a hooker-in-training—

there's no room in her traumatized mind for a few women who'll probably end up splitting entrees and drinking only water.

Steve comes out with a to-go bag and a strange grin on his face, either oblivious to the devastation he's created or relishing it. He gives my mom a kiss on the cheek. "I just made some burritos, if that's okay. It looked like we had enough carne adovada. Sorry we can't stay," he says, grabbing Carmenita's hand and pulling her toward the door. "Rain check?"

"Good to meet you guys," Carmenita says. "Bye, Frankie."

They're out the door before any of us can say good-bye, but their presence lingers, having made the air somehow thicker, so my parents can't move at full speed.

Mom finally takes the order and stumbles back to the kitchen. My dad comes to the booth and flops down as if he just woke up in a strange place and can't quite figure out where he is.

"Way to put the hammer down," I say.

His voice is soft from shock. "How long have they been together?"

I should probably be pissed off right now; there's no way my parents would have let me get away with any of that. But instead of feeling angry, I just feel sorry for them. "Relax, Dad. It's not like he's going to marry her."

Mom serves the women a basket of tortilla chips and a bowl of salsa and makes her way back to the booth. "Rebecca is a nice girl, Chief Sanchez's daughter," she says absently. "Why can't he be more like you?"

Neither one of them has ever said that to me. I perk up and wait for more, like a damn poodle at a dog show. But my mom has nothing else to say, and my dad doesn't know what to say at all. Just about the time I start to feel pissed about that, I notice the women waving over to us.

"They don't have waters," I say. I jump up without complaint from either of my parents, leaving my mom and dad to flounder together in a pool of their own self-doubt.

fourteen

I ARRANGE the better part of Friday so that I'm in the hallway whenever Rebecca walks by. Sometimes I'm at my locker putting my books away. Once, I pretend to read the announcements on the big cork bulletin board outside Miss Reyna's classroom. With Homecoming only eight days away, more court campaign flyers are popping up: JOHN DALTON IS THE MAN! VOTE VINCE PADILLA! GRACIE GOMEZ MAKES YOUR SUEÑOS COME TRUE! No posters for Steve, though.

I may be waiting for Rebecca, but I'm not a stalker. Not even close. There's absolutely nothing wrong with wanting to say hello to a friend. It's not easy, and sometimes I arrive too late, but since I already know her schedule by heart, most of the time I'm able to get in position early enough.

And besides, just calling me a stalker wouldn't be giving me the proper credit for my skill. It's hard to make my presence appear accidental. In order for the trick to work, I have to make her feel like *she's* the one running into *me*. Sometimes I don't even acknowledge her—it's enough for me to see her walk past out of the corner of my eye. I think it's even smoother when I don't say anything. Plus, it's not like I follow her home and press my sweaty face up against her bedroom window while dry-humping the wall.

Once school's over, I don't have to play that game anymore; I told her I'd meet her under the Eagle. About twenty years ago, there was a competition between all the high schools in the state to see which one could design a sculpture that best represented the "essence of the Southwest." Needless to say, Borges High did not win. Our entry—a welded steel interpretation of an eagle taking flight, which to me looks exactly like a ten-foot glob of eagle crap—now sits behind one of the temporaries near the parking lot.

A gust of wind brings the scent of rain. It's distant, still far enough that I can only smell it with the breeze, but it's coming. Steve jogs up—shirtless, blue shorts, cleats. His soccer bag hangs across his chest like a sash.

"What's up?" he says, fidgeting a lot, like maybe he has to go to the bathroom.

"Aren't you late for practice?"

"I'll be okay."

"Was Cheo at school today?"

He shrugs. "I forgot to take attendance."

Not knowing what's going on with them is killing me, but I don't want to sound like Steve's third-grade teacher, like I want the two of them to sit in the Trust Corner and work out their differences. So I change the subject. "I don't think Mom and Dad were quite ready to see Carmenita's ass cheeks."

Steve laughs. "A little shock now and then is good for them, don't you think?"

I'm not entirely sure *that* particular shock was good for them at all. "A little different from Annabelle, I guess."

"A little more . . . outgoing," he says with a wide smile. He raises his eyebrows a few times. "If you know what I mean."

The images that pop into my head are so nasty that I can't come up with words to describe them. "Are you taking her to Homecoming?"

Steve scoffs. "Oh, hell no. What the hell am I going to do at a dance in the damn gym?" He looks over his shoulder and takes a step closer to me. "So what's up with your girl? She's friends with that chick Nicole?"

"They hang out. Why?"

Zach notices us from across the parking lot and waves, with Begay alongside him. Begay is a big fan of Swisher Sweets—those little mini cigars—but he doesn't smoke them on campus because the smell travels too far, too fast. Instead, he just pretends to smoke them, complete with inhaling and exhaling, even though possession is illegal on campus, too. He must think it's cool, but without the smoke, he looks like a two-year-old sucking on a brown stick.

"What's up, Steve?" Zach says.

Steve nods at him, clearly annoyed to have been interrupted, but he doesn't say anything.

I can see disappointment in Zach's eye; he was probably hoping for more of a reaction. Zach turns to me. "Dude, we're going to hit the Rez this weekend—want to come?"

"Are you out already?" It's only been three weeks, but even at the rate we were going, I can't believe he blew up all those M-80s.

"Not even," Begay says. He spits a couple times, trying to get a little flake of tobacco off his tongue. "It's just a road trip."

"You sure you and Mandy don't have a quilting bee to go to?"

Zach elbows me in the side. "That's next Tuesday."

Begay bows his head. "Dudes, you better check the expiration date on those jokes," he says, but the smile on his face tells me that he knows he'll be getting crap for a long time.

I glance up at my brother, who shrugs and kicks the ground. He doesn't seem to be going anywhere. He's probably waiting to get me alone again.

"Did you see her?" Zach asks me.

"Nicole's back," Begay says. "The Caucasian Sensation can't stop talking about it."

I'd heard she was at school today, but I didn't see her.

Supposedly she's been hanging out at home this whole time, watching movies and doing her homework with her mom. Not that I blame her for milking it.

Zach shrugs. "I'm just saying. She looks good."

"How good?" my brother says.

"Damn good." Begay lets the Swisher hang from the corner of his mouth. "I bet Whitey fifty bucks he wouldn't ask her."

"To the dance?" I say. "It'll take more than fifty."

"I don't know about that," Zach says, nodding in Begay's direction. "Pocahontas over here is going with Mandy; you somehow figured out how to get Rebecca to go with you. Maybe there's something in the air."

"That's the crack you're smoking," Begay says.

"Yeah. Ha, ha, ha. But when she says yes, I want a full apology. In writing."

Just now, Rebecca emerges from the other side of the Eagle, and damn if she doesn't bring Nicole Lawrence right along with her. I hope they didn't hear us.

Zach staggers backward a little bit, and I can see why. Nicole does look good. She's wearing a tight yellow tank top that shows off her monster *tetas*, and her blond hair hangs well below her shoulders. She has one of those perfect button noses that looks like she bought it out of a catalog, and her dark green eyes seem to jump out at you. Actually, she looks more than just good; she looks like she belongs in the center of a magazine I won't be able to buy for another two years.

Not that Rebecca looks horrible or anything, but I need to keep my eyes on the right person.

"What's up?" Rebecca says. If she heard us talking, her face doesn't give it away.

"Hey," I say. "How's it going, Nicole?"

"Hey, Nicole," Zach says.

She smiles. "Hey, Zach."

At this point Nicole does something that a lot of girls do, and I have to think they know exactly what they're doing when they do it. She takes a rubber band from around her wrist and dips her head back, gathering all her hair together into a ponytail. Of course when she does this, her chest practically leaps out at us.

I am too smart to get sucked in, so I actually turn my shoulder to her and look Rebecca directly in the eyes. I don't know what to say, because absolutely all my energy is focused on not doing anything stupid. Luckily, my brother breaks the tension of the moment.

"I'm late for practice," he says.

"Laters, bro." I try to shake his hand.

He's a little spacey, so he doesn't notice, and instead of running off to practice, he kind of stands there, shifting his weight from one foot to the other, occasionally adjusting his soccer bag. He's totally staring at Nicole, like her little ponytail trick worked its magic to perfection. She's hot, I'll give him that.

"You glad to be back?" he finally says.

Nicole rolls her eyes. "Yeah, homework and school food. It's like a dream come true."

"You're lucky," Rebecca says. "At least you missed the munch pudding from the other—"

"Did they ever find out who did it?" Steve says.

Nicole glances at him as though she's startled by his question—or by its abruptness—and when she answers him, it's like she's exhausted. "Some fingerprints, I think, but nothing else."

I'm always surprised when Nicole talks—you never really hear older people with lisps. I wouldn't go so far as to say she has a speech impediment, but the way she says "s" has a hint of "th." It's actually pretty cute.

Begay takes an imaginary drag on his unlit Swisher. When he pulls it out of his mouth, the end is all wet and nasty. "You look totally normal," he says.

Nicole narrows her eyes.

Zach hits Begay in the shoulder with the back of his hand. "He means it's good to see you again."

"I heard fingerprints don't do anything unless they're in the system already," Steve says.

"Even if they're not, anyone dumb enough to steal wedding pictures is bound to get caught next time," Nicole says, angry resolve starting to take the place of her fatigue. "And when they do, the cops will bust them for this time."

"Chill, Steve," I say. "You worried your prints will show?"

Steve laughs. "Yeah, *claro*. And Mom's too."

There's no way he had anything to do with it, if that's what you're thinking. No way. He could be worried about Flaco, though, or maybe even Cheo. Maybe that's why they're all weird around each other. Although I have a hard time believing that Flaco's prints aren't already in the system for *something*. But if Steve's worried about them getting busted for this, then he shouldn't be hanging around them. Seriously, respect is one thing, but damn.

"So, Nicole," Zach says. "You're probably behind in all your classes, huh?"

There *must* be something in the air, because I've never seen him like this around her, or any chick, before. Either that or he really wants that fifty bucks.

Steve nods at me. "Hey, I have to go to practice. I'll see you guys later?"

"Bye, Steve," they all say.

He puts on the smooth voice. "Nicole, welcome back."

And then he's gone. We watch him as he jogs toward the practice fields, his bag bouncing rhythmically against his back.

"I did pretty good on the *Julius Caesar* test," Zach says. "I could help you study. If you wanted."

Nicole smiles and glances at Rebecca. "If I need help," she says, "maybe I'll give you a call."

Begay tosses his Swisher into the sage bushes. He chuckles to himself, as if to say, "We should have dangled money in front of his ass a long time ago."

"Cool." Zach turns back to me. "So, if you want to hit the Rez, we're leaving tomorrow morning."

"Come on," Begay says. "I got the keys to my dad's gutless Sierra."

"Nah, I'm good," I say.

Zach points at me with both index fingers. "You sure? It'll be a blast."

I look over at Rebecca, who gives me one of those looks. Those "You boys and your explosives" kind of looks.

And suddenly I feel all self-conscious in front of her, like I'm supposed to be a good citizen because of who her father is. "I said I was good, *ese*."

"You don't have to be a dick about it. I was just asking."

"Meeoww," Begay says, laughing.

"Well, whatever," Zach says, his good eye darting in Nicole's direction. "I got to get out of here. Catch you later?"

I pound Zach's fist and give Begay a backward nod.

"Laters, Rebecca," Zach says. "Nicole, I'm glad you're feeling better."

"Bye, Zach," Nicole says with a wave. I might be crazy, but I think he may actually have gotten to her.

He and Begay take off, leaving me alone with two of the hottest chicks in the entire school. If you had told me a month ago that I'd be chilling behind the Eagle with Rebecca Sanchez and Nicole Lawrence, I would have checked your sorry ass into the nuthouse.

"For real," I say. "Are you feeling better?"

Nicole's face relaxes, and for the first time today I see weakness in it. She shakes her head. "Everywhere I look, I think I see them. I'll think I recognize one guy's walk, or another guy's voice, or another guy's eyes. You have no idea how hard it is not to be afraid of everybody I see."

A new Honda Accord pulls up in the parking lot, and the driver honks the horn.

"That's my mom," Nicole says, glancing over. "She didn't think I was ready yet."

"See you later?" Rebecca says.

Nicole nods. "Bye, Frankie."

I wave good-bye, and as Nicole climbs into the car, Rebecca turns to me and gives me one of her half-smiles. "So, what's up with you following me around all day?"

And I thought I was being so smooth. "What do you mean?"

"Come on, Frankie. I saw you more today than ever before. I'm supposed to believe that it was just a coincidence?"

"Would you be pissed if it wasn't?"

She sits on the concrete platform, stretching out her legs and crossing her ankles. She props her hands next to her waist and leans back. Her chest presses against her light green T-shirt. It's as though she's offering herself to me, letting me know that we can be comfortable around each other, making me aware that, whatever happens from now on, she trusts me. Or, she could just be resting. "Does that mean you admit it?"

I have two options here. I could pretend I have no idea

what she's talking about, but she's already made it clear what a bad liar she thinks I am. The other choice is to be honest, but how am I supposed to admit to something like that?

"What a crazy coincidence," I say, and then, before she can call me on it: "Are you busy right now? I could walk you home, or something."

"You don't have to work?"

"Nope," I say. "Time off for good behavior." On account of the fact that I've never brought a skanky ho into the restaurant.

Rebecca brushes the dirt off her jeans, and we get our books and then head past the gym. The last time I was here with her, my nose was the size of an orange and I could hardly see three feet in front of me; it's amazing how much things can change in just a few weeks.

There is one thing that hasn't changed, though, and that's my inability to come up with something to talk about. It's not far to Rebecca's house—just across Arroyo del Águila and then toward downtown—so if I want to make this last, I have to walk extra slowly. And in order for that to seem natural, we have to be deep in conversation.

"My brother brought Carmenita to the restaurant," I say finally. It's the only thing I can think of. "Almost put my parents in the hospital from shock."

"Are you guys close?"

"I don't know," I say, and it's the truth. "I guess, when we were little. We used to do all kinds of fun stuff together. We made a time capsule once—buried a bunch of things we thought were important back behind the house."

"Sometimes I wish I had a sister," she says. "I never did anything like that."

"And then we weren't close at all, when he started high school."

"But he hangs out with you at school sometimes."

"That's the thing. It feels like we should be tight now because of that, but it's even worse than when I knew he didn't want to have anything to do with me. Like it's not so much that we're on the same side, but that we have the same enemy."

"Enemy is a little strong, don't you think?"

We walk in silence for a while, and then I stop and turn to her. "You know what I can't figure out? Why don't *you* hate Dalton?"

"Why would *I* hate him?"

"I don't know . . . the Tortilla Emporium? The recipes? It doesn't bother you at all?"

"Bother me?" she says, as if the thought has never occurred to her. "My dad was never going to be in the restaurant business, no matter how good the recipes were, so he made a deal. And it just so happens that Mr. Dalton is a great businessman." She sounds sincere enough, but there's something in her tone, something hiding behind the nonchalance, that makes me wonder if these are her father's words, not hers.

"It's not his business."

"It is now, and my dad's proud of it. Who would have ever

thought that people all over the country would be eating his *abuela*'s tortillas?"

"I know, it's just that—"

"And it's not why my mom left, if that's what you're thinking," she says. "She was already gone."

"That's not what I meant." But now that she mentions it, I have to wonder.

"I promise. You don't need to worry about us."

I have to take her word for it, but I still don't understand. It's like the Daltons stole a part of the Sanchez family history. The fact that they paid for it doesn't make a difference. "Okay," I say with a laugh. "I'll check that off my list."

On the other side of the arroyo, we hit a small grove of Russian olive trees and sage bushes. Everything is gray—the leaves, the bushes, even the clouds above. There's a pause in the conversation, and I can sense her slowing down, so I slow down, so she slows down even more, and then we're not moving at all.

A gust blows a couple pieces of paper trash across the road. They dance in the wind, ducking and weaving, one sprinting forward while the other twirls in place. Eventually, they both end up stuck in a bush. A single raindrop strikes the ground in front of me, sending a tiny puff of dust into the air.

This is when I know we're going to kiss. And this is when all the confidence I'd built up over the course of the walk totally disappears. It feels like everything is riding on this—if it doesn't work out, then what's the point of even going to

Homecoming at all, right? She'll just be dreading another awkward kiss from me the whole night, and I'll be hoping she'll give me another chance—and suddenly my eyes are closed and our lips are together, and here we are.

I don't have a whole lot to compare it to, but I've never kissed anyone like Rebecca. She doesn't open her mouth too wide, like Taryn Zamora, so that her lips are on the outside of mine and my face gets wet. And she doesn't have braces, like Maya Bechtel, so I don't need to worry about getting my lip caught on her teeth. Instead, she's relaxed—totally natural—when we press our lips together, our mouths open slightly.

We pull apart, and her lips glisten as she smiles at me. I need to come up with something to say, something smooth, but the only thing I can think of is to tell her how freaking awesome that was. I feel a massive smile building from deep inside my chest. "What are you doing tomorrow?" I say.

"Is tomorrow Saturday?"

"Yeah, I thought we could do something."

"Like a date?" Her face is completely neutral, waiting for me to answer.

"I figure, you know—"

"A *date* date?" she says, and then, unable to keep her poker face any longer, she leans her head back and laughs.

"So that's how it's going to be?"

"You're really not going to the Rez?"

There was a time when a road trip to the Navajo

Reservation with Begay and Zach would have been perfect. I would have loaded up on some Black Cats, maybe even pretended to smoke a Swisher Sweet on the way. Dinner at Begay's uncle's house would have been filled with jokes and profanity and stories about the white man while we all pointed at Zach and laughed at him.

As the rain begins to come down for real, neither of us moves. And there's no way I'm going to the Rez tomorrow.

It's dusk by the time I push open the door. My clothes and hair are wet from the rain, and I find my mom sitting on the edge of the couch, hunched over a mess of papers spread out on the coffee table. She has at least two pencils tucked in her hair, which has been pulled tight into a ponytail. There's a calculator in front of her.

I practiced a long list of excuses all the way from Rebecca's house, considering that Mom freaked out the last time I came home so late. But when she glances up at me, I see in her eyes neither relief nor anger. Just recognition. "Is everything okay?" she says.

It is. I can still taste Rebecca's strawberry lip gloss. "Where's dad?"

"He'll be home soon."

Her weariness creeps me out. I step from side to side. "I should probably go do my homework. I have a lot." I turn around, but she stops me before I reach my room.

"Frankie?"

She's going to ask about Steve again, I just know it. About his girlfriend and his friends and what he's doing and what they should do about it. I can see it in the way her eyebrows rise, like someone waiting for news at a hospital, both hopeful and beaten at the same time. I point to the coffee table. "Bills?"

"Don't worry about it, Francisco. Go on ahead and do your homework."

"Right. *Te quiero.*"

I really do have a lot of homework, you know. I wasn't lying about that.

My desk is a nightmare. My dad always tells me to clean it up, that I'll never really be able to do good work until I have a clean surface to work on, but I can't make a dent. I don't even know what half the crap is—I just know I have a lot of it. Every time I try to clean it up, I just end up moving piles of stuff around anyway, so I've just given up and embraced it. This way, at least I know where to find everything. It's all right there in front of me.

I'm about halfway through Mr. C.'s crazy-ass math homework—something to do with nonlinear equations and cosines that I don't think we ever covered in class—when I hear my dad's heavy footsteps coming down the hallway. Damn. He knocks on the door. I'm about to answer when my mom comes up behind him. Their voices are muffled, but I can still hear them.

"He has a lot of work to do, Jaime."

"I just want to talk." His voice sounds gravelly, like it is in the morning.

I picture them standing in the hallway, sand crushing underneath their feet on the cool brick floor. Somehow, after at least ten seconds, my mom gives up. I wouldn't have thought it possible, but she gives up, and I'm screwed.

"Has lo que quieras," she says. "It's up to you."

She shuffles down the hallway, her steps disappearing into the distance.

My dad knocks again, and I have to think fast. I jump away from my desk as quickly as possible and crawl into bed, where I lie on my side with my back to the door. Another knock, and then the door opens.

"Frankie?" he says. Hesitant.

I close my eyes and try to regulate my breathing. I try to remember the last sleeping person I saw. What did he look like? How did his chest move? Nice, easy breaths. Dad takes a couple steps inside my room, but I'm focusing on my breathing. In, Mississippi. Out, Mississippi.

He comes over and sits down on the edge of my bed. "Frankie, are you awake?"

My eyes are closed, but I can't keep my lids from twitching, no matter how hard I try to control them. I sense him with every muscle in my body. Sleeping people are supposed to be loose, so I take another deep breath and try to relax.

He places his hand on my shoulder, and it takes everything I have not to react. I give a pathetic half-groan and stretch out my legs, but I'm still asleep, of course, so I shrug my shoulders up close to my ears and go back into the fetal position. Dad's hand is still on my shoulder, but he doesn't say anything.

We stay like this for over ten minutes. I know because I count the whole time—counting helps me breathe more naturally. Six hundred and twelve, Mississippi. His hand resting on my shoulder.

fifteen

I ALMOST GAVE Rebecca a dozen red roses, but my brother always says that flowers are guaranteed to scare chicks away. His style is to play hard to get, which works for him because he's so good looking, such a good athlete, blah, blah, blah. But hard to get doesn't really work for guys like me, so I decided to go somewhere in the middle and take advantage of the Saturday afternoon to show her how to make stuffed sopaipillas. I know she doesn't like spicy food, but she has to get over that sooner or later if she's going to roll with me.

Besides, it makes my mom happy. Steve didn't come home last night—again—and she and my dad spent most of the night arguing. Steve has no idea how his nightlife affects *me*.

I'm the one who has to deal with the crap he leaves behind. It would piss me off if it weren't so typical. Anyway, things are a little stressful around the house, so if me bringing my date to the restaurant brightens my mom's day, then that's a bonus.

Rebecca is wearing jeans again, but they're definitely not her tightest pair. I think she's trying to be polite for my mom. Her yellow tank top actually covers her whole stomach, but I'll still get caught staring. She's that fine. As for me, I'm actually dressed up, considering this is sort of a date and all. My chinos are clean and wrinkle-free, and I've got on my short-sleeved, dark red, collared shirt. I also look fine, if I do say so myself.

Right now, however, I'm wearing a flowery pink apron, and I don't *feel* very fine. There's a pot of chicken breasts boiling on the stove, the tomatoes and lettuce haven't been cut yet, and that damn oven is making me sweat. Rebecca leans against the counter, watching this whole disaster with a smile on her face.

"Hey, *Mamá*," I say over my shoulder as I roll out the dough for the sopaipillas. "Could you take the chicken off the stove? I don't want it to get dry."

"Let me do that," Rebecca says, but I stop her with my rolling pin before she can move.

"Wait. You're not allowed to work, remember? I'm cooking."

My mom comes in and lifts the chicken off the stove and pours the water into the sink before filling the pot back up with cold water. She seems more hurried than normal, more on edge. She must still be thinking about my brother.

Rebecca laughs. "You run the kitchen like a pro."

"Yeah, yeah, yeah. So, do you want to learn how to make sopaipillas, or what?"

"I'm so sorry," she says, literally wiping the smile off her face with both hands. "I'm all ears."

"Good. Okay, the first step is the dough. You want to make sure it's not too tough, otherwise it doesn't fluff up like it should, and then you can't stuff it with anything."

"Right. Tough, fluff, stuff. Got it."

"I'm serious!"

Again she tries to stop laughing, but she can't help herself. If she didn't have such a ridiculous smile, I'd be annoyed. She takes a deep breath and holds her hands out in front of her. "Okay, I'm serious, too."

My mom peeks over my shoulder. "Don't you want to make burritos instead?"

I turn to her, beads of sweat forming on my eyebrows, and beg with my eyes. "*Mamá*, I want to make stuffed sopaipillas, okay? Rebecca's never had a good one."

"You think it's a good idea for *you* to make them, then?" Rebecca says, fighting back a smile with everything she has.

"Ha-ha," I say, turning to Rebecca and waving a pair of tongs in her face like a magic wand. "This is the dangerous part, okay?"

I take one of the pieces of dough and drop it gently into

the deep fryer. It sinks for a second or two, and then it starts to fill with air and comes to the surface. I spoon oil on top, then flip the dough over, leaving it in for another ten seconds until it turns golden brown. Finally, I snatch it and lay it down on a bed of paper towels.

"It doesn't seem that complicated," she says.

"That's because I'm an expert."

"Oh, right. I forgot. Can I do one?"

I motion for her to take my place in front of the fryer. "Remember to not leave it in too long—"

"I got it."

"I'm just saying—"

"Do you want me to shove your face in here?"

I'd rather my skin not melt off my skull, so I clasp my hands behind my back and lean over her shoulder, careful to keep my mouth shut. She cooks the sopaipilla to perfection and soon lays it on the paper towels next to mine.

"Very nice," I say. "You pass." I pucker my lips and lean in.

She glances over her shoulder and pats me on the cheek. "Not in front of your mom."

Oh, well. I go over to the sink and start shredding the chicken by hand. "Okay, why don't you cut the lettuce and tomatoes so we can eat before next weekend."

"Thank God. I'm starving."

She shoots a kiss across the butcher table and starts chopping like one of those chefs on the infomercials. I'm not just impressed; I'm a little embarrassed. "Wow, that's pretty good."

"You're not the only one who can cook."

I slice open the sopaipillas and stuff them both with shredded chicken. There's some pinto beans on the stove, so I put a big spoonful into each of the sopaipillas, on top of the chicken. Then I ladle on a nice helping of red chile, followed by a handful of shredded cheese. Finally, I put both plates in the oven to melt the cheese.

"Don't tell me I slaved over the tomatoes and lettuce for nothing."

"Easy, *princesa*, easy. You don't want it to wilt, do you?" I can't help but raise my eyebrows a few times.

"God, Frankie. You're disgusting. Why do you guys always think we want to hear that stuff?"

"Because it's hot," I whisper. She throws some lettuce in my face.

With the cheese melted, I take the plates out of the oven and garnish them with Rebecca's vegetables. "You happy now?"

"*Thank* you."

We bring the plates out into the restaurant and settle into one of the gold vinyl booths near the door. I make sure to bring a big pitcher of water just in case the chile is hotter than it should be, even though everybody knows that water just makes the burn last longer. The only real treatment is to eat a sopaipilla with some honey on it. My mom winks at me as she retreats tactfully into the kitchen.

"Okay," I say, spreading my napkin on my lap, "the most

important part is not to swallow it right away. Let it roll around in your mouth for a while. I promise you'll taste all sorts of flavors you never knew existed."

"If it's too hot, I'm going to kill you." She reaches into her pocket and pulls out a little jar of lip balm. Then she scoops some out with the back of her pinky fingernail and puts it on her bottom lip. Finally, she uses the tip of her index finger to rub it in before smacking her lips a couple times. I mean, how cute is that?

"You ready?"

"Shut up," she says. "I'm protecting my lips from your fire chile."

With her lips sufficiently defended, she takes a bite. I'm happy to see that she doesn't spit it out right away. Instead, she follows my instructions perfectly, chewing slowly.

"See? Is that not the best thing you ever tasted?"

She swallows and licks her lips. "I could get used to it."

The door chimes ring. "Hello?" says a voice behind me.

Rebecca's fork is poised at her mouth, ready to deliver another bite of my spectacular cooking, when she glances over my shoulder. Her eyes go wide and her smile disintegrates.

"Why, Rebecca," a female voice says. "What a wonderful surprise." It's a thick Texan accent, like you hear in the movies. *Wunduful suhpraahs.*

My date lays the forkful of sopaipilla gently back on her plate and smiles once again. "Hello, Mrs. Dalton. It's nice to see you."

I whip my head around at the name, and when I see her and her husband standing in the doorway, a mixture of panic and anger and disappointment courses instantly through my veins.

Mr. Dalton is a grotesque assembly of two entirely different bodies. His waist is narrow, and his legs are skinny, but his chest pretty much blocks the doorway, and his stomach hangs over his belt like he's smuggling a sack of flour under his shirt. His wife stands beside him, wearing so much turquoise and silver jewelry that I'm surprised she's not hunched over. Her red lipstick perfectly matches the sweater tied over her shoulders, and her hair has been styled aggressively into a huge blond helmet.

You can understand how Dalton became . . . Dalton. The apelike torso, the blond hair and blue eyes. It's all right there.

My mother rushes out of the kitchen, wiping her hands on a dishrag.

"Isabel," Mr. Dalton says, "I know we're a little early. Is it still a good time?"

A little early for what?

"Of course, of course," my mom says. "Don't be silly." She waves the towel, as if in surrender, then moves to the biggest table and wipes it down. She's almost frantic, desperate to please, as if her master barged into her quarters unannounced. "Have a seat. I'll be right with you."

When Mr. and Mrs. Dalton move away from the door, they reveal their son. He looks miserable, slouching with his hands jammed deep into the pockets of his jeans. I haven't seen him too much since the Golf n' Goof night, but I don't know if that's because he's been staying away from me or because subconsciously I've been avoiding him.

What surprises me is how the shame comes rushing back. I feel it in the bottom of my spine, like a twisting dagger, the moment I see him. You'd think I would have some power over him, with Rebecca on my arm, but I don't. Instead, I feel his instep against my cheek even more now.

"Frankie, *ven a la cocina*," my mom says on her way to the kitchen.

"This isn't happening," I say under my breath, and Rebecca chuckles in agreement. As I toss my napkin onto the table and stand up, I realize—way too late—that I forgot to do something before I sat down.

"Nice apron," Dalton says as he passes by. He yanks out a chair, and the metal leg screeches against the floor like fingernails on a chalkboard.

"Fuck you," I say quietly, without moving my lips.

Dalton shoots me a look of surprise. "What was that?"

"I said, 'Thank you.'"

As I'm walking into the kitchen, Mrs. Dalton says, "Rebecca, why don't you come sit with us? It's been such a long time."

Can his parents really be that clueless? Don't they have any idea what's going on in their piece-of-crap son's life? It's like they think we're still five years old, coloring in kindergarten, and all the kids get cupcakes whether it's their birthday or not. Maybe it's a kind of self-preservation. If parents actually knew what their kids were like, they'd probably shoot themselves in the head.

As soon as I'm in the kitchen, I take off my stupid pink apron and throw it in the corner. I lean against the counter and watch as Rebecca stands up from the booth and walks over to their table, pulling the bottom of her tank top well below her waist. "What the hell are they doing here?" I say.

My mom opens the oven and pulls out a fresh batch of carne adovada. Steam rises as she stirs the pot with a thick wooden spoon. "Not now, Francisco. This is important."

"Why?"

"Take them waters, please."

"I'm not working today."

"Francisco Torres," she says in a venomous whisper. Her eyes narrow and her chest heaves as she whirls on me. I can tell it's taking all of her self-control not to smack me across the face with the wooden spoon. "You will. Not. Argue."

I can count on one hand the number of times she's given me this look. When I was seven, she caught me stealing a pack of gum. When I was twelve, I told her to fuck off when she wouldn't let me sleep over at Zach's. And, of course, when Zach and I almost burned down the neighbor's house. But I have to say, none of those times even came close to this. If I don't get out of the kitchen right now, there's no telling what she might do.

My fear of her is the only thing that could make me serve the Dalton family waters. And because I have no desire to return to my mom, after I put the glasses where I'm supposed to, I step back into the no-man's-land between the table and the kitchen. The fans' crooked overhead whirring does nothing to combat the sweat on the nape of my neck. Gigantic drops snake between my shoulder blades and puddle at the small of my back.

Mr. Dalton raises his glass to me. "Thanks for the water."

"You got a new bike, huh?" Dalton says.

He must have noticed it leaning up against the side of the restaurant. It turned out great, by the way—almost worth not having a car so I can ride it to school. When the sun hits it, the burgundy metallic paint is almost blinding. Cheo even surprised me by throwing on a skull surrounded by blue flames.

"Frankie airbrushed it himself," Rebecca says. I can only assume that she's trying to stand up for me. Besides, it's partly true.

"Wow." Dalton smiles at me. "That's awesome."

"Johnny used to have a bicycle," Mrs. Dalton says, oblivious to the sarcasm in her son's voice. "We couldn't get him off it. He just rode and rode and—"

"Mom," he says, his disdain obvious in the way he turns away from her. He picks lint from underneath the letter on his jacket.

"Well, you did."

Mr. Dalton scoots his chair back and rests his forearms atop his gut. He scans the room, nodding.

Something must be going on here. This is the first time I remember even one of the Daltons coming to the restaurant, much less *all* of them. "Did you guys want to see some menus?" I say.

"Francisco," my mom calls out. *"Ven."*

When I get back to the kitchen, I see that Mom has prepared sample platters of our signature dishes: chile rellenos, stuffed sopaipillas, and carne adovada.

"What are they doing here?"

"Ándale," she says, motioning toward the door. "While the food's still hot."

It's hard to explain how crazy she's acting. She only gets like this when we're having company over and the house has to be "party perfect." That's when she runs around, her forehead creased with worry, readjusting furniture and checking her hair in the mirror.

"I said, what are they doing here?"

She doesn't even answer me—just shoos me away. Then she puts the carne adovada back in the oven and wipes her hands on her apron. She picks up the phone and dials. "They're early," she says into the receiver.

I load up the plates. After years of waiting tables, I can serve or clear a four-top in one trip. Three entrees on the right arm, one in the left hand, I back out of the kitchen toward my new definition of hell.

Rebecca still has her stuffed sopaipilla in front of her, but she hasn't touched it since she changed tables. I put a plate in front of Dalton, his mom, and his dad. "Where does this go?" I say, holding the last one above the table.

Mr. Dalton taps the empty spot next to him. "Put it here."

"I bet he spits in the food," Dalton says under his breath. But it isn't far enough under his breath, because his mom smacks him on the forearm.

"John," she says as though she's shocked at what an ass-hole her dear baby boy has become.

As I stand behind him, it occurs to me just how much trust we put in other people. Complete strangers, friends. Everybody. Dalton's just sitting there, relaxed, trusting that I'm not going to lose my temper and stab him in the back of the neck with a fork. Every time we get into a car, we trust every-body else on the road. Every time we walk on the sidewalk, we put our lives in other people's hands. We'd never even leave the house if we actually thought about how little control we have over living and dying.

I'd rather risk my crazy mom in the kitchen than watch the Daltons eating our food. I wish I could take Rebecca in there with me, but Mrs. Dalton is peppering her with ques-tions, so I just slump away.

I push the door open just as my mom is taking off her apron. She hangs it on the wall and turns to me, wrapping her hair in a massive bun. "How do I look?"

"Are you going to tell me what's happening?" I lean against the counter. The stainless steel is cool against my ass.

She moves to me and cups my cheekbones in her hands. "I'm so sorry. They were supposed to come later. When you weren't here."

It hits me, and for a second I feel everything slow down as my mind tries to make sense of it all. The fans in the restaurant shimmy with a pathetic tap, tap, tap. My tongue feels heavy and fat. When my mouth catches up with my head, there's almost no breath in my words. "You're selling."

She nods, a melancholy smile on her face.

And with her nod goes any hope that I might have been wrong. I thought maybe she would laugh, pull me to her, and give me a little kiss on the top of my head. I blink a few times. "Really?"

"We're doing this for you."

"How does that make sense?"

"For when you go to college."

"College?" What does that have to do with anything?

"Steve has his scholarships. We want you to have the same options."

I don't even know what to say. My parents are selling the restaurant they've owned for over fifteen years because I'm not as good at sports as my brother. There have to be other ways to come up with that money, like loans and stuff, right?

"I thought you'd be happy," she says. She steps to the kitchen door and pushes it open a crack.

"Happy?"

"I thought you hated working in the restaurant. Now you can find a job doing what you want."

"It's not that bad." Okay, so I've said a few things, but that doesn't mean I hated working here. "Why didn't you just ask?"

"I'm sorry, *mijo*," she says, pushing the door a little more open. She puts one foot through. "I can't have this conversation with you right now."

"We don't need their money."

"It's not just a question of money."

"But—"

"Have you ever thought that running a restaurant may not be what I want to do with my life?"

"Mom—"

"We're a good match for them. The recipes, the local credibility. It's good for both of us."

"*Mamá*," I say, trying to keep my voice under control. "They're going to screw us! The same thing happened—"

"It's a very fair offer, Francisco."

She slowly walks into the dining area, and I follow. "How fair?" I whisper.

"If you really like working here, don't worry," she says. I can hear the fake smile on her face. I bet her lips aren't even moving. "We're going to run the restaurant for a while, and I'm sure you can help."

With that little nugget, she leaves me standing in the middle of the restaurant, my arms limp at my sides. It's funny actually, when you think about it. Now I'll have a chance to work for the Daltons, like everyone else. It's like I'm living in the pages of some lame-ass bilingual picture book, and all the happy pages just got ripped the hell out.

Dad barges through the door, sending the chimes flying almost up to the ceiling. When we make eye contact, he gives me that "holy crap" look, the one I always used to make when I realized I'd been caught in a lie and there was no hope of escape. "Frankie! What are you doing here?"

He opens his mouth as if to explain himself, but then thinks better of it and turns to the Daltons, shaking hands with John and his dad and giving Mrs. Dalton an efficient and businesslike hug. So much for navigating those turbulent waters together.

My dad puts his briefcase on the table and snaps it open, and I can see his hands shaking as he shuffles with whatever's inside. "Could you bring me a glass of water please?" he says without looking at me.

I go fetch his goddamn water, and the walk back to the table is the most horrible ten seconds of my life. I can't look at Dalton, I can't look at my dad, and I definitely can't look at Rebecca. I have a vision, so clear that it nearly blinds me, of Mr. Dalton in the kitchen, ordering my mom around, rubbing that massive Texan stomach up against her, grabbing her ass.

"Here you go, Dad," I say quietly.

He takes the glass of water and downs half of it at once.

I spend the next hour in the kitchen, pretending to clean

things. From time to time, I glance under the heat lamps and see my dad and Mr. Dalton laughing, or Rebecca and John struggling to make small talk. At least I think it's just small talk. At least I hope it is.

At one point, Rebecca excuses herself from the table and comes into the kitchen. She looks at me like I'm a cute little kitten that just got run over by a truck.

"I'm really sorry," she says, grabbing my arm and pulling me toward the side wall so they can't see us. "I was having a lot of fun."

My lips force a thin smile. We should have run out of the restaurant the moment the Daltons arrived. But it's even worse to have her acknowledge the situation. It makes it real. "Don't worry about it."

"They offered to take me home," she says. "I'll stay if you want."

Oh, I want her to stay, all right, more than just about anything I can think of. But my admitting that will only bring attention to it. "No, that's okay. I have to clean up around here anyway."

"I really had a good time." She puts her hands on my shoulders and gives me a quick kiss, as if trying to convince me. Then she disappears back through the double doors and takes her seat again.

Finally, mercifully, the men push back from the table. Handshakes are exchanged, as are pats on the back. Mr. Dalton rubs his fat stomach and chortles, and his jowls shiver. The men step to the door, and the women stand. Rebecca is the last one sitting, but even she gets up eventually. My mom and dad stop at the door, thanking everybody for coming, smiling like they've just had a marvelous Thanksgiving feast. John lets Rebecca pass in front of him and glances over his shoulder as he walks through the door. He grins, and fuck if he doesn't salute me.

A few seconds later, my dad backs through the kitchen doorway holding a plate in each hand. Mom follows with the rest of the dishes. At least they had enough sense not to ask my sorry ass to help.

As I try to process what just happened, I feel a warmth pass over the length of my body. The muscles in my throat tighten, and my heart begins to beat fast, then faster. I sense every blood vessel in my chest. My mouth goes dry. This is what rage feels like. My first thought, as I lean forward against the counter, is that I want to destroy something.

My next thought surprises me: I can't wait to tell Steve about this.

sixteen

IT TAKES US about ten minutes to cover six blocks; we ease through the shadows and sprint under the streetlights. Yeah, we're more likely to arouse suspicion this way than if we just walked naturally, but I'm not cool enough to walk naturally. Plus, we're two teenagers roaming around downtown at one thirty in the morning. We'd arouse suspicion no matter what we did, so we might as well be in the light as little as possible.

On the way, we pass a Dairy Queen, a boarded-up warehouse, and a Mustang gas station advertising a free car wash with the purchase of ten gallons or more. Some graffiti artist with a sense of humor recently tagged the Dairy Queen sign, painting an *F* over the *D*, so now it reads: FAIRY QUEEN.

The Emporium's main entrance is on West Ella, but I'm not about to walk through the front door. The wall is entirely glass, and in the center of the lobby, lit from below and displayed like a priceless museum artifact, sits an antique tortilla-making machine. Dalton once bragged that it's the oldest of its kind still in working condition. I don't know what's more retarded, him bragging about it, or the fact that everyone at school was impressed.

We jog around back to a wide alley where a massive Dumpster guards the concrete wall at the end. A few green beer bottles, almost hidden in the near-black, are scattered around the base of the Dumpster. Halfway down the alley is the service entrance, a large sliding aluminum door that's been padlocked shut.

"It's locked." I say, resting my hands on my knees and gasping for breath.

"No shit, it's locked," Steve says, his attention focused on the wall as he searches for another way in. "This is the Tortilla Emporium, home of the world famous Borges tortilla." He continues down the alley. About ten feet from the door is a large window with panes of glass each about the size of a basketball. Five across and four high. He presses his face against the bottom center pane.

I peer over his shoulder and whisper into his ear. "What are you looking for?"

On the other side of the glass is a handle. Steve flashes me a confident thumbs-up and grabs one of the empty beer bottles. When he gets back, he takes off his sweatshirt and wraps it so that I can still see the mouth of the bottle through the fabric.

I step between him and the window and put my hand on the sweatshirt, feeling intimidated, almost threatened, by the rough texture of the fabric as it stretches against the bottle. "I don't know if this is a good idea."

"Dude, trust me," he says, glancing down the alley. "Do you want to fuck their shit up or not?"

"Yeah, but—"

"Then move."

"What if there's an alarm?" I say.

He shrugs. "Then we run, hop in the car, and drive the hell out of here. It would take the cops at least five minutes to get here, and by that time we'd be long gone."

"What if it's a silent alarm?"

"*Chingao*, Frankie. If you don't want to do this, then go back to the car and wait for me. If the cops come, you can leave me here. If you do want to do this, then chill the hell out. Whatever you decide, just get out of my way."

When I first suggested we get back at the Daltons, I was in the comfort of my own living room. I liked the idea of the two of us doing something to stand up for the family, to show a little Towers pride, but it feels different to be out here, actually going through with it. Steve doesn't seem to notice the difference; it's scary how confident he is. It's like none of this even fazes him. He looks down the alley and then back at me.

Finally, I step aside.

In one quick motion, he brings the bottle against the window, exactly in the center of the pane in front of the handle. The glass breaks—tiny cracks spread out toward the edges of the pane like slices in a pizza, but his sweatshirt muffles the impact. The pane doesn't shatter entirely because he maintains some pressure with the bottle rather than smashing right through.

"Did Flaco teach you how to do that?" I whisper, a mixture of awe and anxiety in my voice.

And suddenly I feel stupidity in the marrow of my bones. How could I not have noticed? Maybe the image of him and me in the backyard—eagerly burying our time capsule, digging and smiling and feeling like brothers, our minds filled with questions about what future generations would think of us— maybe it stopped me from accepting the truth. What if all this time that I criticized my parents for their inability to see what he has become, he has existed on a level that even I didn't want to admit?

He removes the bottle and places it gently against the wall. He pushes the smallest shard back and forth until it pops out and falls inside. It barely makes a sound when it hits the ground.

"You have to be hard to get respect," he says. Now that he can get his fingers around the other pie-shaped shards, he begins removing them one by one and laying them on the ground below the window. He clears out the entire pane in no time.

"Cheo's not hard?"

"Shit, Frankie."

"What are you talking about?" I glance nervously over my shoulders. If he doesn't have respect, what chance do I have? "You have a scholarship! Everybody already respects you."

"Do we even live in the same town?"

"But what difference does it make if you're going to be gone soon? Mom and Dad—"

"Can we not talk about this right now? Would that be okay with you?"

I take a deep breath. "Sorry."

He shakes out his sweatshirt to get rid of any tiny shards before putting it back on. "Are you going to puss out on me?"

Yes, I want to say. Not only am I going to puss out, but I'm also going to shit my pants. Maybe even throw up a little. But I don't say anything, of course. I just shake my head.

"*Vale.*" He reaches through the now-empty window and grabs the handle. "Ready to run like hell?"

He pushes down on the handle. For a second nothing happens, and he has to push down harder. Then the rubber seal around the window makes a hissing sound, and the whole thing begins to open.

I cover my ears with my hands, closing my eyes and bracing for the inevitable shriek.

But there is no alarm. Nothing.

"We're in," Steve says. He finishes opening the window.

Now it's perpendicular to the wall, giving us about a two-foot opening on each side. "Ladies first," he says, stepping out of the way and motioning me inside.

"Hell no," I say, but he stares at me, so I poke my head in. It's pretty dark, but enough light is coming from a few dim emergency-type lighting fixtures on the walls that I can see the outlines of dozens of machines arranged in two long rows.

I hop onto the windowsill so that my waist is leaning over the edge and then push myself up with my arms. I bring my left leg onto the ledge and push off, landing silently inside as if I've cat-burgled all my life. It takes a second for my eyes to completely adjust to the shadows, but when they do, I'm amazed by what I see.

A sign over the chain of machines to my left says, simply, CORN. On the far end is what looks like a huge drum, followed by a conveyor belt that leads up to a rectangular funnel. Below the funnel is a gigantic block with another conveyor belt leading to the biggest machine in the room: an oven about thirty feet long and six feet wide. At the other side of the oven is a rack that holds seven conveyor belts stacked on top of one another. At the end, next to where I'm standing, is a bagging station conveniently placed just ten feet away from the sliding door of the service entrance. The sign over a similar set of machines to my right says FLOUR.

When I was ten, my fifth-grade class went on a field trip to the headquarters of the *Albuquerque Journal*. I remember being in awe of the machinery, the assembly line that churned out newspapers at what I thought was an impossible rate. It's the same thing here: dozens of enormous silver machines arranged one after the other, each with a specific duty. All designed to spit out tortilla after tortilla with as little human involvement as possible.

I'm so into the view that I forget all about Steve, and when he hops down next to me, I almost squeal like a little girl. He takes the sleeve of his sweatshirt and wipes down the windowsill. Smart.

"What now?" I say. If it were up to me, I'd hop right back out the window and run my sorry ass home. No matter how pissed I am about the restaurant, it's not worth a felony.

Four stories' worth of offices line the entire wall on the FLOUR side, with windows overlooking the factory floor. Steve points toward an open staircase to our right, on the other side of the bagging station. "There."

"What are we looking for?"

He shoots me a harsh look. He probably can't believe he's related to me. "Just be quiet. And find the fucking office, *ese.*"

He brushes past me and walks around the flour line, and in my hurry to follow him, I knock against one of the bagging stations, sending half the equipment tumbling, as I fall on my hands and knees. A huge clatter echoes throughout the factory. Steve whirls around as three massive steel trays rattle on the concrete floor. I grab my shin and moan in pain. Jesus Christ.

Steve runs over, but I get the picture and manage to shut

up by myself. We both stand absolutely still, hardly breathing, while the echoes die out. Miraculously, there are no security guards, no Dobermans, no dumbshit-Frankie-activated pig traps.

"Sorry," I whisper. My shin still hurts like a bitch.

"All kinds of sorry."

Steve and I hit the stairs, and I stop at the second floor while he continues up. I push open the door. The same kind of emergency lighting from the factory sends shadows climbing all over the walls of the twenty or so cubicles arranged in two rows down the length of the room. I creep my way through, stopping occasionally to rifle through stacks of papers on the various desks.

Most people have made some sort of lame attempt at personalizing their little space. One guy has a tiny sandbox with rocks and a miniature rake. I stop and rake a little *F* in the sand; I can't help myself. Other cubicles hold pictures of families, cartoons, a plant here and there. In some of the pictures I recognize kids from school; one of them is Rubén Gutierrez. In the gold-framed picture, he and his parents are standing at the top of some mountain, their hair all windblown, smiles on their faces. Clouds in the background. I wonder if his family knows what a punk he is.

I want to get out of here. I want to go home and forget about everything. Forget about John Dalton and the goddamn Tortilla Emporium. Forget about my crazy-ass brother and whatever the hell is going on with him and his friends. I shuffle over to a window overlooking the factory floor, lean my head against the glass, and close my eyes.

"*Pendejo*, what are you doing?"

I snap my eyes open. Steve stands in the doorway with his hands on his hips. "Umm . . . I was just—"

"Yeah, yeah, yeah. Shut it. You need to come up here." He takes off up the stairs and waves for me to follow him. After one last look at Rubén and his unsuspecting parents, I go out into the stairwell and start climbing.

Steve is already inside by the time I get up to the fourth floor, which is basically a classier version of the second. Cubicles line the walls here, too, but they're made out of wood and glass. "Where are you?" I whisper.

He pokes his head out of one of the offices on my right, the opposite side of the room from the windows overlooking the factory. This must be where the big boys sit. When I walk into the office, he's behind a huge wooden desk, silhouetted against the meager lights of downtown, which glitter through the window behind him.

"Come here."

There's something in his face that makes me nervous. He's breathing a bit more heavily than normal, and he seems to be talking to himself, nodding. Like he's psyching himself up to do something.

Slowly, I join him behind the desk. "Whose office is this?"

"Dalton's dad's," he says, pointing a tiny pocket flashlight at the computer. "You want to fuck it up?"

"Like, break it?"

"Hell yes, 'like, break it.' Why else are we here?"

I know the instant our eyes meet, and it shames me. Worse than any beating Dalton could ever give me, worse than being dissed in front of a whole flock of hot chicks. He's testing me. I think about the conversation in Cheo's garage, about Nicole sitting afraid and alone in her closet, and about the way Steve looked at her the other day at school. I know now that Steve was a part of it, and I still can't say no to him. He says that being hard will get me respect, but I feel helpless and weak. I hate who he's become, and I hate myself, and I hate him for making me feel this way.

The "old days" flash before me, like some slow-motion montage in a nasal decongestant commercial. Us sprinting through the backyard sprinklers between intense games of hide-and-seek. Us opening Christmas presents in front of the fireplace. Us spilling flour everywhere while we try to bake cookies in the kitchen. And now look at us. Look at where we are.

I make a move to the computer. I mean to kick it as hard as I can—to smash it, to hear the crunch of metal and plastic, to feel the pain it would bring—but the signal gets lost somewhere between my brain and my foot, and I flail out with my right leg and barely make contact. The computer wobbles meekly and then settles back into its original spot. I can't feel my body.

Steve puts his hand on my shoulder. I knock it away. I lose my balance. My legs give out under me, and I fall, slamming the side of my head against the corner of the desk on the way down. Steve bends over and tries to catch me, tries to cradle my upper body, but I must be too heavy for him because he lets me fall all the way to the ground. I slump against the side of the desk. My eyes close. I want to go to sleep.

My head hurts, so I reach up and grab it. My hand comes away wet. What is that all about? I can hear a faint wailing. Is that me? Am I screaming? I look up at Steve, but he's not looking at me. I must not be making that noise. He's over at the window, staring outside. Why isn't he looking at me?

"Holy shit, Frankie. It's the cops! There must have been a silent alarm!" Steve runs back to the desk, wiping his sleeve on the dark brown wood. I grab the top of the desk and pull myself up.

"What are you doing?" he says. His voice is loud. He pushes me back, and I stumble to the ground again. What an asshole. He wipes my prints from the desk.

"Come on." He puts my arm around his neck, lifting me almost a foot off the ground. "We have to get out of here."

"Where are we going?"

"Frankie, you have to move your legs. I can't carry you down the stairs."

I blink a few times, trying to make sense of everything. I wish he would just stop so we could talk about this.

"Remember what I said before?" He's talking to me like I'm a four-year-old. "Run like hell? Well, that's what we have to do right now."

That sounds like a stupid plan to me, but he's my brother, so I'll do what he says. We stumble all the way down the stairs, and by the time we get to the bottom, my legs start working again.

"Come on," he says, pushing me out the window.

I land on the concrete outside and roll to the ground. Steve jumps out after me and starts to close the window, but even though he's cranking the handle like crazy, it doesn't want to close all the way, so he gives up.

"Can you walk?" he says after wiping down the windowsill again.

I push myself to my feet and nod. Steve grabs my arm and starts down the alley, but the wailing suddenly gets louder, and he stops. "We can't go out that way. There's going to be cops everywhere." He turns around and starts pulling me toward the huge Dumpster. "Come here."

He tries to push me behind the Dumpster, but my head doesn't fit. Then he tries to push the Dumpster back, but it's too heavy. He can't get it to budge. I decide to help him, but by the time I start pushing, he's already gone back to the front and opened up the top.

"I ain't getting in no Dumpster," I say. The sirens are louder.

"My ass!" He grabs me around the thighs and lifts. "Jump!"

Like I said, this is my brother, so if he wants me to get in the Dumpster, I guess I have to get in the Dumpster. I jump up and he helps me, pushing my feet from the bottom until I roll over the edge. I land on something soft. Steve pulls himself up and in, and then he goes over to the side and pulls the top down over us. Now we're inside the Dumpster together.

No sooner does he get the top closed than I hear a car screech to a stop. The wailing of the siren stops as well, but I can still see the flashing lights through a crack where the lid doesn't quite close. My cheek tickles.

"Steve, what—"

He reaches over and covers my mouth with his hand. I try to shrug free, but he won't let me go. "Frankie, just shut the fuck up," he whispers. "I swear to God, if you say one more word, I'm going to knock your ass out cold." He pulls his hand away and rubs his thumb and fingers together. "Holy shit, dude, you're really bleeding."

When I touch the blood dripping from a cut above my temple, it all starts to come back. We just broke into the factory, and the cops are here to get us! Awareness washes over me like those floods you see on TV, where the guy's sitting in a canoe while his house floats by. I don't feel like the guy, though; I feel like the house. As if at any moment I could suddenly be washed away.

A car door slams, followed by another, and another. Men talking. Now that my head is clear, I'm terrified. I try to pull myself up to take a look through the crack, but Steve yanks me back down, and I nearly fall backward into the trash. With my nose just inches from the garbage, it becomes clear to me what we're sitting on: bags and bags of rotting tortillas.

You know that smell when a piece of bread gets all moldy and green? It's like festering mud, but it's sharp and bitter along with being musty. You can almost see the mold particles jumping from the bread and flying directly up your nose. That's what being in the Dumpster is like, except it's so bad that I have to cover my mouth with my fist to keep from tossing my cookies. It's dark, but I imagine a thick cloud of mold particles, like smog, seeping into my clothes, my mouth, and up my nose. Even in the fall, it can get pretty hot, and this steel Dumpster's been an oven all day, baking the fungus. We're probably going to get cancer.

I reach for the top edge of the Dumpster so that I can sneak a look outside, but once more Steve jerks me back down. Instead of going down passively like last time, I whirl on him and grab the sides of his face, squeezing his head tight between my hands. The tortilla bags squeak almost inaudibly under our shifting weight. I move my mouth slowly, so that he'll be able to understand me even though I'm not actually making any noise. "I'm. Fine. Now."

He nods. It looks like he wants to fight me, but that may just be his surprise at having me crush his head. He brings his finger to his lips and nods again. I let him go, and he points to his ears. The men are close enough for us to hear them talking.

"Hey, Carl," one of them says. His voice is deep and gravelly.

"You find something?" another says; this one is much more high-pitched. Younger, I think. I don't know any Carls. Footsteps come toward us, hard-soled boots crunching against the grimy alleyway concrete.

Steve and I are hardly breathing. My cheek tickles again, but I bite my bottom lip, hard, to take my mind off it.

"Some broken glass. Window half open. Looks like someone broke the pane and cranked open the window to get through. I'll go tell the guys out front."

"If this is where he went in, he could still be inside," Carl says. "Or he could be long gone. I'll hang back here—take a look around."

Steve motions for me to be quiet, but I'm not retarded. I concentrate on my breathing while Carl pokes around the Dumpster. The beam of his flashlight pierces tiny cracks in the sides as he waves it around. I'm pretty sure I'll be spending the next couple years in juvie. I close my eyes and wonder if people get boafed in a juvenile facility, or if that only happens in real prison: don't bend over for the soap, and all that. I bet I'll get boafed.

But Carl must not feel like opening the Dumpster, and he walks back down the alley. Maybe my ass will remain a virgin after all. I give my ears a break and start to pay attention to my other senses. There's something making the back of my neck tickle. And my legs, too. I sit up. "Give me your flashlight," I whisper.

"Not until the—"

"Just for a second, I promise."

Reluctantly, he reaches into his back pocket and hands me the light. I cup one hand around the bulb to keep it dim, but the moment I turn it on, I wish I hadn't. Ants are everywhere. Little black ones. Spewing out the tops of the garbage bags like lava from a volcano.

My reaction is immediate and involuntary. I thrash my legs and start brushing my hands all over my body—in my hair, on the back of my neck, my arms, my chest. The flashlight leaps from my hand and clatters against the metal walls of the Dumpster, lighting up our little hiding place like *luminarias* on Christmas Eve.

"Holy shi—"

Steve smacks me across the face so hard, it numbs my entire cheek. He quickly grabs the flashlight and turns it off. "Don't you fucking puss out on me," he says through clenched teeth. "Suck it up."

"But—"

"Someone's coming!"

The footsteps return, and we sit in an impossible silence. I'm not afraid of pain. They're little black kitchen ants, not fire ants. I'm worried about what happens if they get in my ears. Can they crawl down into my brain and start snacking? It feels like my skin is moving. But I try to take deep breaths, and the slower I breathe, the more I relax, the less they run around, and the less I feel them. Maybe they figured out I wasn't food. Or maybe they took some pity on me.

It's really cold, and the fact that we're going to be in this ant-infested Dumpster for the next few hours while the police do whatever it is that police do to investigate a break-in makes me even colder. That's the problem with the desert—hot in the day, cold as balls at night.

It doesn't make much sense, but part of me starts to enjoy being trapped like we are. At least if we get caught, we'll be together. And if we don't get caught, we'll always be able to joke about the time we hung out all night with tons of moldy tortillas and ants crawling all over us and almost froze to death. Although if it were up to me, I'd rather freeze my ass off in an ant-ridden Dumpster with Zach. At least he doesn't judge me.

"Frankie, you awake?"

"Huh?"

"You fell asleep," he says, way too loudly. I put my finger to my lips, but he shakes his head. "They left about an hour ago."

Somehow I've managed to curl up next to an open trash bag. A piece of moldy corn tortilla is stuck to my cheek, and even though it's covered with ants, at least they care more about the tortilla than they do about my brain. I can't believe I fell asleep.

Steve leans back against the metal wall and shakes the ants out of his hair with both hands. "You were dreaming about your girl, am I right?"

"Huh?"

"What's up with her? You getting any?"

"Is this really the time to talk about that?" I give him a nervous laugh. I want to ignore him because the truth is that I haven't been getting much. Or, I should say that I haven't been getting as much as he probably thinks I should have gotten by now. We've made out a bit, but I've never crossed the equator, if you know what I mean. Hooking up is not exactly my area of expertise. Just one more thing for him to make fun of me about.

"I didn't think you were," he says. "Damn, bro, how long are you going to wait? She won't stick around until your balls drop."

Ha-ha. Balls drop. "I'm getting there."

"You're getting there? At least tell me you have a plan for Homecoming. Tell me you're renting a motel room, or crashing at someone's house, or taking a limo at the very least."

I can't tell him any of those things because I'm not doing any of those things. We're doubling with Rebecca's friend Katie, but I don't know how we're getting there. Actually, I never even thought of the motel room. I have a feeling that if I suggested it to my date, she would rip my balls clear off, whether they've dropped or not.

"You think it's safe to leave yet?" I say.

He doesn't answer me right away. Instead, he makes a face like he's cleaning his bottom teeth with his tongue. He stands up and looks through the crack at the top of the Dumpster.

"I just hope they didn't find the Sizzler," he says, and he pushes the lid back all the way.

The sky is dark gray with a hint of pink—the sun will be up in a couple hours—and it's five thirty in the morning by the time we make it back to his car, which miraculously remains unticketed even though it looks like the definition of suspicious: a hand-painted piece of shit parked alone on a street six blocks from a break-in.

"Do you think the cops saw it?"

Steve opens the door. He motions to the street with his free hand. "They're not here, are they?"

I get in the car and slam the door. Steve plops into the driver's seat and starts the car, revving the engine a few times to let me know what a punk I am. He does a quick U-turn, putting the Tortilla Emporium in the rearview mirror, and we set off down the early morning streets.

Today's sunrise is a beauty. Pink light creeping up above the mesas, wispy clouds streaking toward us. And the streets are deserted. We could be the only people in Borges who see it. But as perfect as it is, this particular sunrise reeks of failure.

All that happened tonight is that I disappointed my brother. I pussed out at every opportunity. We didn't get even with the Daltons; we didn't show a little Towers pride. I couldn't even entertain him with stories of how much my girlfriend puts out.

I check my head in the side-view mirror. Just above my temple is a bump about the size of a marble. A trail of dried blood runs down my cheek, but there's also dried blood smudged all over the right side of my face. Blood has dripped onto my sweatshirt, and my palms are crusty and red as well. And all from such a little cut.

"I look like shit," I say, not meaning it to be out loud.

Steve just grunts.

It's just before six o'clock when Steve kills the engine and coasts into the driveway. To my great relief, our mother is not standing behind the front door when we walk in, and I manage to sneak into my room and climb under the covers without making a sound.

seventeen

THE PROBLEM WITH breaking into the tallest building in town is that you can never get away from it. The Tortilla Emporium has taunted me all week, looming on the horizon like a beacon of conscience. There was just a little article in the paper about it, and even though the police didn't sound too concerned because nothing was stolen, I've had a hard time sleeping. I can't stop thinking about what it would be like to be arrested, to have the cuffs around my wrists, to see the look on my mom's face.

All I want is some peace and quiet, some time to myself. But I'm lying on my back with my eyes closed, in the spotty shade of a cottonwood on the edge of campus, when Dalton kicks the sole of my shoe. From what I hear, he's had a good time at my expense all week. Begay said he saw Dalton laughing about how one of these days he's going to have to fire that lazy Towers family.

"Wake up, Spankie."

I crack open my right eye and give him the finger. I don't even care anymore. People suck. My parents sold our restaurant to the biggest dick in school; my brother—who isn't even close to who I thought he was—is ashamed to be seen in the same area code as me. Plus, Zach and Begay are all buddy-buddy, talking about how much fun they had on the Rez. At least Rebecca didn't go all *loca* on me, too. I figure as long as I can make it to tomorrow night, everything will be fine. I'll deal with my life after Homecoming.

"Bite me." I close my eye again and lace my hands behind my head. There's nothing he can do to me that he hasn't done already.

By the way, it's amazing how long you can go without talking to your parents if you really try. Now that I don't work at the restaurant anymore, all I have to do is ride my bike to school and hang out in my room when I get home, and I hardly even see them at all. Not like they've noticed, I'm sure. They're busy "transitioning" the restaurant and talking about how much freedom they'll have. Good for them.

"Where you been all week?"

It's true—I haven't socialized much. It's already Friday and I've hardly said a word to anybody. "Banging your mom,"

I say. It's better than telling him the truth. "She's real nice."

"That's cute." He squats down next to me and lowers his voice. "Come on by Los Torres anytime. Tacos are on me."

At this, I open my eyes and sit up. "Suck my ass, you stupid ape *güero*."

He stands and looks behind him, probably checking for teachers or something. It's nearing the end of lunch, but there are still plenty of people scattered around. "You really want another piece of me?"

I stand up and offer myself to him. "Bring it. You don't even need your two friends to help."

I can see over his shoulder that people are starting to pay attention to us. A few guys stand up and watch. I wonder if Rebecca and her friends can see. My breath is coming in huge gasps now, my chest heaving up and down. I push him square in the chest with both hands, but he barely moves. "Hit me, John!" I'm yelling now. Calling him by his first name for the first time I can remember. "Come on! Don't be such a pussy!"

I see Steve out of the corner of my eye, running toward us. I hear his voice, but he barely registers. Dalton takes a step closer and cocks his fist, and for a second I think he's really going to do it. But then he just spits on me.

My brother jumps between us and pushes Dalton away. "Get back," he says.

Dalton puffs up his chest. "What are you going to do?"

"You'll find out right now if you don't step back."

"You won't do dick. How are you going to play

tomorrow if you get suspended?" Dalton shakes his head. "Homecoming and everything? Wouldn't it suck to miss that?"

Steve moves toward him, but Dalton doesn't budge. They stand chest to chest, breathing the same air, my brother looking down. "The season doesn't last forever, *gringo.*"

They stare at each other for a few more seconds, and then Dalton smirks. He steps back and points at me over my brother's shoulder. "You're pathetic, Spankie."

As soon as Dalton's out of earshot, my brother whirls on me and throws up his arms. "What the hell is wrong with you?"

What's wrong with *me*? How is this my fault? I wipe off Dalton's spit with my shoulder. "He came up to me. I was just lying—"

"The fucking cops are here, Frankie," he says with his teeth clenched. "You can't get into a fight when the cops are on campus."

"The cops?"

"Yes, the cops," he says. "Chief Sanchez and some other guy. The one who busted you and Zach for the bottle rockets."

"Sergeant Rodriguez?"

He scoffs. "You think I give a shit what his name is?"

"What are they doing here?"

"You need to keep your mouth shut. Don't act weird. In fact, don't even look at them if you don't have to. They'll read it all over your face."

"I swear, Steve, I didn't say anything."

"*Cálmate, ese,*" he says, scanning the campus behind me. "I never said you did. If they come up to you, don't turn away. If they ask you a question, be polite. Breathe. Don't stutter or shift your feet. Put your hands in your pockets so you don't fiddle with them."

"I never stutter."

"Just try to stay away from them. You're the worst liar ever." He cocks his head at me. "You okay?"

I need to find Rebecca. Maybe her dad hasn't seen her yet today. Out of everything that's happened to me this week, the one thing I could count on was her. We walked home from school every day, sometimes holding hands, sometimes not. Of course we talked about the restaurant a little, but not on purpose. We talked about her mom leaving. We didn't talk about my brother. Once in a while we'd step behind a wall and make out for a little bit. Nothing major—nothing worth bragging to Steve about, at least. But it was something, and it was real, and he can go fuck himself if he thinks it's not enough.

The hallways are crowded, everyone in post lunch food comas, jostling back to their lockers like melancholy salmon. I wish I could just jump into the current and be swept away, but Zach cuts me off as soon as I walk inside. "What's up, Frankie?" he says.

"You know, you know. Hangin' in there." I peer over his shoulder. Rebecca should be coming around the corner any minute now.

"What are you looking at?" Zach says, glancing around behind him.

"Nothing."

"Dude, you want to come over after school? I picked up some more stuff last weekend. I was thinking we could get some old tennis balls and go to work on the ditch behind my house."

"Is Begay busy or something?"

"Come on, man."

Where is she? "Uhhhh . . . I kind of have, uh . . ."

"Have what, Frankie? Plans?" he says, shaking his head. "What's your problem?"

Like I need this right now. "I don't know what you mean."

"At least Begay didn't stop talking to his friends when he started going out with Mandy."

Okay, so I admit that I haven't really hung out with him in a while. But what does he expect me to do? He's the one who kept telling me to ask her out in the first place. He was psyched about what happened at the Golf n' Goof, and now he's whining about it. All I can say is that if the situation was reversed, I'd be happy for him.

Besides, I've got Homecoming tomorrow, and I need to stay focused. "Dude, Zach, give me a break, okay? I'm chilling with Rebecca today—"

"And yesterday, and the day before, and the day before that—"

Ahhh, here she comes. Who's that guy she's talking

to? I don't know him. Is he a sophomore? Maybe a junior? Damn, I hope he's not a senior. "Don't be so jealous, *ese*," I say, trying to laugh. "You'd be doing the same thing if you were me."

"My ass, Frankie," he says. He leans in, and for a second I think he's going to push me, but then he glances over my shoulder and shakes his head. "You don't care about what's happening to anybody but yourself."

"What are you talking about?"

"Nicole, you dumb-ass. I was going to ask if you wanted to come with me and Begay tomorrow."

"She said yes?" I almost break out into a smile. Almost. "You must really have needed that fifty bucks."

"Go suck on it," he says, shaking his head. "Here comes your girlfriend."

With that, he brushes by me and walks down the hall. He walks right by Rebecca without even saying anything to her. What a bastard.

"Hey, Frankie," Rebecca says without much cheer in her voice. The way she says it makes me feel like I'm being held after class. That can only mean one thing.

She grabs my arm and leads me down the hallway, but instead of talking to me, she just stops next to one of the Spanish classrooms, under a HOMECOMING COMES ONCE A YEAR banner. I don't want to call attention, but I have to risk it. "Your dad's here today."

"Yeah, I know."

"Have you talked to him?"

She grabs my hand and pulls my arm so that my ear is near her mouth. Smelling her strawberry lip gloss is the best thing that's happened to me all day. If only I could stop her before she says anything else. She whispers, "He doesn't want me to go out with you anymore. He thinks you're a bad influence."

It's like all the water in my body evaporates at once. My mouth is a desert, and my eyes are so dry I can't blink. I think I just stepped on my stomach.

"I'm sorry."

At least I don't have to worry about bringing a gun to school. I can kill my brother at home. The one thing I had to be happy about is gone, and all because of him. It doesn't matter how cool we act, it doesn't matter if our prints aren't in the system. Somehow they know it was us.

"Frankie?" she says.

I can't make my mouth form words. "I'm . . . Are you serious?"

"He doesn't normally like to get involved in my private life, but he said this case was different." She lets go of my hand and shrugs.

Was it the Dumpster? Did something fall out of my pocket? Maybe I was fingerprinted for some reason when I was really little, but even so, shouldn't fingerprints change from when you're a baby?

"I'm sorry," she says again. "I was really looking forward

to Homecoming, but I have to do what he tells me. You're too risky."

And here's how boafing just barged its way back into my future: the Chief and Sergeant Rodriguez turn the corner. Fully armed, of course. They wave at Rebecca and walk toward us in perfect synch. Their shiny black boots squeak against the linoleum with every step. A sunbeam pierces the window and reflects off their badges and right into my eyes. I notice polished steel handcuffs poking out of holsters on their utility belts.

"Hey, *Papi*," Rebecca says.

The Chief smiles broadly. This must be the happiest day of his life. "Hello, sweetheart." He bends over and gives her a hug.

Sergeant Rodriguez tips an imaginary hat. "Hi, Rebecca."

"Francisco?" the Chief says. The smile leaves his face as he turns to me. He rests the heel of his right hand on the handle of his still-holstered gun. So this is what it feels like. "Are we going to need a chat?"

It's amazing how much I want to rat on Steve right now. If I'm going down, the least I can do is bring his ass with me. I picture his face, all shocked and upset, when they shove him against the Sizzler's hood and slap the cuffs on him. See how he feels when they take soccer away from him. You know what, though? I bet they'd still let him play the rest of the season.

I don't tell, of course. I guess I'm too much a pussy even for that. I jam my hands in my pockets and staple my feet to the ground. "Why would we need to chat?" I say, peeking nervously at Rebecca.

The Chief dips his head. "Just make sure she's home by midnight," he says.

"Huh?"

"Midnight, young man. Do you think you can do that?"

"I . . . I think . . ."

"You don't have to stutter," Rebecca says, biting her bottom lip. "It's not a hard question."

A small trickle of drool forms at the corner of my mouth. If I don't get it together soon, I'll slobber all over the Chief's gleaming black boots. I glance over at Rebecca and wonder why the hell she's enjoying this so much. I wish she would just tell me what's going on.

The Chief leans in so slightly that I hardly notice it. "Mr. Towers?"

"Uh. Yeah. Midnight."

Instantly, he breaks out into a warm smile. "Good. Then we won't need to chat." He leans over and kisses Rebecca on her forehead. "Bye, sweetie."

"See you later, *Papi*," she says.

The Chief and Sergeant Rodriguez chuckle at me before turning away and strolling back down the hall. Sounds come back. The slamming of lockers, even the flickering of the lights overhead.

Rebecca busts out laughing. She even does one of those snort laughs. "Oh, my God! That was so awesome."

Relief spreads over me one molecule at a time. If she weren't so hot, I'd have to punch her or something. "Did you know he was going to do that?"

"Yeah, we planned it."

"Why is he here?"

"Some antidrug lectures for the freshmen. They do that every year."

I always wondered what it would feel like to be in a noose, about to be hanged; to feel the rough fibers of the rope against the soft skin of my neck; to glance down between my feet and see through the planks of the trapdoor.

My heart pumps pure adrenaline. "That wasn't funny."

"No, it was funny, trust me." She grabs my hand again and pulls my cheek down to her. I get a kiss.

"I'm never trusting you again."

I should find Steve and tell him, shouldn't I? Let him know he can relax, for now. Or maybe I'll just let his punk ass stew for a while.

"So, what was up with Zach? It looked like you guys were all pissed at each other."

"Nothing, just stupid stuff. He's all wounded because I won't go blow up some M-80s today. Don't worry about it."

"Can you believe about him and Nicole? She's so excited."

Every time I hear her name, I think of my brother—was he really there? Did he really do it?—and it takes everything I have to ignore it. Is that wrong? That I just want to push him out of my mind?

I raise my eyebrows at Rebecca. "She is?"

"Why is that weird? He's funny. He makes her laugh. He's kind of cute. Anyway, you should go tonight."

"That's okay."

"No, seriously, I don't want to get between you guys—"

"Trust me, you're not—"

"Besides, I haven't really seen any of my friends this week, and they're getting bitchy. Everyone's going over to Andromeda's house tonight, so it's not like you'll be leaving me without anything to do."

You've got to be kidding me. "No, really, it's cool."

"We're going to see each other tomorrow night anyway, right? Go ahead over to Zach's house. It'll be fun." She cradles her books against her chest and does that thing where she twists back and forth, while looking up at me with her head cocked to the side. I hate that move, and I'm just about to tell her that, when Señora Fernandez pokes her head out of the Spanish classroom.

"*Rebecca,*" she says, "*todavía necesitas tomar la pruebita.*"

Rebecca winces. "*Momentito, Señora,*" she says over her shoulder and then turns back to me. "Oh crap, I have to make up a Spanish quiz I bombed. My dad was right—you are a bad influence on me," she says, reaching up to give me another peck on the cheek. "Bye!"

She's gone before I can convince her not to go to Andromeda's, where they'll probably sit on the bed in their pajamas, holding pillows against their chests, and talk about me. And what am I going to do? Not go over to Zach's, that's for sure. Let him come to my house and apologize for being such a *pendejo*.

Damn. For the first time, I'm glad Rebecca hasn't gone down my pants yet; the last thing I need right now is a bunch of girls chatting about my johnson.

eighteen

"FRANCISCO, we're leaving in forty minutes!" my mom screams from the kitchen. "I put your corsage in the fridge, okay? Don't forget it!"

Yes, my mom's taking us tonight. I called all the limo places in Albuquerque and Santa Fe, but because it was so last minute, there weren't any limos left in the whole state. I can't get a ride with Steve because he's not going—he wouldn't be allowed to go even if he wanted to take Carmenita, given what happened at his game today. So that leaves my mom.

My parents have had opposite reactions to my refusal to interact with them in any meaningful way. My mom still tries as hard as she can to make conversation. She throws on a smile whenever she sees me, makes me lunches, and basically tries to wear me down with her cheer. It's annoying, but it's probably going to work one of these days, and at least she has a plan.

But my dad doesn't seem to have any idea what to do. We haven't really talked yet because I've managed to avoid him all week by eating early and complaining about how much homework I have. I was even hoping that I'd get out the door tonight before he came home.

Unfortunately, I'm in the bathroom with a towel around my waist and shaving cream all over my face when I hear his tires on the gravel driveway. I'm a sitting duck; I can't close the door because there's too much steam in the bathroom and I wouldn't be able to shave. I can't wait him out because I told Rebecca I'd pick her up at a certain time. I may not be the smartest guy in the world, but I do know that picking your date up late pretty much guarantees you won't get any at the end of the night.

The hinges creak—horror-movie style—when he pushes the front door open. I cross my fingers, and his footsteps go toward the kitchen and away from me. "Is Frankie home?" he says.

Come on, *Mamá*, don't tell him. Say you already took me to dinner. So what if it's only six o'clock? Or tell him I'm taking a nap, or sick, or over at Zach's. I just want to get through the night without having to put up with that look on his face when he tries to talk to me. That I'm-trying-so-hard-to-be-a-father look that just makes me sick.

My mom answers him right away. "He's getting ready in the bathroom."

So much for that. I've got half my face shaved by the time he pokes his head in and leans against the doorway. "Pretty steamy in here," he says with an exaggerated wave of his right hand.

"Yeah."

"You know, you shouldn't shave against the grain. The hair grows from the bottom to the top on the lower part of your neck. That's why people get razor burn."

How precious: some helpful tips from my father before I go out on my big night. I half expect him to pull out a banana and show me how to put on a rubber.

You shouldn't get the impression that I hate my dad, because I don't. He's my dad, right? So it doesn't make any sense to hate him. It's kind of like when you're watching your favorite team and one of the players sucks, even though he's trying the best he can. You don't hate that player. Sure, you want him off the team as soon as possible, but how can you hate him if you don't really know him? You just want a forward who can put the goddamn ball in the net for once.

I try to make out my own reflection in the foggy mirror. "I don't get razor burn."

He picks up a washcloth and clears a nice big circle in the mirror for me. "Are you about ready?"

"Just about."

"Your mother's driving you?"

Mom offered to let me borrow Dad's truck and drive myself, but I figured that since Rebecca wants us to catch a ride from dinner to the dance with Katie and her date, there was no need to leave the truck in some parking lot. Plus, I'm more likely to have Rebecca home by midnight if I'm not in control of the driving. That's the one thing I don't want to forget.

"Yeah," I say. "In your truck."

There must be something nasty caught in his throat, because he spends a good ten seconds clearing it. When he's finished, he wipes the mirror again and leans in toward me. "Can I talk to you for a second?"

Like I have a choice? I glance at him for a moment and then go back to my shaving. "Okay."

"Do you have your tuxedo?"

Does he think I'm a moron? Of course I have my tux. Homecoming isn't as formal as Prom, but most people wear tuxes anyway, especially the underclassmen because we're not guaranteed a date to Prom. "Yeah. Mom got it for me this afternoon."

"What color did you choose for the cummerbund?"

I wish he would just hurry up and talk about whatever it is he wants to talk about. "Yellow."

"Yellow?" He wipes the mirror clean again. "You got a *yellow* cummerbund?"

"And tie."

My mom walks by and pokes her head in. "Jaime, don't keep him too long. We have to leave in a half hour."

"Did you know he got a yellow cummerbund?"

She beams at me. "*Sí*. I thought it looked perfect." She reaches in and wipes off a tiny spot of shaving cream that had somehow migrated up to my forehead. "Thirty minutes, Francisco."

I smile at her reflection, and then she leaves my dad and me alone again. He rubs his collarbone while I finish up on my cheeks. "Why yellow?"

"Jesus Freaking Christ, Dad," I say as I whirl to face him, accidentally splattering the mirror, the wall, and my dad with soapy water from the razor blade. "So it's yellow! You want me to take it back and get purple or green or something? Who the hell cares what color it is anyway? Goddamn, you're a pain in the ass."

"Frankie, don't you speak to me that way." Oh, darn. I made him angry; he looks down his nose at me and narrows his eyes. Very convincing.

"Well, you are." Finished now with my shaving, I grab a clean washcloth from the rack behind me and push past him across the hall and into my room. Normally, this type of attitude is enough to make my dad go into the other room until he thinks I've calmed down, but this time he follows me in.

My mom kicks ass, by the way—she's laid the tux on the bed, yellow cummerbund and everything. There's a small folded piece of paper sticking out of the shiny leather shoes. DEAR FRANCISCO, YOU'RE GOING TO LOOK SO HANDSOME TONIGHT. I'M VERY PROUD OF YOU. LOVE, MAMÁ.

"Check it out, Dad," I say, tossing the note back onto the bed. "Yellow cummerbund. Yellow tie. Rebecca's wearing a—"

"Why didn't you go to your brother's game today?"

I wait for the punch line, but he's finished. There is no punch line. He's serious? I can't believe it. He's serious. "What?"

He closes his eyes and pinches the bridge of his nose. "What I meant was, what's wrong?"

"Nothing's wrong." I go to my drawer for a clean pair of underwear and pull them on under the towel. Then I toss the towel onto the floor at the foot of the bed. "I just didn't feel like going, that's all."

"Did you hear what happened?" he says, speaking slowly as if he's learning how to read with Hooked on Phonics.

My mom told me all about it. There was a scuffle, and Steve got ejected halfway through the first half for punching the Albuquerque High goalie in the face. The refs wouldn't even let him on the field for the senior celebration at halftime. I wonder what the scouts wrote on their little clipboards about that one. I have this sick urge to pretend I haven't heard, just so he'll have to say the words. But that's plain mean.

"Too bad you sold the restaurant," I say, pulling on my undershirt. "You could have made him scrub the pots."

"That's not fair."

"Not fair?" I grab the tux and rip away its protective plastic cover. The pants fall into a clump onto my dark red sheets, and I snatch them up and start pulling them on. "You buying him a car and leaving me with his old bike, that's not fair." I can't button these goddamn pants. It's one of those things where you have to button the flap on the inside before you can do the one on the outside. "Me working my ass off while he gets to screw around, that's not fair."

He stares at me for a moment as if stunned by my outburst. Then he walks over to the window and peers outside at the backyard. "He had a chance for something special with soccer. We wanted to encourage that."

"You never say no to him. Ever." I finally manage to get the waist button done. But I probably should have waited until I put on my shirt, because I'm just going to have to unbutton the pants to tuck it in. Fuck.

Dad's losing his patience with me. I think it pisses him off that I won't stop getting dressed. "I do my best."

I have to laugh at this one. "A lot of people do their best, Dad." The tux shirt feels like cardboard against my skin. My mom said it was going to be starchy, but I didn't really know what she was talking about. No wonder people look like they have a stick up their ass when they wear tuxes—I couldn't slouch in this thing if I wanted to.

"You can't imagine how much time your mother and I spend worrying about not making mistakes. We simply—"

"You should have told me about the restaurant a long time ago."

"I kept waiting for the right time." He looks at me like a

death row prisoner finally at peace with his fate. His eyes relax. They seem to lose a little luster. "I'm sorry."

My mom appears in the doorway. "Let's go, Francisco. Hurry up and get dressed. You don't want to make your *princesa* wait, do you?"

I look at my dad and raise an eyebrow. For a few seconds, we just stare at each other. "Of course he doesn't, Isa," he finally says to my mom. "I'll make sure he gets ready."

She gives us both an approving nod. "*Qué bien.* He probably needs a little help with the cuff links anyway."

We're silent for a long time after she leaves. Eventually, my dad walks over and closes the bedroom door. He hands me the little felt-covered box with the cuff links and studs in it.

The studs are easy to put in, and I button up the shirt quickly. By sucking in my stomach, I even manage to tuck the shirt in without having to unbutton my pants again.

"Have fun tonight," he says as he pokes the cuff link through its hole. He takes the cummerbund and wraps it around my waist, fastening the clasp and tightening the strap until it fits snugly. "But be smart, okay?"

"Isn't this too tight?" I say, turning around. "I feel like it's going to snap off as soon as I eat something."

"The strap's elastic—it'll stretch." He picks up the matching yellow bow tie and hands it to me.

I latch the bow tie and look at myself in the rectangular mirror above my dresser. The mirror has a long crack snaking diagonally from one side to the other, thanks to the time Steve threw a silver dollar at my head and missed. My dad's face hovers over my shoulder; our faces are on opposite sides of the crack. How meaningful.

"Can I ask you a weird question?"

He smiles. "You can ask me anything you want."

"Did you even like it?" I say to his reflection. "The restaurant, I mean."

The sad laugh again. He shakes his head and looks away.

I think about the game we used to play in the restaurant. When he would invent stories about people who came in. The old man whose job was to refill the price tag guns at all the grocery stores in Montgomery, Alabama. The twin sisters who lived on a commune in Oregon and were the only girls in a family of fourteen. He always came up with the craziest stories, but they were so detailed they could have been true. Maybe that's what happened to him. Maybe he invented a life for himself, and all the little details made it impossible for him to see it wasn't what he really wanted.

My mom knocks twice and opens the door. "Come on, Francisco, we have to go." She stops in the doorway and looks at us, wrinkles creasing her forehead. "Is everything okay?"

"Yeah. Fine." I take one final glance at myself in the mirror, and then I grab my tux jacket and turn toward the door. "I have to get the corsage."

I brush past my mom and into the hallway, leaving her alone with my dad. Part of me wants to hang out within earshot to see if they say anything to each other, but I go into the kitchen anyway. The corsage is exactly where my mom said it would be, right next to the bottomless jar of homemade salsa, and by the time I've pulled it from the fridge, the engine of my dad's truck roars to life in the driveway. Through the kitchen window, I can see my mom in the front seat. She checks her makeup in the rearview mirror, rearranges one of the barrettes in her hair, and looks straight ahead, waiting for me with both hands on the steering wheel.

nineteen

YOU SHOULD NEVER go on a double date with someone you don't know—you need a wingman, and that's why best friends were invented. Unfortunately, I'm flying solo tonight. I wish Zach were here. I should have just sucked it up and called him.

Don't get me wrong, I love sitting next to Rebecca, feeling her dress against my leg, constantly challenging myself to keep my eyes on her face. But I've decided that I can't stand Katie. She has the most annoying laugh I've ever heard, where she kind of squinches up her face and forces these high-pitched giggles to go through her nostrils instead of her mouth. Normally, I could probably handle it without going insane, but she's laughing a lot tonight because her date is a junior soccer player named Rick Mossman.

I don't know Rick well enough to hate him, too, but he's tall, thin, and white—three things I'm not. Plus, the fact that he's probably Dalton's friend makes me want to keep looking over my shoulder. I should have sat with my back to the wall.

Part of me feels a little sorry for Katie, though, because it must suck to walk around school all day knowing that her best friend is so much hotter than she is. And tonight, Rebecca is as hot as I've ever seen her. Her hair is mostly pulled back, with a few curly strands coming down at her temples, almost like those Jewish people with the flat hats. She's wearing a little makeup, but not too much, and with her hair out of her face, you can really see how amazing her eyes are. Plus, the dress should be illegal—yellow and strapless, it makes her chest look huge.

I know I shouldn't be counting my eggs before they hatch, but I can't see how I'm not going to get a little something tonight. She has to know how good she looks, and she has to know what's going through my mind. And even though we still haven't gone that far, tonight has to be different, doesn't it?

It helps that I get to pay for dinner. Mom wanted to cook us a private meal at Los Torres. I mean, I was touched and everything, but please. I don't ever want to go back there. I don't exactly miss it, but it does feel strange to have the restaurant out of my life, almost like we've moved out of town. Anyway, I wasn't about to have my mom around for my

Homecoming dinner. Instead, we're at the Cooperage, a steak house that's not super fancy, but pretty good for Borges.

When you walk in, the seating area is to the right and the bar and restrooms are to the left. The inside walls are some kind of dark wood, and the lighting is pretty dim, coming from a few green fixtures on the walls. A raised platform goes around the outer part where most of the tables are, next to the walls and windows, but you can also sit at one of the tables in the center of the room. That's where we sit.

I lean in to her and whisper. "You look great."

"Yeah, you've already told me. Like a hundred times."

"Oh, sorry."

"It's okay. I like it." She reaches her hand out and pats me on the upper arm—my guns are pathetic compared to her dad's. I glance over at Rick and Katie, but they're busy talking about the game today. Actually—because really discussing the game would involve mentioning my brother—Rick's talking about how well he played, and she's just giggling as if he's the funniest, smartest, most wonderful thing on the planet.

Rebecca takes a sip of her water and dries her lips with her napkin. "Did you have a good time last night?" she says.

"Huh?"

"With Zach. Weren't you guys going to do something?"

I spent the night at home watching TV. Nothing was really on, so I fell asleep on the couch in the living room. I have no idea what Zach did. "Yeah," I say, raising my eyebrows as if in disbelief at the amazing time I had. "It was awesome."

"I hope he's not mad at me."

"Why would he be?"

"For spending all this time with you recently. Sometimes guys get all weird about that, you know." She raises her arm and pretends to crack a whip, complete with sound effects.

I've never seen a girl do the pussy-whipped thing. It's both hilarious and kind of embarrassing at the same time. "Not at all," I say, shaking my head. "He thinks you're the best."

"Good. You guys are such great friends—I would hate to get in the way." Her hand goes up to one of the curls, and she glances over at Katie, who might as well have forgotten we're here.

"Yeah," I say, forcing a smile. We sit there for a second, not looking at each other, before I change the subject. "What about you? Did you have a good time at Andromeda's?"

And did you talk about me?

"We didn't go to sleep until, like, four in the morning. I was so tired I had to take a nap this afternoon, and I almost didn't have time to get ready for tonight."

Fine, but did you talk about me?

She takes another sip of water and dries her mouth again. "Anyway, it was a good time. Girl talk, and everything."

That's what I was afraid of.

I'd like to sit here and stare at Rebecca all night, but I have to go to the bathroom, and my mom has beat it into my head that it's rude to get up during the meal. "Excuse me," I say, pushing back from the table and standing up. "I'm going to use the restroom before our food gets here."

Rick jumps to his feet. "I'll go with you."

I don't have a lot of experience going out to fancy restaurants, but somehow two dudes going to the bathroom together doesn't seem normal. "Okay . . ."

"What's the big deal?" Rick says, laughing and buttoning his coat—he's wearing a blue blazer and a tie instead of a tuxedo. "If girls can go together, why can't we?"

Katie scrunches up her irritating little face and giggles.

"Whatever," I say. "If you gotta go, you gotta go."

I don't like the eager look in Rick's eyes at all, but I shrug and motion for him to go ahead. I want him to walk into the bathroom first, just in case this is some sort of trap the soccer players have decided to set for me. It feels like I'm in one of those mafia movies: the part where they take some defenseless guy to an abandoned warehouse and shoot him in the back of the head.

Rick pushes the door open and walks inside. I follow him in, and luckily I don't get whacked.

An old guy is washing his hands at the sink; he looks a lot like my mom's dad. Short, round, and well-dressed, with a little rim of white hair around the back and sides of his otherwise bald head. Rick and I stand back while the man dries his hands and tosses the paper towel into the trash. He inspects his scalp in the mirror for a while before running his hand over it a few times.

"Gentlemen," he says as he walks past us.

I nod respectfully. "Sir."

Rick rolls his eyes and smirks at me. When the door closes, Rick bends down and checks the stalls for feet. I assume he finds none, because he gives me a big smile and a thumbs-up.

"What are we doing in here?"

He reaches into the inside pocket of his sport coat and pulls out a little travel bottle of shampoo. "How long have you guys been going out?"

"Why?"

"Just asking."

"Oh." I clear my throat. "Just a little while, I guess."

"She's hot, dude. Smokin' hot."

I don't like the way this is going at all. I put my hands in my pockets and glance around the bathroom. "I know."

"What do you think of Katie?"

I pause. Is this a trick question? If I say she's hot, will he kick my ass for looking at his date? And if I say she's as ugly and annoying as I think she is, will he kick my ass for disrespecting her? I finally just go with it. "She looks good tonight."

His eyebrows dance up and down. "No doubt. I think I'm home free, if you know what I mean, with her being a sophomore, and all. No offense." He offers me the bottle of shampoo. "Check it out."

It's about three inches tall, with a flowery gold cap. A

perfect miniature of some kind of designer bottle. "The Plaza?" I say, handing it back to him.

"It's a hotel in New York," he says, unscrewing the top. "My dad goes there a lot on business. He goes all over the country."

So freaking what? "Cool," I say.

"My mom collects the shampoos he brings back from all the hotels he stays in. She has, like, two hundred of them or something." He tilts his head back and pours half the bottle down his throat. After he swallows, he sticks out his tongue and shakes his head so that his tongue flaps back and forth against his cheeks. "Damn, that burns."

"What's in there?"

"Rum," he says after a short series of coughs. "My mom's got so many of these little bottles that she has no idea if a couple go missing. So I just wake up early, grab some rum or vodka from the liquor cabinet, and snag a couple little shampoos from her collection. You have to rinse them out pretty good or you get that nasty soap taste."

And people are scared of *Mexican* kids?

Rick offers me the bottle. "Go ahead. Finish it off. I have more."

I could say no, of course. It's not like I feel any peer pressure or anything. I mean, there's nobody else here, so it's not like people are going to find out that I didn't want to have a drink. Besides, what's Rick going to do? Run out to the restaurant and tell everybody that I wouldn't have some of his smuggled alcohol?

I accept the bottle and peer inside through the top. Sure enough, dark liquid sloshes around inside. "Did you rinse out all the shampoo? It looks like there are still some bubbles in there."

"Dude, give me a break," he says, checking himself out in the mirror but still keeping one eye on me. "Just chug it. You won't even notice."

Screw it. I tilt my head back and pour it all in. Rick was right about one thing—it burns. It's like someone's shooting hot air up through my nostrils, and I can actually feel the rum go down as it coats the inside of my throat. I still taste the shampoo, though, and I get a little bit of it down the wrong pipe.

"That's the shit, Frankie. You know what I'm talking about?" He comes over and pats me on the back, hard, until I stop coughing. When I finally look in the mirror, I can only laugh. My eyes are all watery, and my face is bright red. I look like I've been sobbing.

"You ready to get back out there?"

I splash some cold water on my face and dry off with one of the stiff brown paper towels. Rick holds the door open for me, and I'm about to follow him when I remember the reason I came here in the first place. "I still have to take a piss."

"Yeah, whatever. I'll see you back out there." He salutes me and spins away back into the restaurant.

As I stand at the urinal, I let the effects of my little rum and shampoo shot spread all the way down to my fingertips. Doing dumb shit feels so good. You could be caught at any moment, and you love it! It's like a little warm spot in your chest. That could be the alcohol, I know, but I didn't really have that much, so there's got to be something more to it. Maybe that's why chicks date the assholes.

I guess I'm one of Rick's buddies now, like he trusted me enough to share his booze with me, and that makes us boys. From now on, whenever I see him in school, we won't even have to talk; we'll just give each other a little nod. I finish up and wash my hands.

When I pull the door open, I almost run directly into my new friend, who's leaning in the hallway with his arms crossed, staring at me.

"Damn, dude, you scared the—"

"I didn't want to watch you take a leak," he says.

"Thanks." I put my hand on my chest; somehow, my heart's still beating.

When we arrive back at the table, our salads are there, and the girls have already started eating.

"You guys okay in there?" Rebecca says. "We waited for a while, but then we just got too hungry."

Rick flashes a smile. "Yeah, sorry about that. Frankie fell in."

I shake my head and walk around to my seat. As I pull the chair back, I notice the old man from the bathroom sitting at the table next to us. Across from him sits a woman I assume is his wife. She's probably around his age, wearing a black sweater and a necklace of huge turquoise stones.

I nod at the man as I sit down. "Sir."

"You look very nice," the woman says. "I've always enjoyed a man in a tuxedo."

"Thank you, ma'am." I feel suddenly paranoid about having chugged that drink. The old man probably waited outside the bathroom and heard everything we said. I bet they can smell the rum on my breath. I turn back around, and Rick rolls his eyes.

The food, when it finally comes, is pretty good. Rebecca attacks her chicken parmesan like it said something about her mom. I love that. It makes me all self-conscious when girls don't eat.

It might just be the soapy rum, or it might be Rebecca's perfume wafting toward me, but the thought occurs to me that the sooner we finish our meal, the sooner we'll be at the dance, and therefore, the sooner I'll have an excuse to wrap my arms around my date. I grab the knife and slice off a chunk of meat.

Rebecca reaches over and stops me from putting it my mouth. "Easy," she says, "I don't know the Heimlich."

My fork holds at least three bites' worth. I put it back down and slice off a smaller piece. "Thanks," I say. "You just saved my life."

"My pleasure." She winks at me. My God, I hope that means what I think it means.

Halfway through the meal, the old people leave, giving our table a wave as they go. For dessert, Rebecca and I end up sharing an order of flan. It's gooey and bland, but I eat half of it so she doesn't feel like a pig. When we're finally ready to leave, I call the waiter over and ask for the check, but he just shakes his head.

"It's been taken care of," he says with a smile.

"I'm sorry?"

"The elderly gentleman asked that your bill be put on his card."

There must be some mistake. I look around, and the entire staff is smiling at me. The hostess covers her lips with the fingertips of both hands. "You're kidding," I say.

"He told me to remember the look on your face." The waiter glances over at the hostess and takes a deep breath. "He said to think of it as a gift."

"Thank you, geezer!" Rick says, banging the table twice as he stands up. "Let's make like shepherds and get the flock out of here."

Katie and Rebecca get their little purses together, but I can't bring myself to stand up yet. Rick digs into his pocket and pulls out his keys and jingles them in front of my face. "Come on, dude, let's go."

"Yeah, just a sec," I say. "I'll meet you out there."

Rick spins away and struts toward the door, and the two girls follow him. When Rebecca reaches the doorway, she looks over her shoulder, but I'm still sitting at the table. She stands in the doorway, her hands clasped in front of her, waiting patiently.

I don't want to exaggerate what just happened—just some people buying dinner for a few high school kids—but there's something about it that floors me. After all the crap I've had to deal with from my family, for a perfect stranger to actually do something nice? I didn't know people like that existed.

I finally manage to push my chair back and stand. I take a very deep breath and turn to the waiter, who reaches out and brushes some lint off the shoulders of my jacket. "If they ever eat here again," he says, pointing to my face, "I'll tell them."

twenty

AS I LEAD Rebecca under a tunnel of black balloons and into the Land of Enchantment, I feel a warm tickle of anticipation growing in my chest. Fake moss creeps along the edges of the walls, and some of Zach's sparkling silver streamers dangle all the way from the ceiling. A combination of dry ice and strategically placed smoke machines creates a layer of fog at everyone's feet. Green and purple lights shine from behind large potted trees, and what I can see of the gym floor is covered with brown paper.

The music is almost deafening, and the DJ has an elaborate colored laser light show going on. Because you can't get rid of the bleachers, there's only so much you can do to spice up a gym, but that doesn't matter once we start mingling. It's hard to believe these are the same kids I see every day—the chicks all look hot, and most of the dudes are just as dressed up as I am.

Begay and his date Mandy, who's sexy as hell even though she's not wearing her glasses, are right by the entrance. Rebecca and Mandy immediately squeal and grab each other's hands and lean back, commenting on each other's dresses, hair, shoes, corsages, and probably dates, too.

Begay has to yell to make himself heard over the thumping bass. "What's up, Frankie? Nice tux." He points to his look, a simple black suit with a white shirt and a turquoise and silver bolo tie. "I would have worn one, but I had to represent the Nation."

"It looks good."

"No, dude." He leans in. "*Rebecca* looks good."

I know that, but it's still nice to have someone else confirm it. The smile on my face must be ridiculous. "Where's Zach?"

"Here somewhere," he says. "But good luck getting his attention. If I'd known Nicole was actually into him, I would never have offered his ass the fifty bucks."

Rebecca comes to my side and grabs my hand. I feel a jolt run to the back of my neck; it's like a warm chill. "Come on," she says. "Let's dance."

I'm as bad a dancer as everybody else, but the shampoo rum works its magic—or maybe it's Rebecca's magic—and I manage to let myself go. We bump a little, grind a little; Rebecca claps when I do a goofy stomp-step, and she flails her arms and bobs her head back and forth.

In the back of my mind, I was worried that Dalton would show up and accept yesterday's offer of a fight. But after a while it becomes clear that he's not here, and that makes me very, very glad. At one point, I catch a glimpse of Zach and Nicole over by the DJ, dancing and laughing like they're the only ones in the room.

Cheo's hanging with some chick I've never seen before, but he's too into her to notice me whenever I try to get his attention. My brother is nowhere to be found, as promised, but I wouldn't be surprised to see him and Carmenita crash the party later.

During one of the slow songs, when I've got my arms wrapped so tight around Rebecca's waist that I should probably be worrying about pressing wood into her thigh, Rick stumbles over to us.

"What's up, bro?" he says. The stench of rum on his breath is almost overpowering. I guess he had more than just a few shampoo bottles stashed away somewhere. The one good thing about my mom picking us up after the dance is that I won't have to get in the car with him again.

"Hey," I say as unkindly as possible. I don't want to be a jerk, but he's attracting attention.

He wraps his arm around my neck and leans in even closer. "Dude, you want to borrow my car?"

I know Rebecca hears this, and it makes me want to kick him in the nuts. I don't know what to say, so I ignore him.

"Right, right. I got it, bro. Keep it smooth." Still holding on to my neck, he leans back and shouts at the top of his lungs, "Frankie Towers in the house! Smooth as hell!"

A few people turn around, but Rick isn't the only drunk one here, so nobody pays too much attention. I notice some of the teachers look our way, which makes me nervous, but they're the younger ones, and they don't seem to be in the mood to enforce any rules. Either that, or they're clueless.

"Take my keys anyway, bro," Rick says, putting them in my pocket. "Friends don't let friends drive, you know? Oh, hey. There's Katie!" With that, he stumbles off toward his date.

I shrug, as if to let Rebecca know that I want absolutely nothing to do with that guy. "Sorry about that."

"It's okay," she says, leaning her head against my shoulder. I swear to God, if that bastard blew my chances tonight, I'm going to kill him.

When the song ends and some hip-hop joint starts bumping, we clear the dance floor and I grab us a couple glasses of punch before joining her on the bleachers. We sit together for a while, watching everyone make fools of them-selves. Part of me still can't believe that she's actually here with me. I feel like any second now her real date's going to show up and lead her out to the dance floor, where he'll be a fantastic dancer, naturally, and he'll freak with her all night while I'm forced to sit on the cold, hard bleachers and watch.

A few songs later, Rebecca wraps her arm around mine. Her eyes are wide open, and I can feel her heart beginning to flutter a bit. "Rick gave you his keys, right?" she whispers.

Um . . . hell yeah, he did. Is she serious?

"Really?"

She must pick up on my total disbelief, because she stands and pulls me to my feet. She squeezes my arm tight and leans in close, so that I can feel her breath way into the inside of my ear when she talks. "I hope you remember where he parked."

I feel as if every single person in the gym watches us leave.

It takes no time to find Rick's silver Jeep, which is parked at the very edge of the lot, far from the gym but near the exit because, as Rick told us earlier, he's always ready for a quick getaway. We gave him a hard time because he made us walk so far, but the fact that it's in a dark corner of the parking lot makes it perfect now.

My heart is beating like a freaking drum solo as I unlock the car and open the rear door for her. I'm actually getting in the backseat with Rebecca Sanchez. Goddamn, if my brother weren't being such an asshole, this is exactly the type of thing I'd want to tell him about—not that he would buy a word of it, unless I stole her bra or something.

I've never been in a situation like this. It's not like a movie theater, or the top of a Ferris wheel, where you have to make your move quickly. We have all the time in the world, or at least it seems like it.

So we sit next to each other and, I shit you not, stare into each other's eyes. I swear to God, if I weren't sitting right here, I would call myself a lying bastard. And as strange as it sounds, there's no pressure. We know what we're here to do, so it's not like either of us is worried about getting rejected. We sit still for at least five minutes, our legs touching, our arms around each other, sharing breath, feeling our hearts beat faster and faster until finally we can't take it any longer and we lean in for the kiss.

I unzip the back of her dress, praying the zipper doesn't get caught in the fabric, and peel the front down, but it takes me a little longer than we both want for me to get her bra undone. My fingers are too clumsy—it feels like they're made out of wood, like the joints don't work. She's wearing one of those strapless bras, so she just pulls the whole thing down to her waist.

"Give me your jacket, Frankie."

"Why?"

"In case people walk by, I don't want to flash them."

I quickly take off my jacket and help her get her arms through the sleeves. "Good idea." It is a good idea, isn't it? She's so awesome.

I have to confess something: my hand feels just about perfect when it's on her *teta*. It's like there's no better place in the world. It's always softer than I expect. I mean, the skin is softer. I almost feel embarrassed that my hands are so rough.

I'm not exactly *experienced* with the ladies, and I don't know how far to push this. I don't want her to get all threatened, and this is the one thing I really don't want to be bad at. Rebecca can't undo the buttons of my stupid tuxedo pants, so she reaches under my waistband, and just the touch of her fingertips against my skin is enough to make me gasp.

By the time we really get going, though, we hear engines revving to life and car doors slamming.

"We should probably stop," I say.

She bites my bottom lip and speaks with it still between her teeth. "I know."

One thing, though: if I'm having the time of my life, why do I feel so insecure? It's like I'm so high right now that there's nowhere for me to go but down. I take a deep breath and savor the moment, suddenly positive that nothing like this is ever going to happen to me again.

Someone whoops and bangs a fist on the hood of the car, and that scares the crap out of both of us. I yank my hand out from under her dress and whirl my head to look out the window, but I can't see anything—whoever did it is gone already.

She turns away from me to pull her bra back up, and her dress is all zipped before I can even think to offer some help. "How do I look?"

I want to pick right up where we left off, but the mood is totally shot. "Perfect," I say.

She fixes her hair and then straightens out my tie. "Can I still wear your jacket? It's kind of cold."

Is she kidding? She's Rebecca Sanchez. She can do whatever the hell she wants. I lean in to give her another kiss, but there's more hollering, and now I hear footsteps. I turn around and press my face against the glass, looking in the opposite direction of the gym. Headlights shine against the trunk and branches of a juniper tree about thirty feet away. I hear the familiar roar of a 340 engine.

"Oh, no." I have no more air in my lungs.

Rebecca leans over my lap. "What's wrong?"

"Come on. Let's go," I say. "Something's happening."

twenty-one

A LOOSE CIRCLE has formed in a dim corner of the parking lot. With all the spectators dressed so formally in suits and tuxedos and dresses, it's like they've come to watch the opera. The moon sits above the horizon, cutting through the trees and bathing everyone in a mix of shadow and deathly white. Pebbles crunch beneath my rented tux shoes as I pull Rebecca to the front. In the distance, a steady bass line pounds a tribal beat.

When I reach the front, I see what I was afraid of. The Sizzler, engine running, is parked next to an old silver Chevy truck. My brother stands in the center of the circle, less than three feet away from Dalton, who holds a half-empty fifth of

Jim Beam loosely in his right hand. Flaco, wearing khakis and a beater, with a baseball cap pulled down low over his bandanna, hangs back a couple steps behind my brother. Carmenita and the other *cholas* aren't here, though. Whatever is about to go down is man's work. Six or seven *cholos*—the guys from the Golf n' Goof—are spread out around the circle, waiting.

Will Burrage emerges from one end with his palms up in the universal gesture of peace and tries to pull Dalton away. "Take it easy, Steve. He's wasted."

"Ain't no excuse for being a bitch," my brother says. "We got some unfinished business."

Dalton leans back and takes a swig of Beam, the side of his black suit flapping up like a wing. Then he slams the bottle onto the ground, sending shards of glass and drops of whiskey scattering over the black asphalt. "Let's finish it, then."

Burrage tries to pull his friend back, but he doubles over when one of the *cholos*, lightning quick, leaps over and knees him in the chest. Another of Flaco's friends yanks Burrage back to the edge.

From where I stand, Flaco is completely silhouetted in front of the truck. Headlights glare in the faces of every witness, but nobody turns away. They're all mesmerized. Bass still thumps from the gym.

I know how this is going to end. I used to want to see them fight, but Dalton can hardly keep his feet right now, and my brother is bulletproof. "Come on, Steve," I say, my voice tinny in my ears.

Steve turns, surprised, as though he didn't expect to see me. "Get out of here, Frankie."

I shake my head. "You don't want to do this."

Dalton turns to me and leers. "I didn't want to fuck your mom last night, but I did it anyway."

And that's when Steve goes insane. In one motion, he leaps toward Dalton with his right fist cradled in his left palm. He whips out his right elbow and connects squarely with Dalton's chin, and the sound is exactly like fights on TV. A perfect *thwack*, like a wooden spoon to a side of beef, and Dalton crumbles to the ground.

Burrage makes a move to help his friend, but two of the *cholos* hold him back. "Damn it, stop!" he says.

"You think you own me?" Steve kicks Dalton in the chest. He flops to his back and tries to roll away, but my brother follows him, taunting him, toying with him. Another kick to the chest. "You like that?"

"Frankie," Rebecca says, tugging on my arm. "Please!"

Everything is happening so fast, I can hardly process it. Dalton tries to crawl out of the circle, but Flaco steps in front of him and pounds him on the back of the neck with his fist. Dalton crashes face-first to the ground.

"Wouldn't it be too bad if you couldn't play in the game next week?" Steve leans down close to Dalton but he's still yelling. He kicks Dalton onto his back.

My dad told me there would come a time when my life would suddenly be right in front of me, like a mirror. And my reflection would be staring at me, waiting for me to make a decision.

But how do I do it? What do I say?

Dalton is a moaning heap. Steve paces back and forth and raises his heel and stomps right next to Dalton's knees. The sound of his foot on the asphalt is flat and empty like a gunshot. "Every time you limp your sorry ass around, you'll think of me."

Steve raises his leg again, his arms spread wide above his head, elbows bent slightly. Except for killing him, it's the worst thing he could do.

"Stop!" I yell.

"What?" Steve says, lowering his leg.

Now my body finally catches up with my mouth, and I run between him and Dalton. "Don't do it."

"Frankie," Steve says. It must be destroying him for me to do this, his little brother so disloyal in front of his friends. "Get the fuck out of my way."

This is it. This is the moment when I always give in. This is when I let his eyes scare me or his popularity intimidate me. My life is filled with moments exactly like this one. So many that if they were bricks, I could build a fortress for my shame, to hide it away in a tower somewhere.

"No," is all I can say. My voice cracks. How pathetic.

"Come on," he scoffs. He pushes me aside, but I get right back up in his face. This time, I root myself into the pavement and hold my fists at my sides.

"No," I say again. And I sound like a man. A peace washes over me. We stare at each other, each breathing heavily.

"Bullshit." A deep voice strangles the silence like a python. Flaco steps toward us and flicks his cigarette at my feet.

Dalton writhes in pain on the ground, moaning to himself. His face is covered with blood from a cut above his eye. All I can do is wish none of this had ever happened.

"This dude beat your ass down and you want to protect him?" Flaco says.

"He's hurt bad enough," I say, my voice quavering again. Rebecca watches me with her hands clasped together in front of her mouth.

Flaco's laugh is filled with scorn. "I seen you the other day looking like a *pinche* raccoon, your face all busted up. Ain't nobody ever going to respect your sorry ass."

I'm scared out of my mind right now, but there's no going back. I've made my decision. I reach over to help Dalton up, and Flaco brings his fist hard against my left cheekbone. I slump to the ground.

"Frankie!" Rebecca cries out.

Steve jumps between me and Flaco. "What the hell was that?" he says to Flaco.

I can't feel an entire side of my face. Twice I try to stagger to my feet, but I'm too dizzy, and I fall to my knees each time.

"Is that what you teach your brother? To lay down like a *maricón*?" Flaco makes a move toward me, like he's going to finish me off, but Steve pushes him back, protecting me.

"It's over," my brother says.

This time Flaco lunges at him, and Steve flinches horribly. Flaco laughs a deep, demonic cackle. "Oh, it ain't over. Not for a while, it ain't over."

The blood drains from Steve's face. There's something familiar in the way he looks at Flaco. It takes me a little while, but when I finally notice it, I almost gasp. I see myself.

"Come on, *ese*," Steve's voice cracks just slightly, and for the first time I can remember, I see fear in his eyes. "Let's just get out of here," he says, unable to meet Flaco's intense stare, not strong enough to protect me.

With everyone's attention on Flaco and my brother, Burrage shakes free and helps Dalton step away. I'd like to think I see gratitude in Dalton's eyes.

"*Híjole*," Flaco says, whistling through his teeth. "I thought you were a *cholo*? You think you're hard, college boy? You think one little B & E puts hair on your *cojones*? Shit, you're just playing *cholo*. You don't know what hard is."

His words hang in the air; the cruel depth of his voice makes time seem to slow. Burrage holds a slumping Dalton at the edge of the circle. Rebecca implores me with her eyes. My brother tries to force air into his lungs. As for the people still gathered around the circle—they can neither leave nor fully bring themselves to watch. A warm evening breeze rustles through the trees, and it's as though the life we all knew before is about to be gone—replaced by a cold, primitive savagery. And everyone feels it.

Flaco smiles—like he was only kidding—and then reaches out as if to shake my brother's hand.

When we first started *Julius Caesar*, Miss Reyna told us that what makes Shakespeare great is that his themes are universal, that even though people don't wear tights anymore, or duel with swords, his plays are as relevant now as they were four hundred years ago. She said we would appreciate his genius once we looked beyond the language and understood what the plays were really about: passion, jealousy, hatred, love.

Betrayal.

My brother's neck snaps back. Flaco's header is swift and vicious, even though the result seems to take forever. My brother's eyes roll up into his head, and blood shoots out from his nostrils. He staggers back and falls to one knee, holding his face with one hand and the ground with the other.

Almost instantly, one of the *cholos* leaps over to me and pulls my arms behind me. I fight him as hard as I can, but the fucker wrenches my shoulders back, and the pain is so strong I can feel it in my stomach.

Rebecca screams.

Steve looks up at me. There is no badass in him anymore. He's just a little boy. Bile rises from my stomach and burns the back of my neck.

I hear shouting in the distance. More and more people show up from the dance. To my right, I see Zach and Nicole push through to the front of the crowd. Zach makes a run toward me, but one of the *cholos* is in his blind spot, and he doesn't see until it's too late. The dude punches him hard in the gut, and he collapses to the ground only two feet from the edge. Nobody else tries to help.

Flaco comes over to me. "Best you learn this lesson while it still does you some good."

At the sound of his voice, Nicole breathes in sharply and brings her hands to her mouth. Her face goes white. She kneels down to Zach and pulls him back to the safety of the crowd.

Flaco and his crew swarm my brother like hyenas on a carcass. The beating is savage. Steve keeps his feet for a few seconds, but he doesn't stand a chance against four of them.

"Somebody do something," Rebecca yells. But it's like we're in a vacuum. The darkness has smothered all hope.

Shadows fly. Now it's just Flaco. Steve lies in a fetal heap at his feet, rolling back and forth among pieces of Dalton's shattered bottle. There is no screaming—not from Flaco, not from Steve. They're both well past that.

I shout and writhe to break free, but I'm not strong enough. Every time I turn to look away, to close my eyes or bow my head, one of the *cholos* slaps me across the face and squeezes my head so that I can witness.

Finally, mercifully, sirens begin to pierce the dull symphony of kicks and punches, of grunting and moaning. I never thought I would be as happy to see the police as I am now. Squad cars squeal to a stop. I'm shoved to the ground when the *cholos* around the circle take off, and two officers give chase into the moonlight. I fall to my face.

Chief Sanchez steps into the circle, his gun drawn and aimed at the back of Flaco's head. "Don't move!"

Flaco gives my brother one last kick and then stands fully erect. Headlights focus on him as though he's an actor alone onstage, his hands and face spattered with my brother's blood. A dark red sash streaks the glowing white cotton of his shirt. He kneels on the ground. He lies face down.

Chief Sanchez glances at his daughter.

"I'm okay," she says.

He nods. "Your hands," he says, and Flaco puts his arms behind his back.

When they snap the cuffs on him, Flaco doesn't resist. He doesn't even seem to mind. They pull him to his feet and steer him toward a squad car.

As soon as there's room, I sprint to my brother's side. I kneel down and put his head in my lap. His shirt is torn. Blood cakes the hair to his forehead, and a large gash below his left eye reveals the pulsating ivory of his cheekbone. His face, swollen beyond recognition, is a cruel cartoon of his former self.

"Frankie," he mumbles. Tiny slits open where his eyes used to be. I can hardly understand him.

When I lean my ear down to his mouth, I see that Cheo has just arrived. He stands at the edge of the circle, his arms limp at his sides, with an expression of pained disbelief on his face.

"You got blood on your tux," Steve says. Then his eyes flutter closed.

Chief Sanchez puts his arm on my shoulder, and I cradle Steve's head against my chest as the wailing of the ambulance drifts closer.

twenty-two

I AM UNPREPARED, to say the least, for the sight of my brother lying motionless on the hospital bed. Tubes and wires connect him to a massive array of beeping machinery. His right leg is raised slightly and encased in yellow fiberglass. A thick layer of gauze wraps his head like a turban. His face, what I can see of it under the oxygen mask, is blanketed by scrapes and cuts and bruises.

I want to talk to him, to rush to his side, to hold his hand like the caring relatives on TV, but it's as though someone has nailed me to the floor. This isn't my brother at all. This is something out of a science fiction movie.

My parents have already seen him today. They brought

him down to Albuquerque last night, but I couldn't come because of the two hours I spent with the police. While the cops interviewed the other witnesses, paramedics treated a small cut on my temple and iced my ballooning left cheekbone.

I open my mouth, but nothing comes out. A clear narrow tube snakes out from under the gauze. Pinkish fluid inside.

Eventually, I stagger to the chair at his side and force myself to sit. Closer now, I recognize him. Under the fresh wounds, I make out the scar below his right eye where one time I accidentally hit him with a football. It's Steve. The machines beep and whirr above our heads.

The door creaks open, and I feel a hand on my shoulder.

"*Órale*, Frankie," says a solemn voice.

"What's up, Cheo?" I say without looking at him.

Metal whines against the linoleum floor as he pulls up a chair next to mine. His hair is gelled back, and he looks nice, pants and a blue button-down, as if he'd been expecting a funeral. "*¿Cómo estás?*"

It's a strange question to hear when you're the healthy one. I really don't know how I'm doing.

Cheo motions to my brother. "He's going to be okay?"

"That's what they say."

"He better. Stupid *pendejo* owes me ten bucks."

"Huh?"

Pride injects some cheer into his voice. "The '65, *ese*. It's done. I drove it down." But then his laughter fades, and we're left where we started: with my brother's machines beeping through the silence. "Too bad he can't play next week. Cibola don't have nobody who can guard him."

"He'll get better," I say.

Cheo runs both hands over the crisp shell of his hair. He empties his lungs and shifts in the seat. Then he looks down. "I'm sorry, *ese*. I wish I could have . . . It's my fault, isn't it?"

I wonder if my mom and dad blame me for this. I bet they think I should have known, that I should have warned them, that I was the one who could have stopped this from happening, and maybe they're right. But Cheo understands the truth that none of us is innocent.

"I want to go home," I whisper.

He pats me on the leg as he stands up. "*Vámonos.* I'll take you."

Back in the waiting room, the anxious relatives of strangers hide behind old issues of *People* and *Newsweek*, and I hate them. I can only think of my own pain, my family's pain, and being reminded that others are also suffering cheapens that pain by making it common. My mom and dad huddle in the corner.

My parents hug me and tell me they'll stay for a while longer. They tell me they love me, and I believe them.

I step into the elevator and turn to face the waiting room. My dad puts his arm around my mom and pulls her close, resting his cheek on the top of her head. The hair on my arms stands on end, and my skin feels alive. This is what they must have looked like twenty-five years ago, before life worked them over like a thug with an iron pipe. I listen to my heart pump the blood through my veins. Not a thump-thump like in the cartoons, but more like a whisper, like a librarian saying, "shhh, shhh, shhh." Mom pulls away and cradles his cheeks in her hands. The elevator slides closed.

An old adobe building sits abandoned in the sage field behind my house. One room, about twenty feet by ten. Dirt floor, no roof. Stuccoless walls weathered and eroding. It's been there for as long as I can remember. Someone built it with his bare hands.

I climb through the barbed wire fence and make my way through a field of huge dark green weeds, prickly and almost spherical, coming up nearly to my waist. In a couple weeks, they'll start dying. They'll break off naturally from the root, dry out, and blow away. Tourists from New Jersey and California will visit the many souvenir shops on the way down to Albuquerque. They'll ship a few authentic tumbleweeds back home in order to give their brick and wood houses a hint of the wild, wild west.

A black widow spiderweb spans the doorway, and I have to duck low in order to get through without disturbing it. The missing roof makes me feel both trapped and free at the same time. One of the small windows looks out onto our backyard, and I can even see our door—in case someone decides to come searching.

I walk to the northwest corner of the small room, kicking

weeds out of my way as I reach a clear spot about the size of a basketball hoop. I kneel down and pull out a few live tumbleweeds from around the edge, tossing them across the room and sending large clumps of soil pattering against the walls. Once I've cleared enough space, I sit cross-legged and begin to wipe away a thin layer of dirt from the top of a flagstone.

I wedge my fingers under the slab and lift up. The earth underneath is moist and covered with bugs—ants, worms, roly-polies—all suddenly swarming around in a panic. This is probably what New York City would look like if you took the top layer of street away. Subways exposed, tunnels, frantic commuters searching for cover, running for their lives. I look around for a stick to dig with, but I can't find anything, so I just shove my hands into the ground.

Back when Steve and I buried our time capsule, we used a shovel. Now, by the time my hands reach the metal Spiderman lunch box two feet down, my fingertips are all bloody. Little piles of excavated dirt surround me. Ants bite my arms and legs, but I don't mind so much. They're entitled to it. Retribution for the years of torture I've subjected them to.

I lean back against the wall after pulling out the lunch box. The latch is rusted shut, so I jam my elbow down on it. Hard. Jolts of pain shoot up to my fingertips, and after the third hit, a gash opens about two inches of the skin on my forearm. Blood spills to the ground. Mixes with the dirt. Finally, the latch breaks free, and I open the lid. Inside is a letter written in Steve's lazy scrawl.

Dear New Mexicans of the future,

I am Stephen Towers, of Borges. My brother
Francisco and I want you to know about us.
Please take these artifacts to your leaders.
P.S. Do you speak English or Spanish?

I place the letter on the ground in front of me and remove our artifacts, the evidence of our childhood together: Steve's Under-10 state championship medal, a drawing of our family I did in kindergarten—stick figures with huge heads standing next to an adobe house—a menu from Los Torres, a pack of firecrackers, a dried red chile.

I bang my head back against the adobe, feel little chunks of wall crumbling down the back of my shirt. My breath comes in short spurts now, shallow, like I'm just under the surface of the water and I have to steal oxygen whenever I can. The tears come suddenly. Pain erupts from deep inside my chest, and my arms tingle. I look down at the dirt on my bloody fingertips. I choke on my own saliva and lean over to throw up, but nothing comes out.

Steve and I used to stay up at night trying to decide which superpower would be the best. Superhuman strength? Telepathy? Shape-shifting? We'd argue about the benefits and drawbacks of Green Lantern's ring, or try to figure out how Iceman moved forward on his floating ice sidewalk.

But now I realize that we missed the obvious. The best

power of all is time travel. You're going to screw up, whether you can fly or not, whether you have spidey sense or X-ray vision or adamantium claws, and the only true superhero is the guy who can go back and fix his mistakes before they happen.

When the tears are gone, I pull the Band-Aid from my temple and lay it into the Spiderman lunch box. Each of the artifacts goes in on top of it. The letter is last. I place the time capsule back in the bottom of the hole, and I cover it up, handful by handful. After I'm done, I replace the flagstone.

twenty-three

BY THE TIME I get to Zach's house, I'm out of breath and sweating like crazy. I lean my bike next to the front door and ring the doorbell. I wipe my forehead on my shirtsleeves as I wait. I can't help but smile when I hear a loud *BOOM!* from the backyard.

Zach's mom answers the door wearing a green apron and holding a pair of bright purple oven mitts. The scent of baking cookies billows from the kitchen. Her face lights up when she recognizes me, and she puts her hands on her hips. "Frankie. You know you don't have to ring the doorbell."

"Hi, Mrs. Mason."

"Are you okay?" she says, opening the screen door, and

when she sees my swollen face, my blood and mud-caked hands, she swallows me in a massive hug. "I'm so sorry, honey. Zach told me what happened." She releases me and holds me at arm's length. "Is your brother okay? How are your parents?"

"Is Zach here?" Another explosion from the backyard.

"Of course he is, sweetheart. Come on in."

"I don't want to bother him if he's busy."

"Nonsense! He'll be glad to see you. Please, come in." She ushers me into the front hall and pushes me toward the back-yard. "Do you want some Popsicles? Or something to drink?"

I can see him through the window, near the back fence, hunched over a pile of dirt. "No, thanks."

"You really should wash your hands. . . ." She drifts off, following my gaze. "Go on ahead outside, hon. I have to check the cookies."

It takes me a few minutes to work up the courage to walk out there. While his mom goes back to her cooking, I watch Zach from the safety of his living room. He moves from the big pile of dirt, holding a large spool and trailing it across the yard. Eventually my curiosity gets the better of my anxiety.

He's so into it, whatever it is, that he doesn't hear me approach, so I take a seat on the old cottonwood stump and wait. "What's up, bro?" I say finally.

"Aaahh!" he screams, and I swear to God, he jumps about three feet. "Holy fucking shit!"

You know how it is when other people trip and fall or something? You know you shouldn't laugh, especially if you're the one who tripped them, but you can't help yourself, and it just ends up pissing them off? That's what's happening right now. I'm laughing so hard my face hurts, but I can't stop.

"Frankie, you asshole, you scared the crap out of me."

Tears stream down my face again. "I'm sorry, *ese*, I thought you heard me sit down."

He bends over and picks up his large spool, which he threw about twenty feet into the air when I freaked him out. "Shut up. I think you actually did scare the crap out of me. I have to check my pants."

Finally, somehow, I'm able to stop laughing. "I'm really sorry. I'll get you a new pair." I stand up, pointing to his spool, and walk over to him. "What's that?"

"What's up with your hands?"

"Is Nicole okay?" I say.

He nods. "Your face is all busted up again."

I wonder sometimes whether real life would be easier if it were just like *Star Wars*, with good and evil so clearly defined. With only two sides to the Force, as if there were a line that you could simply cross, easy as picking teams on the playground.

"You know how they always talk about the Dark Side of the Force?" I say. "But you never hear what the *other* side is called. Is it the Light Side? They never tell us."

"Is that supposed to be deep?"

"If it's so important, shouldn't it at least have a name?"

He stares at me for a second and then shakes his head. "You're one weird little wetback."

"Moistback," I say. "My dad's Wonder Bread like you."

He smiles. "Right, moistback."

A roadrunner leaps onto a wooden fence post and shakes its head, watching us, distrusting. Then it darts off, sprinting under a sage bush and out of sight. The state bird, and it can't even fly—that should tell you something. It's supposed to be good luck if it crosses your path.

I point to whatever he's holding. "Seriously, what is that?"

"Dynamite fuse," he says, tossing it to me. "Check it out."

It's heavier than I thought it would be, and I almost drop it on my foot. The metal spool itself is about the size of a basketball, and the braided fuse, wrapped like thread around the spool, is about a quarter-inch thick and the color of a deep bruise. "Where did you get this?"

"Begay. His uncle had a whole stack of them, so we swiped a couple. He threw it in with the last batch of M-80s I bought because he said I was his best customer."

"Fucking-A! What are you doing?"

"Suddenly you're all interested?"

I hand him back his fuse. "Come on, *ese*."

"Yeah, okay." He lays the spool gently on the ground and walks over to the huge pile of dirt. "I dug a hole about a foot deep. Then I tied three M-80s together with the dynamite fuse and put them in the hole." At first, Zach speaks quietly, but as he gets further into his explanation, he becomes more and more animated. "This is the cool part. I filled up a bunch of water balloons and put them on top of the M-80s."

"Water balloons?"

"I know," he says. "Pretty sweet, huh?"

"What if they leak?"

He shakes his head. "The dynamite fuse is waterproof, just like the M-80 fuses. So then I filled the rest of the hole with dirt and piled up a whole bunch more dirt on top."

We're standing around with our hands on our hips, like architects surveying a construction site. I point to the hill, which is about two feet high. "Don't you think you put too much dirt on?"

"Only one way to find out, isn't there?"

We follow the fuse away from the hill, and Zach picks up the spool and rolls it out until we're crouching behind the big stump. He takes out a pocketknife and cuts the fuse, and then he tucks the loose end of the spool under itself so that it doesn't uncoil. He pulls a lighter from his pocket and offers it to me.

"No, hu-uh," I say, waving it off. "This is all yours."

He nods and sparks a flame. "Here goes." He's trying to be all cool about it, but I can tell that he's excited to see what happens. Jesus, *I'm* excited.

Zach steadily lowers the flame until it touches the fuse. Nothing happens for about two seconds, and then the fuse flashes to life. It's like a moving firework, sending sparks flying in every direction as it burns, advancing at about a foot per second, and leaving in its wake a spent shell like a narrow black snake.

"I hope Steve's okay," he says.

The fuse races toward the hill, and I tear my eyes away and glance at Zach. "I'm sorry."

The fuse hisses. It's ten feet away from the pile now and moving fast. I think Zach notices me, but I'm not sure. After all, I'm in his blind spot. "Yeah, I know. Whatever," he says. "Here goes."

The sparks disappear into the pile, and for a moment all is quiet. I pat him on the back. "Maybe the balloons bro—"

The first two explosions are muffled, coming almost exactly at the same time. Dirt and mud spray everywhere, and we dive to the ground and cover our heads. About a second after the first two explosions, the third M-80 detonates. Because it was launched into the air by the force of the first two, there is no soil or water to muffle the sound of the report, and it nearly deafens me. I even feel the force of the blast against the back of my neck. Little pieces of balloon drift to the earth around us.

My ears ring as we wait for the echoes to die down. I prop myself up on my elbows. "That was awesome."

Zach busts out laughing. "Frankie, you have crap all in your hair."

We lean back against the stump as the cobalt wisps of gunpowder smoke float gently above us. Mrs. Mason appears at the living room window, folding a dish towel with a worried look on her face. To reassure her that our hands are still undamaged, still five-fingered and connected to our wrists, Zach and I raise our arms high above our heads and wave.